Praise for
TOM CLANCY'S OP-CENTER NOVELS

"Rovin capably orchestrates all the players en route to the explosive climax." —*Publishers Weekly*

"Top-notch . . . combining politics, suspense, and action." —*Booklist*

"Intricate plotting, plenty of action . . . will leave you sleep-deprived." —*Defense Media Network*

"A frightening and exciting tale about a very new, but also a very old threat."
—Larry Bond, *New York Times* bestselling
author on *Out of the Ashes*

"Thriller addicts like me devoured every Tom Clancy's Op-Center tale. Now they are back, intricately plotted, with wonderfully evil villains and enough realistic military action and suspense to ruin a couple of night's sleep. Highly recommended."
—Stephen Coonts, *New York Times*
bestselling author

TOM CLANCY'S OP-CENTER NOVELS

ALSO BY JEFF ROVIN

Tom Clancy's

OP-CENTER

GOD OF
WAR

CREATED BY
Tom Clancy and Steve Pieczenik

WRITTEN BY
Jeff Rovin

St. Martin's Paperbacks

This is a work of fiction. All of the characters, organizations, and events portrayed in this novel are either products of the author's imagination or are used fictitiously.

Published in the United States by St. Martin's Paperbacks, an imprint of St. Martin's Publishing Group.

TOM CLANCY'S OP-CENTER: GOD OF WAR

For information, address St. Martin's Publishing Group, 120 Broadway, New York, NY 10271.

www.stmartins.com

Library of Congress Catalog Card Number: 2019058394

ISBN: 978-1-250-20924-5

Our books may be purchased in bulk for promotional, educational, or business use. Please contact your local bookseller or the Macmillan Corporate and Premium Sales Department at 1-800-221-7945, ext. 5442, or by email at MacmillanSpecialMarkets@macmillan.com.

Printed in the United States of America

St. Martin's Griffin trade paperback edition / August 2020
St. Martin's Paperbacks edition / September 2021

10 9 8 7 6 5 4 3 2 1

PROLOGUE

To Dr. Amy Howard, the South African A330-200 Airbus was a long, lovely whisper that forced her to leave her laboratory.

Four times a year, the forty-three-year-old endocrinologist flew from the O'Connell Research Lab at the University of Cape Town to the Australian Endocrine Center at the University of Notre Dame in Perth.

At present, the two scientific research facilities were working on enhanced forms of radioactive iodine for treatment of a hyperactive thyroid. The pharmaceutical firm EndoXX had not only given them a five-year grant, they insisted on face-to-face meetings to keep key research secure. The firm had two mottos. The official one was "Everything for Wellness." The unofficial one was "Everything Important Stays Off-line."

That was fine with Dr. Howard. EndoXX's security concerns furnished her with something that passed for a social life. Her career, her life, was about finding new ways to heal "that bloody gland." Thyroid cancer had taken her mother when she was ten.

The flight had departed three hours late, forty-five minutes earlier, and Dr. Howard had done exactly nothing but sit in the plastic bucket seat in the terminal and now on the comfortably padded cushion here. The business-class seating was quite roomy, the aisle to her left was spacious, and the big, balding man to her right was quietly watching a movie on his tablet. There was a lot of red and strobing white lights coming from the screen. A pillow, firmly but casually tucked against the armrest, blocked most of it.

The visual busyness did not bother her, much. The man was happy. Every now and then he would talk to the screen. He fidgeted several times with the shade, seeking the precise position to cut down glare without blocking his view of the sea. At this time of year sunlight was full and blazing from before 4:30 A.M. until well after 8:00 P.M. Securing some comfortable darkness was always a challenge.

Once in a while the man snuck a look in her direction, as if to make sure he wasn't bothering her. He needn't have worried. As someone who saw fatal cancers every week, she had learned not to let little intrusions bother her. Besides, a seat in a packed aircraft was the price of doing what made her happy. Amy was looking forward to spending time with Dr. Maggie Mui, a Hong Kong expatriate who had become a good friend. Amy was short, thin, and long-divorced. Maggie was tall, athletic, and had a husband and young daughter. Though neither woman acknowledged it, each was doing her own empirical study as to who was the happiest.

Once an analytical medical professional, always an analytical medical professional, she thought.

Beyond the man, outside the now half-shaded window, Amy saw an untextured wall of blue that occasionally glistened with fleeting fireflies of sun. There were also occasional flourishes of distant thunder from somewhere nearer Antarctica. It always astounded her to think that a century ago, explorers used to claw across the surface of the South Pole, freezing and hungry, both nearly to death.

And I'm sitting here with a laptop, an empty bag of peanuts, and a Perrier—

Thinking of the laptop made her feel she should finally be working. Dr. Howard was a few days behind on the latest research and she reached for her carrying case under the seat—

The man in the seat beside Amy coughed suddenly and violently. It was so strong that he doubled over his seat belt and hit his forehead on the seat in front of him. His earbuds went flying and Amy could hear tinny screams coming from the tablet.

She turned to the man as he inflated slowly, like a Thanksgiving parade balloon.

There were other hacking coughs behind her, here and there. She suddenly felt a tickle deep in her chest, like the sudden onset of flu. She cleared her throat. The tickling worsened.

No sooner had Amy's neighbor started to settle back

than a second cough threw him forward again. This time he speckled the seat back with blood.

Amy immediately scooched toward the aisle-side armrest in case there was another spray of blood.

"Sorry—sorry—" the man said in a thick New Zealand accent.

"Don't worry, I'm a doctor." She handed him the small bottle of Perrier. "Drink this. I'll inform the flight attendant. We have to get you back on the ground."

Dr. Howard leaned into the aisle and looked for a flight attendant. No one was about. She felt a tickle in her throat. Dry, recycled airplane air, she decided.

Unbuckling her belt, she rose—just as the tickle became a burning in her gut. She gripped the back of the seat in front of her as the pain intensified rapidly, hotter and more fiercely unsettled than indigestion. It rose swiftly up her throat and blew toward her mouth, causing a violent contraction of her neck muscles. She coughed, an eruption that brought blood and what felt like phlegm to the back of her mouth.

Her mind raced even as her body struggled.

The peanuts? Contaminated beverages? Toxic air circulation? A Typhoid Mary onboard?

Amy leaned her chest against the seat back, swallowing and trying to rally. In the dim light of the cabin she saw that she was the only one standing. As she sought to move into the aisle, the plane suddenly shuddered and dipped forward slightly. She fell against and slightly over the seat back. Below her, a young man was coughing hard into his hand.

"Christ!" he cried as he drew bloody fingers from his mouth.

Beside him, a woman was hacking up blood.

The plane righted itself and the intercom came on. There was no message, only coughing and an aborted attempt by a flight attendant to advise the fastening of seat belts.

Almost at once the plane nosed down again, steeper than before and this time without recovering. There were screams now, interspersed with the coughs. Amy barely heard them as another fire rose in her esophagus. She could feel the inside flesh burning, blistering—*dissolving*? Was that even *possible*?

The woman's knees folded. She fell to the floor between her seat and the one in front of it, landing scrunched in a fetal position. Her head flopped back as she coughed up blood in waves. It plumed up then came down on her face, spilled down her chin. Looking straight up, she saw the big man beside her bent over the armrest, retching.

In the glow of his tablet she saw that it wasn't dinner her companion was spewing. It was *him*. His insides. His eyes were globes, and if the man's airway had been cleared he might have screamed. So would she, but the heat rose again, bringing more than fire. Her throat and nasal passages were both clogged with a substance, thicker than blood and more metallic-tasting. She tried to turn over so her head would face down, so the *stuff* might drain, but the downward tilt of the aircraft and its screaming descent pressed her into the under-seat storage. She couldn't scream, she couldn't breathe, she couldn't clear the liquid mass that filled her solidly from the stomach to her sinuses.

Then she heaved and hacked and the blockage surged forcefully from her mouth and nose. Her neighbor's blood and tissue did the same, and everywhere around her she heard the gagging and retching and moans of the passengers.

She could no longer breathe. Tauntingly, an air mask dangled above her. Her insides cooled somewhat and her body was chilled and trembling on the outside.

Rapid . . . onset . . . pneumonia . . . Ebola . . .

That wasn't medically possible.

Sarin gas . . . she thought *. . . terrorism?*

Whatever this might be, it was quickly lethal. In her final moments of consciousness, the doctor thought to try and get her phone to record what was happening. Her right cheek was pressed against her bag. She struggled to snake her hand inside—

She retched dry heat, nothing more. At the same time, blood began to cloud her vision and clog her ears. She could now hear her own rapid, erratic heartbeat thudding in her blood-clogged ears.

Her fingers were shaking as she pushed them forward. She tried wheezingly to draw breath but her chest felt hollow, as though her lungs had been removed.

That was what her neighbor had regurgitated? Liquefied *organs*?

Amy Howard died without thinking any more about that possibility, without reaching her phone. She died without feeling the impact as the jetliner nose-dived into the rocky shoreline of the barren southern coast of Marion Island. The power-dive collision caused a three-hundred-foot-high fireball that melted the permafrost and obliterated overgrown storage shacks near the crash site. Rolling outward, the blast killed the seabirds nesting on the rough coastline along Crawford Bay.

CHAPTER ONE

MARION ISLAND, SOUTH AFRICA

November 11, 1:33 P.M., South Africa Standard Time

The population of Marion Island consisted of three South African seamen, thousands of birds, and tens of thousands of mice, all of whom were shocked from sleep by a ground-shaking concussion. Occasionally, there were research teams in residence at the science station at Crawford Bay. But not now.

Officially named Point Dunkel but referred to as "Point Dung Hill," the large cinderblock bunker rattled for several seconds, cups falling from counters and pictures tilting on walls. Dressed in uniforms with thick thermal linings, the men raced from their windowless, prison-sized rooms to the one door and two north-south–facing windows of the blockhouse.

"Fire to the east!" fifty-nine-year-old Commander Eugène van Tonder alerted the others from the open door.

Shivering, the team's helicopter pilot, forty-year-old Lieutenant Tito Mabuza, joined him at the frost-coated entrance. The localized flames were at least a mile away but the men felt wisps of heat. The driving wind was so swift and forceful that the heat barely had time to dissipate.

"Volcanic, sir?" he asked.

"I don't think so," van Tonder answered, sniffing. "I mean, it's unlikely without any warning, yeah?"

"We had that notification this morning," said twenty-year-old Ensign Michael Sisula. "The faint glow, likely outgassing."

"On Prince Edward, not here." Van Tonder shook his head. "Anyway, that's jet fuel burning."

"I'll contact Simon," said Sisula.

Simon was Simon's Town, home of fleet command for the South African Navy.

"Let's have a look," van Tonder said to Mabuza, pointing up. "There may be survivors."

The men rushed back to their rooms, neatly avoiding the half-dozen mousetraps in the corridor. As he pulled on his outer gear, Commander van Tonder was processing what they had seen and heard and felt. Silently, he prayed to God. The crash was likely a passenger flight. Prince Edward and Marion Islands were at the fringes of the commercial airline routes between Southern Africa and Oceania. Research planes typically flew along the Antarctic coast to maximize data gathering, and there was no tactical value for military aircraft to be here. When the South African Air Force tested their Umkhonto short- and medium-range missiles, there was no reason to travel over one thousand miles to the southeast.

Mabuza finished first and ran out to the black Denel AH-2 Rooivalk helicopter. He removed the insulated tarp from the main rotor swash plate and the tail gearbox and stuffed them behind the seats. Then he warmed the aircraft up. The commander followed quickly, pausing to holster his Vektor SP1 semiautomatic with a fifteen-round magazine. He had only used it once on the island, to end the suffering of a sick albatross. Given the nature of their assignment here, Simon's orders were that both crewmembers should carry firearms during a flight. The pilot's Milkor BXP submachine gun was in a brace behind his seat along with a shared M1919 Browning machine gun. That powerhouse could also be mounted on the helicopter in the unlikely event of an invasion by pirates or the military. They could destroy a target the better part of a mile away.

Before leaving, van Tonder told Sisula to monitor communications between the chopper and Simon. Depending on where they flew, the mountains could make the direct uplink to Simon spotty. It was strange that, just a score of years before, they would not have been able to communicate at all, not in a straight line. Signals had to go up in space and down so they could talk.

Van Tonder left, buttoning the greatcoat that had been given to him by his sister. A member of the Methodist clergy in Durban, she had been expedition pastor on several South African National Antarctic

Expeditions and had said he would need the coat. She was correct. The standard wool-lined flight jacket provided by the military would not have gotten the job done. The winds here were not only constant, they were brutal. Albatrosses were smart birds, and van Tonder could not understand why so many of them *chose* to live here.

Perhaps it's their laziness, he had thought, watching them when there was nothing else to do. *If you're a bird with a wingspan of up to twelve feet, you want to live where there's constant and substantial lift.*

The helicopter was parked on a large, naturally flat rock fifty yards behind the bunker. There was room for two small helicopters. During warmer months, scientists were ferried here from the mainland. During the late fall and throughout the winter, educated folk stayed away.

The pad was stained with the oil of six decades of helicopters coming and going at the outpost. Because it was set back from the high, rocky coast, the rock wasn't stained with bird droppings. Walking anywhere to the front or sides of the outpost, a person had to watch their step.

The rotors were just starting to spin as van Tonder made his way toward the bubble cockpit. He was still praying, still asking the Lord to look out for the souls of the dead; there were sure to be many. Squinting into the wind as he looked to the left, he saw the horizon aglow with what looked like a second cloudy sun in the sky, yellow-orange flame mushroom-capped with roiling black smoke. He could smell not just the fuel but the burning plastics, rubber, and flesh—both human and avian, he suspected.

The commander climbed into the three-crewmember cockpit, stepping over the food chest, rescue net, and medical footlocker just inside the door, behind the copilot's seat. With weather conditions and geography as extreme as they were here, a crew did not leave unless they were sure they could sit out a storm or provide first aid.

The third seat was above and behind the first two. Though van Tonder was not a flier, he wanted to sit beside Mabuza. Sometimes—and this was certainly the case with the pilot—a man's expressions revealed more than his words. Also, from here, the commander could point and be seen.

Van Tonder donned a headset so he could talk to both the pilot and Sisula. The team was airborne less than five minutes after the crash.

Mabuza ascended to two hundred feet and flicked on both the underbelly spotlight and the cockpit camera before nosing toward the flames. The familiar rocks and their permafrost coating flew by. Van Tonder even knew where the small, slimy, caterpillar-like *Ceratophysella denticulata* lay their eggs.

He was beginning to think the long periods of calm were not as bad as he had imagined.

The three men were career men of the South African Navy Maritime Forces, Ships and Naval Unit Ready Forces. They had been sent to the long-abandoned British outpost three months earlier to investigate reports of illegal drilling on the protected island. In previous eras, invasive species had wreaked incredible ecological damage, in particular the mice and cats that came with whalers. Balance had been restored by both South Africa and nature. The leaders of the parliamentary republic—both from personal conviction, public fanaticism, and international pressure—insisted that order be maintained.

And then, foolishly, an aquatic sciences and fisheries survey in 2019 published a paper that mentioned, by the by, that the islands were likely rich in diamond-bearing kimberlite. The wintertime, evening-hours prospecting began. The navy responded with van Tonder, Mabuza, and Sisula.

The soft-plumaged petrels and Kerguelen cabbage must be preserved, van Tonder had thought when he received his orders.

The response was only partly cynical. Van Tonder believed in the mission. It was just unfortunate that the military invariably had to clean up preventable messes made by their own nationals at the behest of politicians.

Once each month, the fleet replenishment ship SAS *Drakensberg* arrived with supplies and fuel. In the event of a medical emergency, an aircraft could land on the flat plain between Johnny's Hill and Arthur's Hill, just to the northeast. Except for missing his nieces and nephews, and dating—Lord God, he missed women most of all, and the Internet was only a taunting reminder of just *how much*—van Tonder had no objection to being here. He liked the quiet and the time to pursue his studies of history and languages. Except for twice-a-day helicopter circuits of the two islands, his time was his own. And those trips were short. This island, Marion, was just 112 square miles. Prince Edward was even smaller, at just 17 square miles.

The tall, slender, white-skinned, tawny-haired man was frankly pleased to be anywhere in the military. A Boer, he had survived the 1994 transition from the apartheid government under Frederik W. de Klerk to the Government of National Unity under Nelson Mandela. He achieved that by being invisible. He was still invisible, only now it was by inhabiting a region where most of the observers had feathers, scales, and occasionally fur.

"We're not hearing Simon," Mabuza informed both the commander and Sisula. "It's a little bit the wind, but mostly the metal particulates in that smoke are interfering. I'll elevate and go out to sea a little—should clear up the dusting issue."

"I'll relay anything important," Sisula replied. "If it were military, we would have heard the chatter."

"But not a word from SACAA?" van Tonder asked.

He was referring to the South African Civil Aviation Authority, which was as tight-lipped as any similar department worldwide. First they checked with the towers, then they checked with the airlines, then they "revealed" what dozens of social media postings had already announced, often with video or images and the disbelieving commentary of observers: that a commercial airliner had gone down.

"I'm not on their channel, but there's nothing that I've been told," Sisula said.

"Simon knows we're on our way, though."

"Of course, Commander," Sisula told him. "They said they would relay the information to SACAA."

"Thank you. Civilian authorities can be stupidly jurisdictional and I want a record of the chain of reporting."

"Understood."

"Bloody bureaucracy," Mabuza remarked.

It was lunch hour, granted—well into it, in fact—and those bloody bureaucrats liked their afternoon drinks. But someone from the SACAA should have been in touch with the only personnel who were on site. Though their response could be clogged in military channels. Simon liked to be in charge of its own missions. The military bureaucracy was itself formidable.

Mabuza was not as content to be here as van Tonder. There were two things he longed for. One, he openly and frequently declared, was a yearning for the nightlife of Port Elizabeth. The other was a desire to do something with his skills—test new aircraft, even fight in a war.

"To fly so it matters," as he put it.

He loved everything that flew. He designed and built model planes and studied avionics. In terms of his overall desires, the post was a wash. The only females he noticed here had wings. But because they had wings he studied them.

Sisula, the unit's communications and tech expert, was the most content of the three. He loved anything digital and didn't care where he was. Van Tonder was grateful for him. If Sisula were any less able, the outfit would lose Internet access on an hourly basis. The dish on the roof rattled in the near-constant wind, but the brilliant ensign had written a program to compensate for the vacillation. He was always creating uplinks and hacks that provided rich global access to one of the most desolate spots on the planet. Just before bed tonight, Mabuza had delighted to the view from the security cameras inside Boogie Heights, a popular nightclub in Hong Kong.

Van Tonder looked out through the glass-bubble nose of the helicopter as they closed in on the crash site. It looked to him as if the fire was burning across roughly a quarter mile of flat scrub.

Mabuza's maneuver had worked. The next message was from Simon.

"Dunkel, we have SACAA's reply that a South African Airbus went off-radar at zero one hundred hours, eleven minutes, and five seconds local," the Simon radio operator said. "It left Johannesburg at eleven forty-five—it was one hundred miles northwest of you at the time. What is approximate location of presumed wreckage?"

"Location forty-six degrees, fifty-four minutes, forty-five seconds south, thirty-seven degrees, forty-four minutes, thirty-seven degrees east," Sisula replied. "Helicopter en route."

"Is it patched in?" Simon inquired.

"This is Commander Eugène van Tonder. Lieutenant Tito Mabuza and I are approximately a half mile from the site." He pulled off a glove and pushed a pulsing circle on the digital display. "Video should be coming through now. Expect interference proximate to the crash site."

"Un . . . stood . . . ank you, Com . . ."

"Sorry," Mabuza said to his companion. "That'll break up the images as well."

"I'll see what I can do about that," Sisula said. "Simon is talking to SACAA now—reporting to us that there was no mayday. They're looking into any other communication from the cockpit. They want to know what we saw or heard—I'll tell them and get back to you."

"Thanks." Van Tonder turned to his pilot. "So they fell off radar. A sudden descent from thirty-five thousand feet."

"More than sudden, I think," Mabuza said. He pointed ahead at the wreckage, its jagged angles and hidden recesses illuminated by its own fires. "The way the fuselage is separated from the nose section—you see the cockpit there?"

Van Tonder saw the conical structure—what was left of it—angled upward from the ground, the cabin broken off behind it around the galley.

"That came down in a power dive," Mabuza said.

"Powered? Full throttle?"

"Yes, as if someone leaned or fell against the controls," Mabuza said. "That suggests either willful destruction or complete and sudden incapacitation."

Sisula cut in. "Sirs, Simon says Johannesburg tower received no communication from the Airbus whatsoever."

"Then that would seem to rule out pilot suicide or a struggle in the cockpit," van Tonder said. "Someone would have heard something, the shouts of the flight crew."

"It also rules out sudden depressurization," Mabuza said. "The tower would have heard the alarms, even during the descent." The pilot pointed toward the crash site. "Look—four equal, separate fires."

"What's the significance?" van Tonder asked.

"It tells the story of the nose dive," he said. "The flight deck hit at nearly a ninety-degree angle, and the rest of the plane, still carrying the momentum, crumpled behind it—you see the front of the first-class section? Where the outside looks like an accordion?"

"Yes—"

"The structure was compromised there, snapped, and the rest of the plane just crashed down flat. Each of the fuel tanks ruptured at the same time."

Van Tonder heard another communication from Simon.

"I am sending . . . flight path, Dunkel," the voice said. "See if . . . seems unusual to you."

"Thank you, Simon," Sisula said. "Sir, Simon—"

"We got most of it," van Tonder said. "Ask them if they're looking for some kind of sea-based event, like a rocket-propelled grenade."

Sisula forwarded the message.

"They have requested satellite images from Europe and America to look for just that, yes," Sisula said. "But I had a thought. Commander, do you remember that call we received this morning?"

"The fisherman?"

"Yes," Sisula said.

"I included it in the daily briefing. Presumed thermal activity off Ship Rock on Edward."

"I'm looking at the flight path that just came in from Simon," Sisula said. "The point where the Airbus disappeared from radar is a latitudinal match with Ship Rock."

"How many miles away?"

"Let's see—two hundred and twelve."

"That's a slim and pretty distant connection," van Tonder said.

"True, sir," Sisula said. "But when you factor in— just a second, removing height differential so the event and the plane are at the same height—when you factor in the speed of the Antarctic easterlies and the westerlies north of it, something happens."

"What?" van Tonder asked.

"Whatever was above Ship Rock ran smack into the path of the jetliner."

CHAPTER TWO

FORT BELVOIR NORTH, SPRINGFIELD, VIRGINIA

November 11, 7:45 A.M.

Chase Williams had always been an early riser. That had not just been true during his military career, where it was enforced, but also since coming to Washington, D.C. The sixty-one-year-old lived alone at the Watergate and commuted to Virginia. As much as he had little patience for the speed bumps of bureaucracy, he also disliked traffic.

Rising with the sun gave him time to do push-ups and jumping jacks in its comforting orange glow. Then he would shower quickly, put on a seasonal suit, make a thermos of coffee—the vending machine at the DLA was sinister in operation, refusing bills as if it suspected they were all counterfeit—and drive on relatively empty roads.

And there was something ironic about arriving at his new place of employment as the new sun still caused the walls of the building to glow with angelic innocence. Williams imagined that God was in on the joke. The DLA was anything but.

Built on the site of what was once a plantation, and named for the first director of the Defense Logistics Agency, Lieutenant General Andrew T. McNamara, U.S. Army, the nine five-story structures that comprise the McNamara Headquarters Complex are part of the sprawling Fort Belvoir complex. Among other assets, the base includes Davison Army Airfield, tactically located just fifteen miles southwest of Washington, D.C.

A division of the Department of Defense, the DLA is a cornerstone for global combat support, both open-warfare and covert activities. That constant, busy, roiling function is belied by the serenity of the setting. The buildings form an embracing semicircle that includes a large reflecting pool as well as tennis and basketball courts. The façades of the bottom two floors are white, the higher floors are reddish brick. By design, the overall impression is that of a college campus, a home of theory and think tanks, not action.

One of the first things Chase Williams discovered when he came to work here—using the president's own access codes—was that the DLA had active files for the assassination of every major political, military, and theocratic terrorist on Earth. Most of those he knew about. What he had not known was that every category had domestic targets. They were not necessarily enemies of the nation or the executive branch. These were culled—"hacked," as Matt Berry put it— from the black ops groups in this very building.

Many of these files were updated daily. That included a slim dossier on Mohammad Obeid ibn Sadi, a Houthi terror financier who was ancillary to Williams's own first mission here.

Not now, but one day, was the note attached to the file. The note was signed *B*—Matt Berry, the deputy chief of staff to outgoing President Wyatt Midkiff. Berry was the man responsible for moving Williams, the one-man Op-Center, to his new home here. A hard-nosed, pragmatic, unimaginative, self-interested pain in the ass, Berry was nonetheless one of Williams's biggest boosters.

Williams knew from his tenure at the original Op-Center that the DLA was rumored to be the federal government's largest repository of black ops and dark ops activities. It was said—very quietly—that Director Stephanie Hill had more power than anyone in government, including the president. Hill was not hobbled by the high profile and accountability hurdles of the commander in chief.

There was a reason for the secrecy. The Central Intelligence Agency, the Federal Bureau of Investigation, and the National Security Agency were populated with deep state leakers, anarchists, contrarians, and spies. Because of that, the DLA did not truly exist as a unit with a broad command structure. Beneath Hill and her few deputies, no one knew anyone else.

Williams was neither naïve nor shockable. His career embraced thirty-five years of military service, most of it at Pacific Command and Central Command. For the last five years he had run the National

Crisis Management Center—informally known as Op-Center. His dozens of team members had operated lawlessly at times, and lethally on occasion. So had he, himself. Williams never went to confession over any of it.

His late wife, Janette, whom he had lost to ovarian cancer, had been his confessor, when one was needed.

His personal and professional mission had always been to protect these United States from injury. He had done so, putting America before both of those, professional advancement and personal safety. He had sacrificed the approval of his rivals at the FBI and CIA, or even the security of his field personnel. Some of them had paid with their lives.

Still, the Op-Center based at the DLA was nothing like the Op-Center that Williams had been running until eleven weeks before. As Berry called it, Op-Center 2.0 had invited a certain necessary tedium to set in. Williams was one of thousands of sets of eyes that watched Web sites and data to make sure the homeland was safe.

The frustrating truth of it, though—the thing that kept Williams from settling in or enjoying the work— was that he did not understand why he was doing it. The deeper reason. Berry had to have one. So far, nothing the deputy chief of staff had said struck him as even remotely honest, let alone transparent.

Williams knew that the need for Op-Center to go into action was limited to jobs no one else wanted to be caught doing. It wasn't that Delta Force or SEAL

Team Six feared any mission. The opposite was true. But the charters of those and other units were the same as their parent forces.

In short, they played by certain rules. What he understood was that officially, the Op-Center team Black Wasp did not exist. Restrictions did not apply. They were so no-profile, in fact, that Williams had no contact with them. He knew that after their first and so far only mission the three members of the team had moved from their separate commands to Fort Belvoir. However, at Berry's instructions, he was not to have any communication unless and until they had a mission.

"Less chance of anyone recognizing you and asking who, what, why questions about them," Berry had said. "If they know the president gave you a personal combat team, they'd all want one."

That made some sense, but not entirely. Williams had command skills the team could probably use. Why had those been carved away?

Maybe that was part of the plan, he had wondered. To keep the two key combatants as semi-loose cannons. That was part of what had been baked into this experiment. Berry had once described Black Wasp as an autonomous collective.

"Or, as it is referred to in the argot, a 'situational command,'" Major Breen had said when they met. SITCOM was an apt enough acronym. Rank had nominal sway. The members were three soldiers with specific skills working together. Any of them could make a command decision, for him or herself, at will.

It had worked on the first mission. But that was the only empirical data they possessed.

Not a deep sample on which to build a policy, but then they—and I—am expendable the first time it doesn't work, Williams reflected.

The veteran commander was still adjusting to his new reality. He had gone from being a leader of a vitally integrated team to being the sole employee of an Op-Center that was now a subsidiary line item in the budget earmarked for logistical export support. That cost was folded into the Executive Branch Discretionary Fund, a so-called exploratory budget that was conveniently requisitioned and approved by the same person, the chairman of the Joint Chiefs of Staff.

"It's like being buried in a tomb built of UNICEF pennies," he had told Berry when they met over drinks for their weekly face-to-face.

The younger man did not get the reference.

"Halloween," Williams had explained. "Orange milk containers. You'd collect coins with your candy to help needy children around the world."

"Ah," Berry had said. "The ones who grew up to hate us?"

"I can't answer for them," Williams had replied. "I was raised to do the right thing."

Nonetheless, the image stuck: a penny from one trick-or-treater, a penny from another, and you had enough milk for a dozen kids. A dollar from one line item, a penny from another, and soon you had an annual operating budget for Chase Williams's new Op-Center. Most of that money went back into the DLA system to pay for the office overhead. Berry called it "dark financing," officially known as zero-sum operational expenditures.

"That way," Berry had said, "the DLA never has to rely on congressional funding for ongoing operations. Ms. Hill uses each new allocation to expand her power base."

So Williams was buried alive, but he was all right with that. He was single, he had no interest in retirement, and he was always up for new challenges. He was not just undercover but he was underground, in a clean, efficient, well-lit but windowless basement. He spent his days reviewing intelligence data, largely without human interaction. He missed his team, their input, their quirks, their smarts. Everyone he had met here in the corridors and at the vending machines was pleasant in a neutral sort of way. They used words like "hello" and "good morning" smartly and with a smile. But he could never tell if they were having a good day or managing a global crisis.

For some of these operators-perdu, he imagined that an end-of-the-world scenario probably *was* a good day.

Outside his defiantly open door, the crescent-shaped central corridor of the basement level matched the curve of the building. It was uncommonly quiet today, as most of the people here had just learned of the crash of a passenger jet over the Southern Indian Ocean. Given the subantarctic location, Williams was not surprised that the mainstream media had very little information about the event. The only "certain status," as the Federal Aviation Administration called crash details, was that it had happened, and that no reports on fatalities, possible causes, or crewmembers had been issued.

Terrorism had not been ruled out, though it seemed unlikely. South Africa was not on any global terrorism map, save for the sporadic activities of ISIS cells in Durban. And those were typically jihadi sympathizers who were looking to launch attacks outside the nation. And taking down a plane to kill one passenger was tactically more complicated than a car bomb or shooting.

Even as he considered that possibility, the passenger manifest came up on his computer. There were no red flags. Johannesburg to Perth was not a route political activists, religious radicals, or hostile journalists tended to travel. Military commanders did not usually fly commercial.

What kept most of the intelligence and DLA personnel at their desks was no doubt the same material that Williams had just received from Matt Berry. It had originated from the NYPD Counterterrorism Bureau and had been shared with all networked agencies. Which meant that, by now, everyone in Washington *and* the media had it.

The item was an audio file, the recording of a 911 call from Joseph Lewein in Manhattan. The message had a time stamp of 9:16 A.M.—just minutes after the crash and too soon for him to have seen, heard, or read about it anywhere.

Williams listened with headphones that kept any external noise out and internal sound in.

Dispatch: Nine-one-one, what's your—

Lewein: My name is Joseph Lewein and I think . . . I'm *sure* something is wrong, badly wrong. I was—

Dispatch: Mr. Lewein, where are you calling from?

Lewein: Huh? 330 West Forty-fifth Street, apartment 5K, but that doesn't matter! I was video sharing a movie with my uncle Bernard on South African flight—Christ, what's the number? It's two eighty, I think. He was traveling from Johannesburg to Perth and we were watching—Doesn't matter. He suddenly started *convulsing*!

Dispatch: Sir, is this an emergency at your loca—

Lewein: *No!* I'm reporting some kind of emergency on the *plane*. I don't have the FAA on frickin' speed dial! I saw my uncle coughing blood and then his tablet must've fallen because then I saw a woman throwing up—blood, guts. I heard *everyone* choking and screaming!

Dispatch: All right, sir? I need you to calm down and tell me—

Lewein: I *can't* calm down and I *am* telling you! I saw an oxygen mask hanging down! There was a ton of blood on the seat!

Dispatch: Sir, I need you to tell me if you are reporting a terror incident. If so, I will send officers of the Strategic Response—

Lewein: *Goddammit, I don't need help!* It's not *me*!
It's a plane that went down somewhere in the
Indian Ocean! *Christ!* Idiot! Connect me with the
FBI or Homeland Security. Get me *someone,* any-
one who can *do* something! To hell with this—

The caller hung up. That was the entire recording.

Less than a minute after Williams finished listening to it, Matt Berry called on the secure landline.
Williams closed the door before answering. He had
rarely done that at the old Op-Center office.

"Good morning, Chase," Berry said. "What do you
make of it?"

"Same as you, I imagine. Terror attack—usual MO,
early in the flight and out of an airport that's been quiet
for years, maybe a little lax with security."

"Cause of deaths?"

"From the apparent speed, I would say a biological
agent—ricin, maybe *Clostridium botulinum*."

"Not a gas?"

"Not likely," Williams said. "It would require too
much to conceal in a carry-on, and if you want to ven-
tilate it through the aircraft—it takes access and time
to set up before takeoff. Acoustic analysis will probably find nothing underlying the normal sound of the
vents."

"But the fast-acting biotoxins aren't airborne, and
they don't act uniformly."

"No."

"Then it's got to be something else," Berry said.
"What about the baggage handlers?"

"Airports Company South Africa is looking at that," Berry said, adding, "though we'd like to get the FBI over there, establish better relations."

"Not doing more to end apartheid is a big cross to bear," Williams said.

"So was wiping out Indians and ignoring the Holocaust and—let's not go down that road."

"Sorry," Williams said in earnest. "Just some context. I asked about the handlers because a radiological agent in someone's luggage might have caused something like the caller described."

"They've got radiation scanners at Oliver Tambo International. But—good point. I'll make sure they were operational."

"It needn't have been onboard," Williams added. "It could have been a cloud from an aboveground test or nuclear leak."

"Uh-uh," Berry said. "There was nothing like that anywhere in the flight path."

"Then maybe a Russian or Chinese satellite with a plutonium power source failed to reach orbit, penetrated the cabin."

"Imaginative, Chase, but what's that—a billion-to-one chance?" Berry said. "Besides, the NRO, the air force, even NASA would have detected something like that."

"National Reconnaissance Office shift-changes at eight A.M.," Williams said. "Maybe someone was getting coffee. Or checking the classifieds."

Williams was only half joking. More and more, computers were being programmed to watch—and

catch—the large volume of data streaming in from satellites, listening stations, computer hacks, and human
intelligence. A rocket abort, particularly a domestic
satellite—and not necessarily Russian or Chinese,
but Indian or Japanese—might not attract careful scrutiny.

"I'll make sure that didn't happen," Berry said.
"Meantime, I'll be kicking over whatever we learn
about the flight. Midkiff is phoning President Omo-
toso to offer condolences and resources—I may learn
something then."

"I'm sure you'll have the passenger list and security footage under a microscope," Williams said. "I'd
like to look into external factors."

"Seems unlikely—other planes use the route."

"All the more reason to rule it out," Williams said.

Berry considered that. "I need your instincts more
than your skills. Have at it."

"Do we have eyes on the region?" Williams asked.

"SoPo7 is being turned in that direction," Berry
said, referring to the polar-orbit climate satellite.
"First image it took was dead barn swallows on a
mountain—should be able to tell us something."

"You are a font of bizarre information."

"It impresses the ladies," Berry said. "I'll let you
know when there's something new," he added, then
hung up.

Williams thumbed off his phone. As always between the two, a moment of tension could be for-
given by a moment of levity. Still, Williams felt a little
guilty for having goaded him. He had been respond-

ing to an impatience in Berry's voice—stronger than usual—and it had nothing to do with the plane crash. The minds of every functionary in Washington—including Berry, and including the NRO—were focused on finding employment. Midkiff had been president for two terms and his party was voted out of office less than a week before. Like every president-elect, Pennsylvania Governor John Wright would be bringing in his own people.

Berry himself would be unemployed in less than seven weeks and Williams couldn't help but wonder if the new Op-Center had been set up partly so Williams could hire the soon-to-be-ex–deputy chief of staff.

Not that I would mind giving him this desk and going back out with Black Wasp, he thought. As dangerous as that mission had been, it had the qualities of challenge and purpose that had first drawn him to a military career.

Pouring black coffee from his thermos, Williams opened the door and went back to work. He did not go to the linked databases of the organizations that had already reported in. Instead, he went to the daily reports filed by U.S. Geological Survey. Despite Berry's assurances, he looked for seismic activity that might indicate nuclear tests anywhere along the air currents near the plane.

There was nothing.

Williams next went to the weekly updates from the National Oceanic and Atmospheric Administration. Winds crossing the airliner's path at 35,000 feet would have been the Cape Horn Current, the Antarctic Circumpolar Current, and the Falkland Current—westerlies just after takeoff, easterlies when they went down. There were nuclear power plants along all three, from South Africa to the Falklands.

"The path is right, and there's enough distance for radioactivity to rise," he thought aloud.

Assuming, of course, there had been a leak.

He went to the U.S. Atomic Energy Commission alerts. There were notes beside every power plant on the planet. There were no reports of difficulty at any plant along those southerly currents.

That was it for the nuclear option.

He went back to the USGS file. His geology training consisted of a single semester as an undergrad at Tufts, but he remembered that the region was volcanic and that volcanoes released a variety of gases into the atmosphere.

"Maybe a quick, freak incident jetted—what, methane?—into the air? It got sucked in by the engines?"

There was no volcanic activity anywhere that fit with the atmospheric patterns. He accessed NASA's Autonomous Sciencecraft Experiment, which circles the Earth taking tens of thousands of images. After each orbit, the artificial intelligence program on Earth analyzed those images, compared them to the previous pass, and created streams of data concerning observational changes.

This morning, the ASE had spotted an "anomaly" on Prince Edward Island—about three hours before the jetliner would have been taking off from Johannesburg.

He clicked the link to a satellite image. It showed a white dot on the northern side of the island, no explanation. It clearly was not an eruption of some kind.

"What the hell is a white dot?"

Williams went through an up-to-the-minute file from the space agency's Earth Polychromatic Imaging Camera, which failed to show a similar anomaly. He then went to the databases of other land-scanning satellites and found no corroborating or explanatory information. He went back one day, two days—there were no obvious "traumatic events," as they were classified, such as a rock fall, a chunk of space debris striking land or water in the region, or Chinese artillery tests—though he did see a handful of boats near the coast in DNI surveillance, none of them anchored at the nearest natural harbor. He grabbed and saved those images, sent them to Berry for analysis. If the Chinese or Russians were using fishing boats or science vessels as fronts down there it was something worth noting.

But it did not help the current investigation.

This process reminded him of the poker games he used to play with Op-Center's senior staff. Whenever intelligence director Roger McCord had the deal, he would offer a running commentary.

"No help there . . . busted . . . denied. . . ."

The imaginary McCord was right. This wasn't solving the problem of the crash. That was when he came up with a better idea.

Looking at the time on his phone, Williams searched for a contact and then punched the phone icon.

CHAPTER THREE

November 11, 2:46 P.M., South Africa Standard Time

Van Tonder and Mabuza were nearly above the wreckage. The pilot took them higher to avoid a choking stall from the smoke. Van Tonder reached for the binoculars in the side storage compartment.

"Michael, check any updates from the GSSA," the commander said. "We'll look at it when we get back."

"Will do, sir," Sisula replied.

The Geological Society of South Africa provided daily satellite reports of all seismic activity in the region. Both islands were of volcanic origin, and Marion was one of the peaks of an underwater shield volcano. That was one reason van Tonder hadn't given the fisherman's report much attention. Thermal venting in the region was not uncommon.

But not reaching 35,000 feet, van Tonder thought as Mabuza hovered above the blowing smoke and van Tonder raised the binoculars to study the parts of the wreckage that weren't obscured by the churning black clouds.

The aircraft's disjointed, shattered remains were an abstract caricature of something functional. The commander saw at once that nothing moved—except to collapse or pop, like a seat he saw burst and spew melted foam droplets into the air.

There was a brittle, blackened corpse still belted to the chair. It startled both men by jerking when the cushion exploded. Another lay on the ground nearby, curled tightly in a fetal position—either due to rigor mortis or some effort to protect itself, he imagined.

"I don't know if you can see," van Tonder said to the pilot. "The remains I'm looking at are burned but otherwise proportional and intact. Does that tell you anything?"

"Yes, sir," he said. "Decompression at that height would likely have burst a lung. Also, do you see anything stuck in the bodies? You know—cutlery, personal devices, any flying debris?"

"Nothing. Why?"

"That also would have happened if there were a hole in the aircraft, sudden decompression—either from a bomb or a collision."

"I have my doubts, but you mentioned that report from the fisherman—"

"I know, but volcanic gas at that height and intensity that the big boy geologists missed?" Mabuza shook his head. "Unless it was a major eruption—and we surely would have heard and seen that—effective contamination would have disbursed well below the jet's cruising altitude. If it were a heat plume, the air would have cooled it sufficiently to prevent damage."

"That's all I can think of," van Tonder said. "Do you have any theories? Any at all?"

"Not a one," the pilot admitted.

The men continued to scan the site, looking for some detail they might have missed—even a hole punched by a meteor.

"Do you want to go down?" Mabuza asked.

"No. We'll wait for the fires to die a little so we can go lower. What I want to do is head over to Prince Edward. Let's have a look at that vent, see if there's anything to it. Mike?"

"Still here," he said.

"Are you getting the video feed?"

"I am."

"Jump in if you notice anything or if Simon needs another flyover."

"Yes, sir."

Steering the helicopter to the northeast, toward the Southern Indian Ocean and into a black wall of night, Mabuza programmed the GPS for the thirty-mile trip.

The sailors who first braved these waters in the middle seventeenth century had a name for the wind that blew here. They called it "Hell's Bellows." Whether the air was cold or colder, it blew like something infernal. Along with the sound of the rotors, the wind pushed a steady howl as well as tangible pressure against the cushioned headset.

Mabuza was a fine helicopter pilot. The Cape Town

native had joined the navy instead of the air force because there was less of a waiting line to fly the hot, new helicopters, of which the Rooivalk was one. He had quickly adapted to the unforgiving conditions of the southern polar region. But even he was having trouble keeping the aircraft steady in the eastward-buffeting fifty-mile-an-hour winds of the Subantarctic Front.

Fortunately, the journey to Prince Edward was a short quarter hour. The night was clear, and well before they arrived the men picked out their target: a faint, eerie glow rising from the northern coastline, visible only because it rippled the air behind it. They could not see the point of penetration, only a gossamer ribbon suspended above.

"Never seen anything like that," Mabuza remarked. "Like a sliver of the aurora stuck in the sky. In daytime."

It was an apt description. The light was a pale, yellowish strand with a similar translucence.

"You've still got the spotlight on," van Tonder said suddenly. "Kill it."

The pilot switched it off. The glow vanished.

"Incredible!" Mabuza remarked. "Whatever we saw was not burning on its own."

"That rules out magma, hot gas, or vapor hot enough to self-illuminate," the commander said.

"What we saw also doesn't tell us how high it goes, because it was beyond the light," Mabuza said.

"Invisible gas—methane? Carbon monoxide? I'm at a loss."

"Sir, even if it reached all the way to the plane—that doesn't make sense," the pilot said. "We're just twenty-seven miles from where the jet went down. It would have had to drop straight down over the iridescence to hit where it did. That didn't happen."

The pilot switched the spotlight back on. The faint column returned, like a ghost. The men approached in silence until Mabuza coughed.

"You all right?" van Tonder asked absently.

"Throat tickles suddenly."

"Commander!" It was Sisula, urgently on the radio.

"Yes, Mike?"

"Turn back!" he said firmly. "Turn back *now*!"

Van Tonder had learned to trust these men completely. "Do it, Tito," the officer said.

The pilot swung the helicopter south as he tried to clear his throat.

"What's going on, Mike?" the commander asked.

"Simon says the plane passengers apparently came down with some kind of coughing or reflux condition that killed them in minutes," Sisula said.

"Jesus," van Tonder said.

As he spoke, the commander reached around to the medical locker. He threw open the lid, drew out a mask, and put it on. There was a portable oxygen container inside the locker. He took that out for the pilot.

"Commander—" Mabuza rasped. "I'm sorry. I . . . I have to set down."

"Understood," van Tonder said. "Mike? Inform Simon we're landing on Edward. Tell them why."

"Yes, sir."

"Also inform them that I'm putting the lieutenant on oxygen to see if that helps." As he spoke, van Tonder pulled the mask over the pilot's head and turned on the flow of air.

The helicopter wobbled as Mabuza inhaled deeply then coughed into the plastic mask. There were faint spots of blood.

Rallying, the pilot did not bother searching for a landing spot. The bulging mask created a blind spot. Using the altimeter, he simply descended to whatever ground was some fifty feet below.

The helicopter landed hard but evenly and Mabuza immediately throttled down.

"Don't shut down," van Tonder said. The glow of the cockpit illuminated tall grasses around them. The wind was blowing northeast—away from the door.

"How does your throat feel?" van Tonder asked.

"Not . . . worse . . ." he gasped.

Van Tonder patted the man on the arm. "Mike? Tell Simon that there's some kind of—an infection, an abrasive mineral, something that is apparently coming from the pit. It hasn't hit me. I'm using the—what is it, N99 high-filtration breathing mask. It may be enough to keep out whatever this is. I suggest they put all resources into finding out whether this is a natural event or a drilling. If someone was here, they better find whatever they may have taken with them."

"At once, Commander," the ensign replied.

"Oh, Mike? I also suggest they keep aircraft off that

route," van Tonder added. "In case this hasn't played out."

Sisula acknowledged and van Tonder turned to the pilot.

"I still tickle but I don't feel like coughing," Mabuza said.

"Good man." He looked at the illuminated digital instruments. "We've got—an hour of air there and if we just sit here and idle we've got that same hour before we have to go back. You okay with the heat on?"

The pilot nodded. "Feels good. But . . . no chills. Not flu-like."

"You got that, Mike?"

"Yeah."

Van Tonder gave the pilot another reassuring clap on the arm, then looked out at the dark ocean.

Even as a navy seaman, he had never had to face death. Not directly.

Not until now. It scared him to consider how close he and Mabuza had come to dying. Just a few yards in either direction, including up or down—

And they still had no idea what this affliction was just a few dozen yards distant. Not its shape or, if alive, its life span, how far it had already traveled and what vehicle—or city—it might strike next.

CHAPTER FOUR

After a long career in the military, Williams learned that when you were not in a position to give orders you had to be affable. Not that he was ever unfriendly. A high-ranking officer was supposed to be decisive and that did not always make him popular.

But there was a quick learning curve after Williams replaced the ailing Paul Hood as the director of Op-Center. The former banker and mayor of Los Angeles was such a skilled bureaucrat that he offended no one and rightly earned the nickname "Pope Paul."

Williams had agreed to take the job and deal with highly sensitive matters, not knowing those matters would as often as not be age, gender, race, sexual orientation, and an aggressively suspicious human resources department.

He liked it better when subordinates in uniform were treated equally regardless of any consideration.

He wondered, more than once, how HR would deal with an organization that had just one employee.

However, that on-the-job training had paid off this morning when he contacted his alma mater. Using what charm he could muster, he persuaded the alumni director at Tufts to hook him up with a professor he had found on the university Web site: the chair of the Department of Earth and Ocean Sciences, Professor Jeanette Goodman, a sedimentologist. His self-respect took a broadside to effectively go begging, and so did his wallet in the form of extortion—an overdue donation to the school. But he got the professor's private number. A direct question-and-answer would not only save hours of scouring government and public Web sites, collating information, it would prevent his leaving a digital footprint. In a building full of spies, one took reasonable precautions.

Williams vaguely introduced himself as a counter-terrorism specialist with the government and said he was investigating the crash of the South African airliner.

"A horrible event but a turbulent, active environment unless you know it," she said in a raspy voice that sounded like it had inhaled decades of rock dust.

"How so?" Williams asked.

"The upper-atmosphere crosscurrents," Goodman replied. "The potential for a sudden deep freeze."

"What about the geology of the Prince Edward Islands in the Indian Ocean?" Williams asked.

"Ah—I've been to the islands several times. What would you like to know?"

"To begin with, is the area geologically active?"

"Very much so," she said. "Not in the way, say, Hawaii is strewn with volcanoes but closer to the Pacific Northwest or Alaska in terms of tremors."

"We were wondering if there might be a connection between the missing airliner and satellite images showing what appears to be geologic activity in that region prior to the event."

"What kind of activity?"

"We don't know," Williams said. "Light from fissures."

"Not today, no," she replied. "There have been no major eruptions there. That's the first thing I do when I wake. I check the USGS update. If there were something major, then, as you probably know, all airlines would have been barred from the region immediately."

"What about—I don't know. A thermal vent? A geyser of some kind? The image I saw clearly indicates a glow, column-like, that wasn't present in previous images."

"Without seeing the image, I cannot say. In that region it would be a 'white smoker,'" she said. "Very low temperature, remote from the heat source, generally sending up plumes laced with calcium, silicon, other local minerals. Nontoxic at those concentrations, I might add. But I assure you there is nothing of that kind able to reach more than, say, one thousand, maybe fifteen hundred feet. And even that would be increasingly diluted by atmospheric currents."

"I see," Williams said. It sounded very much like a dead end. "Would it glow?"

"Dimly, perhaps. As I said, the heat source would not be near the surface. What about a meteor strike?" Goodman asked.

"I would think the odds are pretty slim, no?"

"Not really," Goodman said. "That is a historically active area. The minerals and organic material date back three hundred million years, with a high percentage of it of extraterrestrial origin, including fragments from the moon and Mars."

"You're serious?" he said.

"Entirely."

Williams was writing everything down on a yellow pad, making sure he highlighted key words. He did not know why he was bothering: Matt Berry would dismiss every word of this, and perhaps rightly so.

"Where are you located, Mr. Williams?"

"Washington, D.C."

"There's quite a collection of planetary specimens at the Smithsonian. An object of that kind, traveling at a high rate of speed, would not have to be larger than a walnut to cripple an aircraft."

"Also, you said organic," Williams said, looking at a word he had underlined. "Microbes?"

"Potentially. Many microbes are dormant in the cold, so something like that would definitely liven things up. Not my field, though there is a belief that microbes, in particular from Mars, may have come to Earth on rock blasted from the surface of the Red Planet. Some would have been hardy enough to survive the journey through the cold vacuum of space. *We* may be Martians, Mr. Williams."

"I see." Williams could not help but reflect, briefly, on just how much information he picked up in this job for which he had no further use. That idea was not something he was keen to share with Matt Berry. "What about the glow," he said. "If not this 'white smoke,' what then?"

"Sunlight reflected on ice? Airborne chlorine?"

"The bleach ingredient? Isn't that toxic?"

"Not in this state," she said. "What you're talking about is—the lye it's combined with is caustic to the throat and skin, and chlorine creates a deadly gas when mixed with ammonia. Straight from the ground there's no risk."

"Why would it glow?" Williams said.

"Presume a rockslide or, more likely, melting ice," Goodman said. "That might expose an ancient rock surface and millennia of deep, deep cracking. A natural gas pocket might be breached and release helium, which rises."

"Helium," Williams said. "The balloon gas."

"Correct. There are also vapors that glow yellow in light but they would not be occurring naturally."

"Such as?"

"Certain kinds of acids. I'm not a chemist—"

"No, of course. Battery acids or something purer?"

"Purer. Your average Subaru would not be responsible for that kind of luminescence."

But a submarine might, Williams thought.

Goodman went on, expanding on every idea as if she were enthusiastically lecturing a freshman class.

"In that region," she said, "the helium would likely

pass through densely packed salt layers, eroded halite. If the event is close to the waterline, the exposed salt would quickly dissolve in seawater. The result—sodium chloride gas, or chlorine. Both gases rise, appearing yellow-green in sunlight or moonlight due to the chlorine. That could explain the glow. And there's no limit to how high in the atmosphere the helium would push the chlorine."

"How would that affect the jet?" Williams asked.

"I have no idea," Goodman admitted. "You asked for a possible phenomenon to explain a glow."

"I did," Williams replied, his mouth twisting. *You've got to love academics,* he thought. The woman's open delight was exceeded only by its failure to solve Williams's problem.

He thanked the woman for her time and hung up. He looked at the scramble of words on his pad. The words "microbe" and "helium" had ended up one on top of the other. He laughed.

"Yeah," he said. "I don't think I'll mention that to Matt."

The phone pinged. It was Berry.

"We've got another one," he said gravely and without preamble.

"A plane?"

"No, worse," he replied. "Sea level. I'm patching you into the live DNI intercept."

Berry hung up. The deputy chief of staff was not just in a hurry, he sounded uncommonly alarmed.

Williams put on his headset and, a moment later, he was listening to the feed from the Department of Naval Intelligence. The file on his computer was stamped "Open Distress Call via the USS *Carl Vinson* in the Indian Ocean." The voices he heard were Afrikaner. The man who was speaking was soft-spoken, almost serene.

The man who came on after him was not.

Johan Krog was locked by deadbolt into the tiny radio room of the 230-foot Lürssen shipyard yacht. He was trembling from fear and from the cold. The heating system was failing and he was naked save for his thermal underwear. Every other item of clothing was presently in use. He had closed the door, hard, with his trousers between the side of the door and the frame. His undershirt was on the top, creating what he hoped was an airtight seal. He had shoved his white sweatshirt, hard, along the small space at the bottom of the door. He bolted the door shut. Then, using a pair of scissors, he had cut himself a small face mask from the sleeve.

Krog did not know what had caused everyone else in the sleek, modern vessel to cough up blood and drop to the floor, and he did not care to find out. He had been nodding at his post in the radio room when he heard the cries and moans, had woken and poked his head out to see what was amiss. When he found his friend and relief radioman Quentin Botha white-faced and throwing up gore in the corridor, a few steps from the radio room, he closed and jammed the door shut. He immediately contacted Claude Foster at his company office in East London, northeast of Johannesburg.

"Have you seen Katinka?" Foster asked after listening to the disjointed account. "She is not answering texts."

"No," Krog replied. "And, boss, don't ask me to go and have a chat with her. She's probably dead!"

"Then—just so I understand—let me review the timetable," Foster said. "You arrived at the destination at 8:22 P.M. local time, two days ago, and an expedition team was dispatched, by raft."

"Yes—*Jesus,* I'm gonna *die* here!"

"People die when they lose their wits," Foster snapped. "You have to stay calm and *we* have to understand. Can you do that?"

"I'll try. I'm scared!"

"Quiet—"

"I liked our other trips better!"

"Be quiet and *listen*!" Foster yelled. "You did what you were supposed to do, yes?"

"We did. Over two days. That part—"

"Quiet! Just answer questions. You said the team worked for approximately ninety minutes each time. Three samples each site. This was done along the northern headland, as planned."

"Yes."

"Tell me again what happened after that. You weren't making it clear."

"I'm not *clear* because I'm bloody *scared*!" Krog shouted. "Okay, calm, calm," he cautioned himself. "The team reported a faint glow coming from the final site. First they thought it was the sunset off the water. But then the sun set and it was still there."

"A dull column of light," Foster said.

"Yah."

"They returned on the dinghy with the others, and the vessel departed. Six samples were opened yesterday after the boat was underway. There were three more left for today. Sometime thereafter—you don't state exactly when, because you were at your post listening to naval traffic, you say—"

"It was after that plane crash I heard talked about. I wanted to find out more!"

"All right, after midnight a 'strange affliction' began striking crewmembers. Your relief man was pale and gasping and regurgitating blood—"

"He didn't *regurgitate*," Krog declared. "He was spewing out his guts is what it was, just a few feet away! I swear, I never seen a thing like it!"

"And then he was silent, everyone was silent, within minutes," Foster said. "Crewmen who were still ambulatory retreated quickly to secure areas—"

"No, sir, judging from their shouts and footsteps they *ran!*"

"—and the ship is drifting."

"Yassir," Krog replied. "I'm assuming we haven't got a pilot anymore. Or a captain."

"Johan," Foster said, "I want to be very sure of something. The, uh—the science crew did not perhaps find something that made it desirable to dispose of the other men aboard? Maybe three or four of you turned on the others?"

"*A lie!* And sir, I don't want nothing except to live!"

"All right, then," Foster said. "If something happened, and if we are to send a boat to assist you, we have to determine what it was. Which means you have to find out for us."

"Sir, if I leave this room I will suffer what the others did," Krog protested. "You've got to bring me a breathing mask, something to protect me. And gloves, in case they all touched something. I just don't know what's going on!"

There was muted conversation on Foster's end—and coughing from the corridor of the yacht.

"Do you hear that?" Krog asked with alarm.

"What?"

Krog's heart was beating fast. It drummed harder when he heard the heavy footsteps outside the door, which was to his left. That sound was followed by someone turning the knob.

"Who's out there?" Krog yelled.

The answer was not a voice but a gurgling sound. It was followed by a thump. Then, as Krog watched wide-eyed, the white fabric of his sweater, under the door, began to turn a seeping, crawling expanse of red.

The radioman breathed heavily into his improvised mask. The rubber band he had used to hold it in place snapped. Gasping, the radio operator slapped a hand on the fabric to hold it in place.

"What is happening?" Foster asked.

"Crewmen are still dying!" he cried. "There is blood coming in under the door!"

"Johan, do not panic—stay exactly where you are."

"So damn *scared*!" he said and moved the swivel chair up against the wall to his right. Suddenly, he coughed into the sleeve in front of his mouth.

"Aw Jesus, no . . ."

Krog froze, but only for a moment. He coughed again, then doubled over and threw up into the cloth.

"Sir . . . my *stomach* . . . !" he gasped. *"It burns!"*

The seaman threw away the sleeve, which was soaked with stomach acid and blood. He returned to the phone then hacked hard once again, falling over the shelf that held the radio console. Dark red blood spilled from the sides of his mouth with small flecks of internal tissue bulging from the pool.

A final cough filled his throat with a mass that burst from his mouth, onto his bare chest, then cascaded down between his legs. A moment later, the radio operator slid from the slickened seat to the floor, where he suffocated.

"Johan?" a voice said over the radio. "Johan, are you there?"

Foster waited. Then he terminated the call.

Chase Williams sat for a long moment with the headset on, thick silence in his ears. He wondered who these men were.

They had to know they were on an open line but did not seem to care, Williams thought. They had only used first names. That would not tell an eavesdropper much. Most likely veterans at some illegal game—smugglers or pirates, perhaps.

Their identity was not Williams's immediate concern. He was sure Department of Naval Intelligence would be on top of that. He was suddenly very fearful about the cause. The talk with Dr. Goodman no longer seemed so theoretical.

The jetliner had been in the sky. The boat had been at sea—35,000 feet below but in the same general geographical region. Whatever had happened killed easily, and quickly, in both places.

A core sample. He thought back to the conversation from the doomed vessel.

The spitballing conversation with Dr. Goodman suddenly took on significance. Something *taken* from that site had been brought to the ship and spread—by air. Something still *at* that site had at least the theoretical means to rise into the atmosphere and be drawn into a jet the only way possible—through engine intake. That air is shared with the ventilation system.

The phone beeped.

"Ever hear anything like that?" Berry asked.

"Actually, I have," Williams told him. "In old films of decompression tests of high-altitude flight suits. But those were at sixty-five thousand feet coming on an hour. Submarine simulations at never-exceed depth might produce that kind of response."

"Which leaves us with nothing."

"Not entirely," Williams said. "They were a seasoned team, whatever they were doing, with a hierarchy. You're checking satellite photos for boats?"

"We are now. But it's the South Indian Ocean. There's a lot of shipping. We'll filter by proximity and those known to have dinghies—which will also be a lot. Seems like it's got to tie in with the plane, but *how*?"

"A local Earth event perhaps."

"What do you mean?" Berry asked.

"There was a NASA report about ground glow close to the flight path, so I called a sedimentologist at my alma mater," Williams said.

"Sediment? As in a doctor of *dirt*?"

"That's right."

"C'mon, Chase—"

"Matt, I'm looking for answers too, so just hear me out," Williams said.

"Sure. Sorry. Got to look under every rock."

Williams let the dig pass. "Dr. Goodman told me that the island is made of ancient stone and organic matter, including meteors from the moon and Mars—"

"Oh, Christ," Berry said. "I need something solid and you give me ETs? I'm checking those boat-grabs you sent me but Harward's on the warpath protecting Midkiff's legacy. Don't ask me to sell them space germs—"

"Okay, forget that part for now. Let's just say it's a bug that's airborne and instantly fatal. Goodman said a lot of the substrata in that island group has been locked in tight for up to a couple hundred million years. No living species would have seen anything like it. And hell, let's *not* forget outer space. Now that I think of it, we quarantined our moon walkers when they came back to Earth in case they were contaminated—"

"And they weren't," Berry said.

"Fine, but reasonable scientists were concerned about the possibility, and we should be too. Because if something *is* loose, something that was hibernating in the cold—"

"Yeah, we already know the rest."

"It's also something that rose thirty-five thousand feet on what Goodman thinks may be helium gas, and it may still be following the currents in our upper atmosphere."

"Hewlett already informed the Federal Aviation Administration to reroute aircraft."

Abraham Hewlett was the secretary of Homeland Security, a highly influential advisor to the president.

"I'm assuming we weren't the only ones listening to that distress call?" Williams said.

"Very unlikely."

"So we should probably be talking with the Russians and the Chinese to contain whatever it is. That includes the crash site, when we know where that is."

Berry sighed. "The secretary of state called from Japan and urged caution on that, and Midkiff agrees."

"Because?"

"You understand that not everyone will want to kill the thing," Berry said. "Dr. Rajini also pointed out that many microbes cannot survive for very long without a host."

Dr. Shahrukh Rajini was the president's science advisor. Williams liked her. She put facts before politics in both senses of the phrase.

"Bottom line, we're going to let that play out," Berry

said. "The *Vinson* has a fix, and so, we guess, do the Russian and Chinese ships in the region. And by the way, the navy is not rushing in, and I don't think anyone else will either."

"I suppose that's wise, if not solution-oriented."

"I said 'rushing,'" Berry said.

"Meaning?" Williams asked.

"This could affect you," Berry said unhappily. "If you and the two doctors are right, and this is a virus or bacteria, we are going to want a sample."

CHAPTER FIVE

November 11, 3:21 P.M., South Africa Standard Time

It was either by divine providence or accident that Katinka Kettle had survived.

Possibly both.

The twenty-five-year-old gemologist—"our special guest," Foster respectfully called her when sending her on these journeys—was not a devout Pentecostal. Her mother had been and her father was somewhat, enough so that she believed in God and Jesus Christ and that she belonged to their holy family. So maybe those great, benign, salvaging figures had a hand in this.

But there was also the possibility that it was dumb luck. Katinka had intended to wear an ordinary surgical mask while examining the first of the three core samples she had collected from Ship Rock on Prince Edward Island. That was how she typically worked with Claude Foster and his Mineral Exploration and Acquisition Survey Enterprises. In most cases, MEASE went—without permission—to protected public lands in search of small supplies of diamonds. Typically, the yield was small but worth harvesting for markets that were not big cities or resorts. These would be extracted in darkness, in rain or dust storms, under conditions when no one was likely to notice them. If gems were discovered, either officials were bribed or clandestine digs were executed at night with armed security. These geographically separated teams were former members of death squads who had killed anti-apartheid activists and dissidents. The crew of the *Teri Wheel* had been comprised of several of these people. Adanna had been the worst of them. She had wanted to shoot the patrol helicopter and its black pilot down instead of hiding.

"No one will find out it was us and maybe they won't even bother looking," she had said.

Katinka had learned to operate every van, jeep, dinghy, autogyro, and small plane they had traveled in. Just to be sure she could get away from them in the event of a general mutiny. The team members were, nearly to a one, sociopaths. The sole exception was her lover Dawid, who worked as a security supervisor for the Pebble-Holmes Diamond Consortium of Durban. He was the one who fed them information about potential mining sites. He was now the director of a former prison that had been converted into a museum of apartheid-era atrocities. It provided a perfect cover for his other activities.

Katinka had done calculations on her own. Foster found and discovered a sufficient number of diamonds every year to pay very handsomely, in cash, but probably not enough to afford and maintain a fleet of exotic search vehicles including a helicopter, a jet—and this fifty-eight-foot-long yacht. From snippets of talk she had heard at his East London headquarters and among the various teams, she suspected that he was involved in other illegal operations, including arms smuggling. It was not to say whether he was right or wrong. To the north, in Mozambique, the National Resistance rebels were no more or less bloody than the government forces that committed random executions and rapes. Their actions caused a massive refugee crisis in neighboring Malawi.

No one was clean.

Foster's other activities were not her concern and, since she knew little about them, they did not bother her. She liked her life and her lifestyle. She also liked her prospects. They depended entirely on her skill and determination.

And she liked Claude Foster. She admired, even envied his confidence, respected and trusted his sharp intuition. It was a barometer that had never failed them, not in any major way. He was creative in that way, an artist.

The fieldwork Katinka did, sometimes in a van, sometimes in a tent, occasionally at sea, was fairly straightforward. Scientifically, it was similar to the prospecting she had done with the University of South Africa to obtain her master's degree. Rock samples or mineral cores were examined and diamonds, sapphires, and rubies were either found or not.

The difference was that her work then was legal. Her work here was not. But growing up poor in Cape Town, she had learned at a young age that poverty was for someone else. She had pursued this career because scientists who worked with gemstones were guaranteed a good living. Scientists who did so without the oversight of the Department of Public Enterprises became wealthy.

Katinka Kettle wanted to be rich. Every time she went on a new sampling mission for Foster, the prospect of a big strike was always there. And when she returned, she always felt closer to her employer. He, too, longed for bigger and bigger strikes; hoping ultimately, as he often told her, "the biggest." He praised her work, he seemed to respect her, and she found in him the strength to overcome her own innately timid nature.

She had dreamed about that after taking a long sleep after the expedition. Prince Edward Island, at night, in the cold and wind, was not conducive to comfort. The earth had been hard and progress with fluorosulfuric acid and the hand-turned auger had been miserably slow. She had done the drilling herself: masked against the dust as always, like the other members of the party, she judged the ground as much by what she felt through the metal-and-wood tool as by what she saw in the dim, dim light.

Tonight, after resting, she had gone to her station, taken a clean lab coat from the locker, and sat on a stool beside the small worktable. When she removed the plastic, non-rotating core from the steel housing, Katinka saw a great deal of very fine powdered halite—more than she had expected. The mineral was undoubtedly crushed ages before by the movement of ice or by tectonic activity, perhaps both. Even this finely granular in a wind-battered environment, the particles were held firmly in place by the frozen ground.

That was the reason she'd used the half-mask respirator before transferring the materials to the portable crush cell apparatus for analysis. She was actually grateful for the sound of her own breathing in her ears. It drowned out the often raucous activities of six of the other eleven persons onboard. The remaining five crew members were sober-tempered members of the security team. They rarely smiled, let alone partied.

"And now they're dead," she said to herself. Talking aloud was a habit she had acquired working alone in the field. Her father once said she enjoyed the company. He should know. He did the same thing fixing cars.

Katinka had heard the first loud cries over her breathing apparatus. Her first thought was that the South African Navy had boarded them. She replaced the core in the container and sealed it. Then she moved to a small electronic panel at the right side of the table, just beneath a porthole. In that eventuality, she had a standing order from Foster to destroy the contents of the lab. That would be accomplished by activating a chute in the lab table that opened directly into the hull and the sea. After showing her how it worked, Foster joked, "Only dead bodies float."

After a few moments it became clear to the woman that the sounds were pain, not panic. Moving tentatively, and slowly undoing the elastic strap of her mask as she walked, Katinka left the small white room with its bright fluorescent lights and went to the darker wood-paneled corridor to see what was going on. She stopped sharply and froze, startled to see a body clawing toward her on the carpet. It was Adanna, one of the security team members. The woman's wide, strong face was contorted into something pinched and sallow, the mouth leaving behind a slime-like trail of brownish blood. Adanna crawled over the fluid, smearing the trail. She was apparently headed for the infirmary in the next room over, her wide eyes moving up toward the gemologist, searching for assistance.

Katinka stopped fussing with the mask strap. She pulled it tight again and thrust her arms straight down by her side, away from the mask. She looked from Adanna to her left. Their medic, "The Major," who formerly served with the Seventh Medical Battalion Group of the South African Military Health Service, was lying faceup, his chest covered in red. A medical mask was clutched in his hand.

The infirmary and the lab shared ventilation systems with the rest of the ship. But the air moved from fore to aft—from her station to his.

Katinka's breath came more rapidly, fearfully. Over

it she could hear the cries of others. She followed the sounds, stepping around Adanna, and saw five members of the crew in the large galley. All were dead or dying, sprawled wherever their knees had given out. Blood and chunks of viscera everywhere upon and around them. In the rear of the yacht, the relief radioman, Botha, lay sprawled in a ghastly puddle.

She noticed, then, that the boat had slowed.

"No, I don't hear the engines," she muttered. "It's drifting."

There was no point going to the bridge. Whatever this was must have reached there. Captain Van Rooyen was a careful man. As soon as a problem arose, he would have ordered the *Teri Wheel*—named for his wife—to stop and gone to investigate.

She thought she heard a voice in the radio room, but there was no reason to stay. Something deadly was about and only her mask had protected her.

But from what?

Whatever it was, she did not want to risk the mask failing. It had fine-particle filtration but she was still breathing the ship's air.

Adanna managed to push off the floor and get to her knees. Blood ran in a steady flow over her lower lip as she went thumping down the hallway, toward the sound of the voice—Johan Krog, most likely. He would be calling Foster.

Until he, too, was dead.

Katinka returned to the lab and shut the door. As much as possible, she wanted to block the sounds and sights of a miserable death. She had to think.

Everyone had been masked at the island, but not here. The drilling had uncovered something lethal and the core she had opened was the likely source. It was not a gas. Nothing that concentrated could spread so far. Radiation would have killed her as well. It had to be biological.

She stood at her lab table trying to grasp the enormity of what had happened. They had come here for diamonds. They had found something more valuable than that. Instant, invisible mass murder. And only she and Foster knew where it came from.

First, she had to cover their route, their deeds, completely. Then she had to get to East London with the samples.

Katinka took a portable burner from the table. Usually, she used it to identify unknown minerals, grinding them with a mortar and pestle, exposing them to the burner, and examining the color of the flame. Now, she took a beaker and filled it with chlorine trifluoride. When exposed to fire, the chemical would destroy the glass and ignite everything it touched.

The woman pulled her personal backpack from under the lab table. She did not want to go to her cabin for her coat, and donned a sweatshirt she kept in a locker. Placing the core samples inside, Katinka slung the bag over one shoulder. Then she turned the burner on its side, lit the flame, and set the ClF_3 two inches beyond.

She had about five minutes before the chemical heated sufficiently to break the beaker.

Running through the corridor, careful not to skid

on the wide puddle of Botha's blood, the gemologist made her way to the stairs and up to the main deck. The motorized dinghy was moored astern. Katinka knew how to work the dinghy, though she did not know how far it would take her—or how long it would take to get home. All she knew was that she had to get off the *Teri Wheel*. She would contact Foster once she was away.

For that purpose, there was the autogyro. Parked at the wide stern, the swift, tiny craft was used by the captain to pay quick visits to Foster when it was too risky for anything but face-to-face contact—or when he had to deliver the occasional strike of uncut gems. Big ones, not dust. Katinka's fear of the crew had paid off since she knew how to fly the craft.

The curtains in the galley were drawn, no light emerging, and Katinka had to negotiate the deck largely by feel. She started to fear that she would not get away in time. The coated wood under her feet was slick with sea and the winds were pushing against her.

Finally reaching the pushpit railing, Katinka ran to the autogyro and started it up. Her breath was coming fast again. She saw a dull orange light blossom across the sea on the portside of the yacht.

The fire had begun.

The autogyro had a two-minute start-up time. She checked the compass as the two rotors began to turn, one above and one pinned to the back of the cockpit, forward the tail section. Above all things, she did not want to go back to Prince Edward. Not if whatever this was had started there and was still loose.

"Northwest," she said aloud, forcing herself to focus as she watched the digital needle.

The woman settled into the seat and, her palms cold and slippery, she lifted off from the deck. Less than five minutes later the arrowhead-shaped red vessel was zipping low across the ruddy, restless water, away from the *Teri Wheel*.

Then, with an enormous, puffball flash that was sure to be seen in Port Elizabeth, the yacht exploded. The sound and shock wave reached her moments later, rocking the aircraft and even warming the cabin with its ferocious heat.

But she had survived.

Katinka flew on at an aggressive speed, hoping the flame and heat had destroyed any biology that was alive onboard. If any had survived on the smoke, it would likely be borne aloft and not toward any population centers.

Again, she thought of the plane crash. She flicked on her smartphone and looked at the news.

There it was, the only headline. A commercial jetliner had gone down, cause unknown, no cries of distress, no hint of danger—

Sweet Lord Jesus.

If there had been a cause and effect, Katinka felt no guilt. The Earth, its bounty and its dangers, its riches and its poisons, were not for humans to control or contain. With one exception, everything, even life, was on loan. The exception was the soul, and if she committed a sin against God, she would repent. She did not hold human law to the same standard.

She saw, reflected in the glass dome of the cockpit, flaming pieces of the yacht throw off steam as they returned to the sea. She had survived that too, well beyond the tumbling, burning shards.

It is time, she decided.

With the shoulder bag on the passenger seat, Katinka kept her left hand on the controls, tucked the phone up her left sleeve for now, and put her right hand behind her head. She found the plastic latch on the elastic band.

She felt like she did, once, before stealing a banana from a food stand. That, too, had gone up a sleeve. There had been a moment of fear and hesitation followed by action.

You have to do this, she told herself.

Her fingers pressed the catch and the mask dropped on top of the bag. She inhaled deeply. She smelled the salt air. She did not want to think of death, a *horrible* death, and had resolved only that if she felt sick she would throw herself into the sea and drown.

But she did not cough. She touched her nose, her ears. There was no blood. She tasted none in her throat or mouth.

Looking down at the dark shape of the bag, Katinka Kettle smiled.

She was alive.

Her find, her treasure, was secure. For the first time she had a taste of the kind of self-assurance Foster himself must possess. So much so that one thing more entered her brain.

He did not know how many core samples were taken

from Ship Rock. No one alive did, but her. They were
from the same spot, within inches . . . were identical.
There was no need to turn them all over.

CHAPTER SIX

November 11, 9:05 A.M.

Five people in the Oval Office had been listening to the exchange. They had been gathered around the rectangular conference table, eyes on the black speakerphone, expressions grave as the saga played out.

Only three of those people were present at the moment: President Midkiff, Chief of Staff Trevor Harward, and Angie Brunner. The forty-nine-year-old intellectual property attorney was heading President-elect Wright's transition team and was expected to be his chief of staff. She had been invited to spend several days with the outgoing president.

Angie had not expected to be faced with a crisis, which was the point.

Two other key persons were listening in: Dr. Rajini and Surgeon General Becka Young.

Matt Berry had walked into the chilly Rose Garden to call Williams. Secretary of Homeland Security

Abraham Hewlett had gone to make a call, with permission, in the president's private antechamber. The adjoining office was warmer, but not by much, than the Western Colonnade. The sun only set on the West Wing.

President Midkiff was perched on the corner of his desk, looking down at the silent phone. Finally, he stood and walked toward the table.

"Becka, thoughts?"

"My first reaction is that the symptoms that were described are consistent with radiation poisoning," Surgeon General Young replied. "Sudden, excessive bleeding, nausea and vomiting."

Harward was sitting on the couch with his leg crossed, foot shaking.

"Radiation—from where, Dr. Young?" he asked. "I think if there were a leaking nuclear reactor or submarine in the region, we would have heard about it."

"Matt said he had someone looking at radioactivity in the region regarding the plane crash," the president said.

"Is there evidence that those passengers were also ill?" Dr. Young asked.

"No," the president replied. "Just an angle of a terror investigation. In any case, there have been no official alerts. Shahrukh?"

"I am very concerned about that core sample," Dr. Rajini replied. "Drilling in Antarctica has brought up living microbes from time to time, not all of them familiar to us."

"That's Antarctica," Harward said. "This is the South Indian Ocean."

"Something may have been there since the land masses were joined, or been released by ice melt or calving and drifted," she said.

"The dread Antarctica Strain, plaything of the climate change fanatics," Harward said dismissively.

"Hypothetical does not mean nonexistent," the woman pointed out.

"I want to hear about it, Shahrukh," the president said.

The chief of staff fell silent. He went to work on his laptop.

"It *is* a hypothesis about the potential danger represented by some incredibly hardy, anaerobic infectious agent that is capable of a long dormancy," the science advisor said. "The theory holds that such a microbe may essentially have been freeze-dried in the past and released today, as lethal as ever."

"To infect a brontosaurus, which they will be hard-pressed to find today," Harward said. He read from a file on his laptop. "Mr. President, the white paper *South Polar Core Analysis Microbial Study*, dated January 20, 2020, dismissed as very remote the idea that a germ trapped before there were people on Earth would suddenly emerge to infect people on Earth. The report cited the unlikelihood of a long life in the open atmosphere, without a mechanism to feed or reproduce or whatever microbes do—"

"Exotic problems are always remote until they

happen," Dr. Rajini said. "Over twenty years ago, scientists with NASA's Marshall Space Flight Center found ancient microbes in a core sample from the Russian Vostok base at the South Pole. Neither American nor Russian scientists could dismiss the possibility that unfamiliar germs such as these were capable of cross-species transmission."

"What year was that discovery? Exactly?" Harward asked.

"June 1998," Dr. Rajini replied.

"Right," Harward said. "A period of decreased funding for NASA. Scaremongering is always a solution for that. But all right, Doctor, let's follow that theory. How deep was the Vostok core?"

"Just over four thousand feet," the science advisor replied.

"The better part of a mile," said the national security advisor. "If these clowns we just heard went ashore somewhere and came back an hour and a half later, the sample was probably—what, a few yards at most? Those islands are environmentally protected, I believe. The squatters would have been in a hurry." As he spoke, Harward's fingers flew across his keyboard. "There's a South African naval outpost there doing daily sweeps of the region. No time for deep drilling. Or noisy drilling, for that matter. They may have used a hand-turned auger."

"A sample need not be deep to be potentially deadly," Dr. Rajini said. "Permafrost in polar and even subpolar regions is what we call a 'highly conducive medium.' Microbes like the water and decay."

"The plane was in the air and so was most of that boat," Harward noted.

"Trevor," the president said, "can you suggest an alternative cause?"

"Sir, I'm just devil's advocating so we don't jump to wrong and embarrassing conclusions that waste time."

The president was distracted as Hewlett returned.

"I just spoke with Jim Grand at the FAA," the secretary said. "He wants to restrict American carriers from flying all southern routes that come near the polar easterlies or lower westerlies until we have a handle on this. Mr. President?"

"Reasonable precaution," he said.

Hewlett texted those words exactly to Grand. Berry stepped back indoors just then, blowing on his phone hand to warm it. His thoughts seemed to be stuck outside.

"Matt?" the president asked.

Berry took a moment longer than necessary to make sure the old doors were firmly shut. The president likely knew that Berry had called Williams. Midkiff himself had already told John Wright about Op-Center. The others did not know, nor did they need to. He turned, expressionless, still not sure what he was going to say.

"I was talking with an associate who knows something about the region," Berry said. "He has a feeling that this may be biological in nature."

"Thank you," Berry heard Dr. Rajini say.

From Harward's sour expression, Berry could tell

he had obviously missed something, no doubt one of Harward's contrarian diatribes. The man was a professional skeptic, as befit his years in a foreign policy think tank before becoming an undersecretary at the State Department.

"Is this associate a scientist?" Dr. Young asked.

"A sedimentologist," Berry replied, pleased to say the word as if he had actually heard it prior to five minutes ago.

"I thought you were talking to someone about radiation?" Harward said.

"That came up dry," Berry informed him. "My geologist has some additional thoughts. He, uh—he believes that in addition to releasing helium gas that would have shot into the air, some kind of clandestine drilling could also have released some very old and unknown superbug."

Harward made a face. The president stood over the phone, looking at Berry, but remained silent.

"Mr. Berry," said Dr. Rajini, "did your associate speculate as to the origin of a biological cause?"

"He did," Berry said, hesitating once again. "My source believes that the ancient sediments may contain biological matter from prehistory or, possibly—these are his words, not mine—from space."

"War of the bloody worlds," Harward scoffed predictably.

The president sat stone-faced for a moment, then said, "Doctors?"

"Mr. President, it's fitting that Matt said what he did," Dr. Rajini said. "It's possible that microbes from another world—in a torpid state in the cold vacuum of space—came to Earth on meteors either recently or in prehistory. Or they may be homegrown, prehistoric. It's possible that there are microbes inside the Earth that have not been to the surface in millennia. I'd like to read something I pulled from the shelf. It's an essay written by the Greek historian Thucydides."

"Mr. President, do we have time for *lectures*?" Harward implored. "Dr. Rajini, if you want to talk about bioterror, an Ebola patient, a Typhoid Mary—"

"To find such a one, Mr. Harward, everything must first be put on the table," the doctor said.

"Not when it's a morgue table we're talking about. Lots of them."

Midkiff scowled him to silence. "Go on, Doctor. But do make it brief."

"Yes, sir. Thucydides recounted a plague that struck Athens in the summer of 430 BCE. He called it an 'infernal fever' and wrote, 'The disease descended into the bowels and there produced violent lesions; at the same time diarrhea set in which was uniformly fluid and passed gradually through the whole body.' He goes on to explain in detail how portions of the body literally came apart. This is a famous account, sir, and medical science has not yet found a disease to match what this respected scholar described."

"Nor any corroborating data, I'm guessing," Harward said.

"You're not quite right," Dr. Young contributed. "According to our own geologic database, volcanoes have regularly erupted in the region as far back as one hundred and sixty thousand years ago, and intense earthquake activity there dates back to at least 226 BCE. Any of them could have coughed up ancient microbes."

"This was a *soil* sample, Doctors! Not Mount Vesuvius!" Harward said.

"That's in Italy," Angie Brunner contributed.

Berry was suddenly sorry he had not voted for Wright.

"You know what I'm saying," Harward snapped.

"Let's assume that Matt and the doctors are correct," Midkiff interrupted. "What do we do?"

"Obviously, we have to notify the Centers for Disease Control and Prevention at once," Dr. Young said.

"Agreed. Brief them, Doctor," the president said. He looked over at Hewlett, who had just finished his call. "Everything good?"

"The FAA is acting, but so is the State Civil Aviation Authority in Russia and the Civil Aviation Administration of China. So, sir, are our respective navies."

"So everyone knows," Midkiff said without surprise in his voice.

Trevor checked his laptop to see if the secretary of the navy had filed a command protocol brief. It had just come in, based on intelligence provided by *Carl Vinson*. There was also an urgent request for a meeting from General Paul Broad, chairman of the Joint Chiefs of Staff.

Harward rose and showed Broad's e-mail to the president.

Midkiff nodded and looked at Berry. "Matt, you

and I are going to talk. Everyone else, please give us a few minutes. Doctors, let me know if you hear anything from the medical community, however speculative."

"Yes, Mr. President," the women replied.

Except for Harward pausing to shoot Berry a look of disapproval, the Oval Office was cleared without delay. Midkiff punched off the speakerphone. He sat on the couch. Berry was still standing and the president motioned for him to sit across from him.

The deputy chief of staff sat heavily, found an unused china cup, and poured coffee from a thermal carafe.

"I assume your geologist was someone Chase Williams talked to?"

"At Tufts University, his alma mater."

The president nodded. "I'm not going to bother to talk to the Joint Chiefs about this. I know where they would stand. If this is a bacteria or a virus, someone—no doubt a number of someones—are going to go in and look for samples."

"Sir, to weaponize a thing like that—"

"I know." Midkiff cut him off. "It's insane, not to mention illegal. But God help us, we have to have it, if only to find a cure. Fast. Do you disagree?"

"Not with that particular action under the vaccine and immunogenicity guidelines, sir," Berry said.

"Fair enough. What do you think about giving the acquisition deployment to Black Wasp?"

"They've proven themselves both covert and adaptable," Berry said. He did not add "and expendable," though that would have to factor into the president's thinking. Any branch of the military would gladly undertake a mission like this, but then there would be oversight and accountability.

Midkiff nodded slowly. "Get Williams's people on it ASAP," he said. "We need assets in motion."

"I'll take care of it, sir," Berry said.

The deputy chief of staff took a swallow of coffee and went back out to the Rose Garden. He had no idea what Midkiff would tell Harward, if anything. A president was not required to share all things even with his closest staff. Often, omission served to temper an aide's rhetoric.

With things set in motion, Berry finally had a moment to contemplate everything that had happened. The Oval Office was usually so thoroughly caught up in managing an event that the shock of it never found purchase deeper in the soul.

Now, suddenly, this one did. As he considered the possibility of an instantly fatal airborne contaminant quickly sweeping the globe, Berry was suddenly very afraid.

CHAPTER SEVEN

November 11, 9:14 A.M.

There was a time when Major Hamilton Breen loved his life and every day that comprised it. That time ended just three months and one week ago. Sitting in the back of a nondescript white van on a dirty, winding street in Little Afghanistan, Breen could not believe how his life and outlook had fallen into such a gloomy state.

It's a good thing you are, above all, a patriot and a professional, he thought.

Breen had loved, deeply, where he lived and worked at the University of Virginia campus. He adored the woman he was dating, an American history professor who challenged if rarely changed his traditional views. They both enjoyed his motorcycle on the weekend—a Yamaha Star Eluder, big transcontinental job, not a Harley. They loved the feel of the wind in their faces. Breen was excited by his work, teaching. An attorney and a criminologist, he had joined the Judge Advocate General's Corps because he loved his country and took its laws and responsibilities very seriously. He wanted to have an active hand in shaping the next generation of Constitutionalists.

So what did the United States Navy do with me, he thought. *They sent me on a mission where we executed a man without a trial.*

Maybe they sent him as a counterbalance. A conscience in a business that did not need or want one. Without being asked, he was made an essential part of a fledgling dark ops team known as Black Wasp. Not that the thirty-seven-year-old wasn't given a choice. Either he participated in the open-ended prototype counterterrorism project known as WASP—Wartime Accelerated Strike Placement—or he went on a sabbatical and did nothing until the army forgave him.

The navy was not forgiving.

The transfer wasn't quite that cut-and-dried, but that was the heart of it and it was abrupt. The team needed a law-and-forensics member and he was it. Of course, he was not told, at first, that he would be seconded to Fort Belvoir as a "tenant organization." The Black Wasp unit was attached to the Headquarters Battalion, where they were listed as "support personnel for worldwide military contingencies."

Maybe the army did not know that at the time. If Black Wasp's first mission had failed, the team would probably have been disbanded and forgotten.

Cut down by success, he thought bitterly.

Success had meant moving to Virginia—away from his dear Inez, away from JAG, away from everything except the two warriors who made up the rest of the team. He had always missed Inez Levey when she went on her field trips to explore some forgotten part of history. Soon the FaceTime sessions slowed and then . . . stopped.

Stop thinking about it, he reminded himself. It didn't help.

Right now, those two soldiers were busy. Lieutenant Grace Lee, twenty-six, of the U.S. Army Special Operations Command, Airborne, and Marine Lance Corporal Jaz Rivette, twenty-two, were making their way through a courtyard house built on a slope of Sher Darwaza mountain. Breen watched their progress via a link with the heads-up display in their helmets. Metal was automatically outlined in red by the threat detection system, a variation of facial recognition software. So far, the TDS had identified keys, an old flip-style cell phone, and a grapefruit knife.

Rivette was on the right, Grace on the left. Their mission was to free a Sikh family—parents and two young daughters—who were held hostage by bandits searching for jewelry and cash.

The major's job was to watch for any outsiders who might be coming their way. He was not to lend any other tactical support. He eyeballed passersby, visible through video cameras hidden around the vehicle and providing a 360-degree view of the exterior. In case

Grace and Rivette were trapped, or in the event the enemy sent out a "moving hostage"—someone who could reconnoiter but also be shot in the back if they tried to flee—his job was to help extricate them. If something went wrong, his only job was to extricate himself.

The day was bright and cloudless and the two had approached on the shadowed courtyard side of the home. That was the side overlooked by the mountain. Using an acoustic receiver designed as a windshield sunscreen, they had ascertained that the captive family had been divided. The children were in the tiny kitchen and the parents were in the living room, tied and gagged. The sounds were extremely muffled, suggesting they were also lying on the mattresses that would typically cover the floor.

A tall man in a black keffiyeh appeared from a doorway on the left. In his hands, pointed down, was the unmistakable outline of an M16A2 carbine.

Lieutenant Lee—who carried no firearms, only an eight-inch camo knife—jumped at the man with a high forward kick. The toe of her boot caught him just under the jaw and knocked him against the doorjamb. She came down beside him, crouching. With her left hand she grabbed the hand holding the gun while with her right hand she swung the knife up and buried it deep in his gut. The Afghani moaned as she rose, still holding his hand and pulling the blade toward his sternum.

He dropped without another sound. While Grace

extricated herself from his chest, Rivette had moved ahead, toward the kitchen.

"Bathroom!" Grace hissed into the helmet comm.

Rivette spun. They had already noted that the bathroom door was closed and the marksman knew just where to look. His Colt .45 automatic pistol was up and aimed even as the TDS identified a Russian AS Val assault rifle being raised in the marine's direction.

Rivette fired once, putting a bullet between the man's eyes. The enemy went back and then dropped, the gun falling to the carpet.

Now that Black Wasp had announced itself, it was time to move.

"Target A!" ordered Lee, who was in command of the incursion.

Grace took the lead so she would have a clear path to whoever came from that direction. Rivette moved ahead while covering their rear.

Suddenly, a text message appeared in both heads-up displays and on Breen's monitors:

```
Report to Briefing Room A
```

Both combatants swore. Breen pressed a red button on Lee's screen. The dead men vanished. So did the citizens of Little Afghanistan who had been milling around him. The Afghanis were all holograms programmed into the heads-up displays. The simulation in the small training village built north of the Tulley Gate was over.

"I liked the last one better," Rivette said as he and Grace walked from the house. "Pulling out the wounded marine made me feel connected, y'know what I'm saying?"

"Sikhs were not part of your experience growing up," said the five-foot-two Lee.

"Maybe . . . yeah," the San Pedro, California, native replied. "Neither was rock climbing and gymnastics, but I like that too. And SCUBA."

The pressure of a body, simulated weight, was provided by sensors in the fine, wireless gloves the two wore. The fabric did not interfere with dexterity or the operation of their weapons. Shoulder pads and boots with shifting gel in the lining simulated physical hits. The guns were real, firing blanks.

Major Breen wasn't convinced this setup was more effective than the cardboard cutouts that used to spring up suddenly for quick-shoot, no-shoot calls. But he had to admit that, inconsiderate of the cost, there were only two places where bleeding-edge technology like this was being fielded, and that was the U.S. military and Disneyland.

Breen emerged from the van. He was wearing fatigues and a leather jacket, which comprised the bulk of his wardrobe since he got here. Grace and Rivette emerged from the structure as they always did: helmets tucked protectively under their arms as they critiqued themselves and each other. It was necessary, he knew, but Grace and Rivette had taken on a sibling quality that turned every discussion into a debate.

". . . should maybe have hung back at the bathroom," Rivette was saying. "Instead of shooting long, I could've pushed him back inside and muffled the report in his gut."

"And if his accomplices heard anyway, I might have faced two or more kidnappers while you were still in the loo," Grace pointed out.

"Nah, I'd've been out," Rivette insisted. "That Colt's got a back kick, helpful if you use it right."

Breen remained silent while the two entered the van, secured their quasi-VR helmets in a foam-padded footlocker, then plopped into the two seats that hadn't been removed for Breen's equipment. It wasn't just the back-and-forth between his teammates that caused him to withdraw. The major was not quite sure how he felt right now. As much as this drilling had gotten familiar, even old, and as curious as he was about why the meeting had been called, he was not the same kind of warrior as these two. He did not need to see action.

Rivette had already pivoted to the next topic as he fell into one of the seats. "I'll bet it's that plane crash," he said.

Grace was still thinking about the drill and seemed to have no opinion; Breen had not thought about it until the lance corporal had mentioned it. He could be right. The matter was South African, and the U.S. was impatient when it came to potential terrorists.

Not that I blame them, Breen thought as he shut the door behind Lieutenant Lee. Even if Washington weren't obsessive about combatting its enemies, Pretoria had limited resources to apply to an investigation of this type.

Their destination was Building 247, the Army Force Management School off Mount Vernon Road. The drive took ten minutes, during which Breen remained silent, Rivette ranged over a variety of topics that included monologues about the firearms the Afghanis had been carrying, and Grace sat mostly watching a replay of the drill from Rivette's head cam. The woman liked to know what she had missed, just off to one side, because she was so present during a confrontation.

The three-story brick building had an appropriate collegiate look and feel.

There was no insignia, no indication of rank, and no name patch on the uniforms of the three Black Wasp members. They had the focus and demeanor of MPs on a mission and the three received—but did not return—only brief looks from the personnel they encountered. The glances were largely because Grace and Rivette carried weapons on their hips. Typically, the only guns and knives in the building were used for instruction or security.

They had never been to this building before. A security guard was seated behind a desk, facing the doors. Before her was a sign that said VISITORS. After sternly eying the Colt and eight-inch blade, the corporal rose, asked for ID, and demanded that the weapons be surrendered.

Her hand was on the butt of her own sidearm, a Sig

Sauer 9mm XM17. When he saw it, Rivette nodded approvingly.

"Helluva pistol, especially with the extended-capacity magazine," the lance corporal remarked.

"Mister, I gave you instructions—"

The radio looped to her belt crackled. "Corporal Franklin, they're cleared as-is," a voice said. "Please direct them to Briefing Room A."

"Yes, sir," the woman replied.

The corporal's hand came off her gun. Sitting, she tapped a button on her laptop then removed three visitors' passes from a credit-card-sized printer. She handed one to each guest and watched while they put them on.

"Make a right turn behind me and continue to the end," the corporal said. "You will know Briefing Room A by the black letter on the door."

Breen could not tell, and did not care, if she was being sarcastic. It was not unknown for soldiers entrusted with localized commands—like a gate or parking garage—to turn into generals.

Grace and Rivette walked ahead of Breen. Whatever this was about, they were both going to be itchy today. Grace followed the morning drills with breakfast and then a ninety-minute martial arts workout. She trained in the gym just a short walk from Little Afghanistan. Her targets were practice dummies, heavy bags, and leather pads on the walls. She used *bo* staffs, *katanas,* throwing stars, *escrima* sticks, *nunchucks,* and her knife to attack imaginary foes. Occasionally, someone who did not know her kung fu skills challenged her to spar. Whatever was thrown at her in the gymnasium ring invariably failed to land. Whoever threw it was invariably thrown.

After breakfast, Rivette went to either the indoor or outdoor shooting range. Regardless of whatever outfit was at the gunnery, a thumbprint scan gave Rivette unlimited access to the field and arsenal. His first words to the officer in charge were always the same: "Surprise me." The young man always preferred to be alone, since the only competition he cared about was with himself. If others were there, they invariably struck up a rivalry—typically announced without words but with looks and then pops of a handgun or rifle.

Just as inevitably, the challenger was bested.

In their time here, both Grace and Rivette had found more admirers than fist- or gunslingers who were looking to take them down. The military was also quick to appreciate skill. Especially when your life might depend on it one day.

They arrived at Briefing Room A and Grace knocked.

"Enter."

She opened the door and the three stepped in. The shades were drawn and the fluorescent lights had a dull, ivory tinge. The room was neither as spacious nor as welcoming as the first place they had met the man inside, the Officer's Club not far from here.

But the man was the same. And so was the serious set of his expression. He was standing beside a round conference table and waited until Breen had shut the door before addressing the team.

"Good to see you," he said, the hint of a smile cracking his strong, resistant jaw. "We have business."

CHAPTER EIGHT

November 11, 4:18 P.M.

The distant flash on the sea, and the rumble that followed a few seconds later, was not lightning. The fact that he could not hear anything caused van Tonder to put the distance at forty or fifty miles to the northeast. Possibly farther, depending on the size of the blast.

Another plane? he wondered. It might be, though he had not seen anything in the sky, heard the shriek of a nose-diving descent.

Lord, he hated this utter sense of helplessness.

Mabuza was still on the oxygen tank, which was nearly depleted. So was the pilot. He seemed to have chills and a fever, and van Tonder had turned up the heat. But he was not considerably worse—or better—than he had been when they touched down.

Sisula had managed to get the situation booted up to Lieutenant Colonel Gray Raeburn, commander of the South African Navy's Military Health Service based in Simon's Town. Through whatever tricks the atmosphere enjoyed playing in these parts, van Tonder was finally able to communicate directly with the sixty-three-year-old pulmonary specialist.

Through Sisula, Commander van Tonder had already recounted what happened and where. He also described what they had briefly seen in the wreckage of the jetliner.

"There is a report from the American FBI that a passenger onboard was reported to have been seized by a possible pathogen," the doctor said. "Lieutenant Mabuza's symptoms seem to reflect that, with some unknown connection to Prince Edward."

"If it helps, I still hear birds . . . there's night life moving around outside the helicopter."

"Cross-species contamination is extremely rare," the doctor informed him.

"That isn't what I mean, sir. It seems to support that theory. Radioactivity or chemicals would have killed them."

"Very good, Commander van Tonder. I'll try and keep up."

"Not at all, sir. You've got a lot to try and figure out. I'm just sitting here playing nurse and offering recon. Which reminds me, there's something else," van Tonder went on. "I saw an explosion of some kind at sea, maybe twenty minutes ago."

"Approximately where?"

"To the northeast, well into the horizon. There was a yacht out there when we did our evening flyover yesterday. It was north of our jurisdiction and nothing out of the ordinary. It may have nothing to do with the fire."

"Name?"

"Sorry, sir. We could barely see the boat in the evening fog."

"Of course. You say you are wearing a surgical mask?"

"Yes. And Lieutenant Mabuza, now."

"Commander, can you look at his mask, read me the specifications? It will be on a tag on the elastic or tieback."

Van Tonder turned on the cockpit light and leaned toward the pilot. He found the blue label. "It says EN 149 FFP3."

"European standard for pandemics," the doctor said. "Very good."

Van Tonder sat back. It took him a moment to reply. "Are you saying that's what we have here?"

"I don't know."

That was a heavy thought for a man whose biggest challenge was trying not to slip on bird droppings. "What do we do, sir?"

"I will try to get a quarantine medical team to you at least by morning."

"What about the aviation investigators? They'll be headed to Marion Island, surely—"

"They are preparing an expedition," Lieutenant Colonel Raeburn said. "There was some debate, I'm told, about going by sea instead of risking an approach that tracked the doomed flight. But they feel it is worth the risk, especially with sensors trying to ascertain what caused this."

"Can they help us?" van Tonder asked.

"As civilians, I believe their priority will be the crash. I'm sorry."

It made sense, van Tonder had to admit. It stank to have resources on the way that couldn't help them—but he couldn't dispute the caution.

"Doctor, we only have the water and medical supplies we brought, which isn't much," van Tonder said.

"I know and I'm sorry, Commander. This is not, you know, something for which we are properly or even improperly prepared."

Van Tonder looked around. It seemed not just desolate out here but ancient, as though human existence was either a blip or a fantasy. He might just as easily have been a time traveler, the helicopter his ship, visiting some antediluvian era.

"You can take heart about one thing," Lieutenant Colonel Raeburn said. "It does not sound as if your pilot has gotten any worse. Either the infectious agent cannot survive long in the air, or else did not possess sufficient numbers. These are matters to be investigated further."

"Then you don't think Lieutenant Mabuza will get worse?"

"Couldn't say. From what you've described, he sounds like any patient who is fighting pneumonia or a similar malady."

"Dr. Raeburn, forgive me, but 'malady' doesn't quite seem to fit this. He's sweating like a footballer and shivering. Yeah, he's fighting now, but what do I do when the oxygen runs out? I don't suppose opening the vents is a good idea."

"If you're serious, no," the lieutenant colonel said. "But only because you will suffer hypothermia."

"I don't follow, sir."

"I assume the heater is on?"

"It is."

"I want you to bundle the lieutenant up as best as possible and turn off the heat," Raeburn instructed.

"Sir, it's close to zero outside."

"I appreciate that, and it's one reason he may still be alive. This is apparently a bug that prefers a cold environment—permafrost, upper atmosphere. That's not uncommon. You probably swept it up the same way the airliner did, by flying into it. Give it cold air to go to. As long as your bodies are warmer than the environment, it may not go back. I also want you to keep the lieutenant's forehead damp so it cools as well."

"For the same reason?"

"Exactly that. Draw it out with cold. And there's one thing more," the doctor said. "How far are you from this glow you saw?"

"I'd say it was about a mile. It was Ship Rock, I know that for sure, though I can't say exactly where we've set down." Van Tonder had already leapt ahead of the doctor, again. "You want me to go there."

"Commander, I do not 'want' that," the doctor said. "But I may need you to give me firsthand intelligence. I'm going to consult my superiors. For now, just kill the heat and keep yourself warm as well. We'll try to get help out to you somehow."

"How about using a missile?" van Tonder joked.

"Not the worst idea I've heard. And Commander, keep the mask on even when the tank runs out."

"Affirmative," van Tonder said.

"I'll get back to you as soon as possible," Lieutenant Colonel Raeburn assured him.

"Thanks," van Tonder said. "I'm glad I apparently got the right man for this call. For once, the navy did something right."

"For once," Raeburn agreed.

The officer signed off and van Tonder cut the heat. Within seconds, the temperature had already chilled. And they still had hours of darkness to go. He took the water bottle and—

"Shit."

He had not asked if he could touch Lieutenant Mabuza. He decided against it. Rather than pour water into his palm he took a shimmy from the toolbox under the seat and folded it across the pilot's head. Then he dribbled water across it.

The commander killed all the lights so he did not have to look at his own reflection in the glass. The sky was deep and near—but also vast and endless. The sense of timelessness, of eternity was something unique down here.

"Okay, Lieutenant," van Tonder said. "I want you to fight this. We may just be blips in the cosmos, but two motes are better than one. You hear me?"

"It's . . . beautiful," the officer said in a raw, gravelly voice.

Van Tonder smiled. "You're awake!"

"Somebody was making a lot of noise, sir."

"Sorry. You usually sleep through anything. Remember that rockslide?"

Mabuza did not reply. He was shivering, his teeth clacking hard. Van Tonder did not have a blanket but he did have the insulated tarps Mabuza had removed. He dragged them over the seat back and bundled first the pilot, then himself beneath them.

Then he sat back and waited.

A ruddy glow played against the blue sky where the explosion had been. Most likely burning fuel.

As he thought back over the conversation, he found himself less encouraged by what he had heard than unsettled.

Those were some pretty specific instructions from a man who was coming to this cold, van Tonder thought. The lieutenant colonel was either a very good or inordinately intuitive doctor, or there was one other possibility.

He had a very good idea what was going on.

Just then, the stars low on the sky were blotted by something moving along the horizon.

CHAPTER NINE

November 11, 10:00 A.M.

There were nods and glances but no pleasantries as the three Black Wasp members entered Briefing Room A. Chase Williams was dressed in civvies and had not removed the blue windbreaker he wore on the walk over. He was standing behind the circular conference table.

Williams seemed, to Breen, to have lost weight. *Not as much socializing as when he was doing something else,* the major suspected. Williams was also paler, no surprise in the late fall. His clothes were sharply pressed and his shoes polished; he expected no less from former navy. But those were small things. The larger difference, big as a billboard, was the absence of fire. When Black Wasp had gone after Salehi, it was a crusade for Williams. Whatever this was, however vital, Breen already knew it was a job.

"Good to see you all again," Williams said with amiable sincerity. "We are going to where the South African A330-200 Airbus went down this morning," Williams said without preamble. "The Twelfth Aviation Command will Huey us to Langley and a USAF-RICOM C-21 will get us to Air Force Station Port Elizabeth in about eighteen hours with four stops for refueling. Your passports will be onboard, along with local currency. NAVAF will take it from there. We do not yet know our precise destination, but it is likely the Prince Edward Islands. Briefing materials and updates will be sent en route."

The United States Africa Command was based in Kelley Barracks in Stuttgart, Germany, and had jurisdiction over the United States Naval Forces Africa. They were responsible for that continent and all points south, to and including Antarctica.

"We have reason to believe that the flight deck, at least, was taken down by an airborne germ of unknown origin or type," Williams went on. "Satellite recon suggests a possible geologic component, not volcanic but also of indeterminate nature. If we have deduced that, then other powers have likely done the same. Our mission is to determine if such a toxic agent exists; if so, to secure it; and without starting a war, to prevent proliferation. Protective gear is being brought aboard the Huey, along with your go-bag gear." He grinned at Rivette and Lee. "Minus what you already have on your persons.

"South Africa does not know the reason for our coming, but we will be arriving under cover from

National Transportation Safety Board personnel who *have* been requested. Any questions, save them for the chopper. We are airborne," he glanced at the wall clock, "at eleven thirty. See you all onboard."

The group rose. Rivette took the bottle of water that had been set out.

Grace shook her head.

"Hey, it's free," the lance corporal said. "I don't leave 'free' behind."

Breen noticed that Williams had made his presentation without notes. The man was impressive. He had not been briefed by anyone. He had been living this since the crash.

"You walking over?" Breen asked Williams.

"To and from is the only exercise I'm going to get today," he said.

"Mind if I join you?"

"Welcome it."

The men followed the two younger Black Wasps back through the corridor. Williams had already pulled on sunglasses and a snapback ball cap that covered his close-cropped gray hair. To Breen, he was a man who did not want to be recognized. They did not speak until they were outside. Apparently, Williams also did not want to be heard.

"May I ask why you are joining us?" Breen asked.

"I'm used to being behind a desk," Williams said. "But not working alone."

Breen did not want to push. He was not even sure he wanted to help—if help were required. That was just the professor and defense attorney coming out, with a smattering of criminologist. He liked to *know* things.

"How have you been?" Williams asked. "I understand that being here was not part of the original plan."

"It was not. Sacrifices had to be made."

Breen's tone was convivial, but Williams saw past it.

"Military service," the retired officer said. "As they used to say during the draft, 'You can't beat it.'"

That was the extent of their talk. Whatever Williams did not want to talk about was going to remain unrevealed.

The walk to the airfield took a brisk ten minutes, the sun taking the bite from the air. The ground crew had already loaded the UH-1N and the four passengers climbed in. They made sure everything they needed was onboard before giving the all clear. Each Black Wasp always had their weapons and either warm- or cold-weather gear packed in two cases each, ready to depart at any time.

The crew consisted of a pilot and copilot. Rivette, Lee, and Breen sat in the row of three forward-facing seats behind them, their bags at their feet. Williams took one of the two side-facing seats. By noon, the team was airborne on the C-21. The DLA kept a small fleet for clandestine missions. They were flown by retired air force pilots and paid for by whoever needed the ride. Williams had quickly realized that was the reason Op-Center remained a valuable commodity to any president. Still funded by Congress as if it were a fully functioning if downsized spy agency, it could pay its own way on missions like this. Transport had an eight-passenger capacity, but Black Wasp and its gear were the only occupants.

Each of the Black Wasps took their own seat.

Berry had sent Williams a briefing on the region and the status of the operation. Williams received the updates in a series of bullet points:

* Distressed yacht exploded 3:43 P.M. East African Time, South Indian Ocean. Likely self-inflicted.
* Dinghy departed area; satellite image attached. One occupant, bearing northeast.
* SA Civil Aviation Authority headed to Marion Island by surface ship.
* Foreign vessels and aircraft not approaching.

Not yet, Williams thought. *No one wants to leave a state-of-the-art military vessel with a dead crew in open waters.* Unlike Black Wasp, they were waiting for more information before venturing into the region. *Or perhaps, like Black Wasp, they had their own special ops teams preparing to launch.*

There was a primer on the history and geopolitics of the region, which all of the team members had received. Williams remembered all of it from his studies at Tufts and the world-changing events that followed.

Apartheid—Afrikaans for "apart" and "hood"—was a policy of racial segregation established by the white minority of South Africa in 1948. Roughly 80 percent of the population were people of color, including those of Indian and Pakistani descent. They were forbidden from living or operating businesses in white areas, or even interacting with white citizens. Jobs that could be held were restricted, and their political interests were represented by whites. The national tongue was the Afrikaans language, also known as Cape Dutch, after the seventeenth-century Dutch, German, and French colonists.

Slowly, the international community was roused against apartheid, culminating in the United States and the United Kingdom imposing sanctions in 1985. Laws were slowly, reluctantly relaxed until they were ended in 1990–91. Though the regulations were no longer on the books, they remained in the hearts of many locals. Centuries of conditioning and a sense of ancient roots, particularly among the proud Boers, the descendants of the Dutch, died hard and often not at all.

Williams wondered how much of this history was known to young Jaz Rivette and how he would take to it. The young man seemed to be engrossed in his reading.

The Prince Edward Islands were discovered by Dutch sailors in 1663 and attempts to go ashore were made by the French a century later. Marion took its name from the surname of the French captain. The British seaman Captain James Cook named the other island, and the group, after the son of George III. The islands were visited largely by sealers, who continued to hunt through the early twentieth century. The islands were annexed by South Africa in 1947–48 and became a nature preserve in 2003.

When everyone had had a chance to digest the material, Breen put himself into the seat across the aisle from Williams.

"Do you remember the dustup about South Africa and AIDS in the mid-1980s?" the major asked.

"I do." He smiled. "You weren't born then."

Breen's mouth twisted. "No. But I studied a variety of legal claims—both slander and libel—in which government officials and scientists were charged with having created the virus in order to eliminate the nonwhite population."

"You understand I was teasing you just now."

"I do. I—This was a hot-button topic, had its own course, because a number of the individuals were high-ranking military figures. The idea was that, as future military officers, attorneys would be faced with similar cases. All of which is beside the point. The legal claims spurred a crash program in South Africa into tracing the origin of HIV. The conclusion among researchers on point at the navy's Military Health Service was that HIV was the mutation of a chimpanzee virus that originated in Cameroon and jumped to humans through hunters or vendors handling monkey meat meant for consumption. That finding was not without precedent. Both Ebola and Marburg originated in monkeys and passed to humans. Subsequent genetic studies placed the first mutation into HIV around 1910, when African colonists established the first large cities. This created a fertile incubation and mutation environment for the virus.

"The bottom line is that the cases against the military were dismissed," Breen said. "But I am wondering if any of your sources can tell us what happened to the navy's bio-research program."

"I can ask, but what reason would South Africa have to conduct that kind of research?" Williams asked.

"The cynic in me says that they'd already been investigated—why not go ahead with exactly what they were accused of? There were citizens of South Africa who were passionate about *not* ending apartheid."

"And why the navy?" Williams asked.

"It had a history of being white," Breen replied. "When people think of South African land forces, the Zulus are still the standard-bearers for heroism and tactics."

"All right, I'll look into it. What I'm going to be asked, then, is do I have any reason to believe this may be true? Because if so, there's a very large implication—"

"That someone released something that may or may not have been created," Breen said. "Yes, that's a big statement and long reach. But there's a strong Afrikaner Resistance Movement, partly in response to the pendulum swing of lawlessness and land seizure against whites, and it seems prudent to rule anything like that out at the start."

"I buy that," Williams said. "And I'll be interested

to see if the South Africans are looking into it. That would be an investigation fraught with peril, home terror attacking an essential hub of transportation and commerce."

"Peril for more than just the South Africans," Breen pointed out as he went back to his seat.

Williams had gotten so accustomed to considering big-picture plays at Op-Center that he did not see that microcosm. It was Black Wasp that would be on the ground looking out for American interests. Unlike the pursuit of Salehi, this mission did not presently have definition or an objective.

Twenty-four hours from now, we may be pursuing some genocidal biologist through the mountains of KwaZulu-Natal, he thought.

Williams used his secure uplink to transmit the request to his computer at the DLA. Berry would be pinged to access the request there. Within the half hour, he received a call from Berry.

"Ten minutes ago, South Africa's minister of health, Barbara Niekerk, sent a private, not government, e-mail to the Australian minister of health, Bryan Cocquerel, urging him to ban flights from the Great Victoria Desert and Great Australian Bight."

Williams was not surprised that U.S. intelligence was monitoring private as well as government e-mails. Other nations did the same to Washington. He looked at a map.

"A reasonable precaution, given the easterlies from the crash location. That would be ground zero."

"Agreed," Berry said. "It's what she said after that which got our attention. She wrote, 'Will advise when hold may be lifted.'"

"She knows something," Williams said.

"Seems like it," Berry replied. "Find out what it is."

CHAPTER TEN

November 11, 5:27 P.M.

General Tobias Krummeck, chief intelligence officer of the South African National Defence Force, woke with a start when the smartphone played the nineteenth-century hymn *"Nkosi Sikelel' iAfrika"*—"Lord Bless Africa." He picked up the phone and squinted at the time then looked at the caller ID. Only the number had come up. It was local but he did not recognize it.

He got off the bed where he and his wife had just exhausted themselves for the better part of an hour, and headed toward the adjoining bathroom as he tapped the Answer icon.

"What is it?" Krummeck said thickly from under his woolly white mustache.

"General, it's Raeburn."

It took another moment for the name to bore through the remnants of sleep. Krummeck was instantly awake.

"Hold," the senior officer said.

There were not many things that the medical officer could be calling about. It had been at least a year since they had spoken last, a chance encounter at a cocktail reception for veterans of the first and second battles of El Alamein. The men had said very little and barely looked at one another. Like illicit lovers, each was a little afraid of the secret they shared.

The general shut the bathroom door, lowered the lid on the toilet, and pulled a bathrobe from its hook behind the door. He threw it over his stooped shoulders, suddenly very chilly.

"What is it?" the old soldier asked as he sat.

"We appear to have had a containment leak, sir."

Tinnitus and an echo in the bathroom made the general mistrust what he had heard. He asked the caller to repeat it. He had heard correctly.

"What happened?" the general demanded. Though the words were calm, it took effort to get them out.

The general had been asleep and had missed the news of the jetliner crash. Raeburn brought him up to date. The senior officer sat like something broken, helpless and still. The horror of it all—and the dread of what might follow—sank into his soul even as his brain was still wrestling with it.

"Still active?" Krummeck said when Raeburn was finished. "In that cold? And a *leak*. How are these things possible, dammit?"

"Corrosive salt water, an underwater geologic event, possibly currents knocking the canister against the wall—"

"You're talking about five inches of steel-reinforced concrete!"

"Sir, I told you at the time that all the bug needed to escape was a vent four micrometers wide—"

"You also told me it would be—the words you used were 'contentedly inert in the cold'!"

"Sir, I've been thinking about that. The truth is I've never stopped thinking about it. We engineered the bacterium to seek a specific target, one that was itself evolving. Maybe the mutagenic properties we built in were more versatile than we imagined. We did not exactly run exhaustive exit-strategy tests when we aborted."

No, Krummeck had to admit. *The goal was to get rid of it as soon as possible.* The military and political situation was too volatile.

"All right, let me think a moment," the general said. "Survival in the air," he said. "What about that?"

"One hour maximum but, again, we don't know what may have changed. We are talking about many, many generations of bacterial life having passed."

While the general thought, Dr. Raeburn sat in his small office listening to the silence of indecision, looking into the past. He was not ashamed about what they had done. But by his soul, he regretted the mix of eagerness followed by urgency that had brought them here. . . .

Just over a dozen years ago, Raeburn's nation was in chaos. Migration, illegal and legal, had strained South Africa's infrastructure. The system was already stressed by the AIDS pandemic and the lingering resentment and petty political vengeance on both sides that followed the end of apartheid. Riots killed hundreds and displaced over one hundred thousand.

A specialist in communicable diseases, Raeburn thought he might have a solution to one of those problems.

The military was a microcosm of the split and combative civil government. The old guard sought a resurgence, rising leaders sought to crush it. There was no middle ground to either side. Because of that, the medical officer had circumvented navy channels with his idea—and, thus, went off the radar.

Raeburn had requested, and easily secured, a meeting with Minister of Health Barbara Niekerk. The pulmonologist had been a fellow student at Stellenbosch University in the Western Cape Province. Raeburn knew her to be a person of conscience and suspected she would sidestep protocol for peace.

"It will be good to see you," she had told him, "but understand that two white doctors, even when they are helping the black population, will be perceived as throwbacks."

Raeburn did not doubt the truth of that. He also did not care. It was one of those reactionary, ultimately fatal idiocies for which he had no time or patience.

When they met for dinner, just old schoolmates, what Raeburn had to say surprised her. Sitting in a quiet corner of a quiet restaurant, he began by asking her security clearance.

"Level Two," she had replied, surprised.

"Higher than mine," he had replied, then smiled. "There is nothing I'm about to tell you that you cannot know."

"About the state of medicine in our own nation?"

"That's right," he had replied.

She had asked, only half-joking, "Because I am white, because I am a woman, or both?"

"Remember when pendulums only swung from side to side?" he asked. "We live in a complex society."

Now she was surprised and mildly offended, but also intrigued. "Go on."

He told her that his plan had come about because of events more than four thousand miles away. A year earlier, in 2007, the United States and Iraq had signed a status of forces agreement that required American troops to withdraw from Iraq in two years. In a rare show of internal accord, the South African administrative capital in Pretoria, the legislative capital in Cape Town, and the judicial capital in Bloemfontain were all concerned about warlords and renegades throughout the region suddenly having access to stockpiles of biological weapons.

The Military Health Service was charged—not by the then-minister of health but by the commander in chief of the South African National Defence Force— with establishing a group of scientists to seek cures to diseases suspected of being weaponized. Chief among these were anthrax and Ebola. Because of his training and fieldwork, Raeburn was placed in command.

"Someone in Pretoria possessed a dark sense of

humor or self-importance, possibly both, when they named the program," Raeburn told Niekerk.

It was called the Bio-Weapons and Necrotic Actinism Program. "BWANA" was East African for "master."

Barbara Niekerk was surprised by two things. First, that she knew nothing about the program. Second, that the military had managed to keep a secret.

"But you're not telling me all of this out of fellowship and school loyalty," she had said over dinner.

"No," he had said. "I've stumbled upon something that requires a separate research group—and funding."

"Something you cannot share with the military, your superiors?" she had asked.

"It's a domestic matter and a potentially explosive one. It is specifically on the list of diseases the military was *not* asked to . . . 'solve,' was the word used in the written order. It was actually footnoted as, 'This is a problem that falls squarely and solely under the jurisdiction of the Public Service and Administration Department of Home Affairs in Pretoria.'"

"AIDS?" Niekerk had asked.

Raeburn had nodded. "We may have found a cure."

"Not a vaccine," she clarified.

"No. I think we have created something to extract the virus itself. We engineered it from *Campylobacter jejuni,* which is drawn to cold. We believe we can 'train it,' if you will, to grab the virus and depart a feverish body."

Niekerk was flabbergasted, momentarily mute, impressed, proud, hopeful, and scared for her classmate's breach of the chain of command.

"You could go to prison for life," she had pointed out after recovering slightly.

"At least I will still have a life," he had replied. "And a soul. If I don't do this, or at least try—"

Niekerk said she understood. She did not have to consider the proposal. She told him that she would pull money from a discretionary fund. Two days later, answering only to Raeburn, BWANA had a pocket team working on the problem.

Six months later—having had little communication— Raeburn and Niekerk had another dinner.

"There is good news and bad news," he had told his sponsor.

The good news was that they had indeed come up with a bacterium capable of clearing the AIDS virus from patients in 100 percent of cases.

"It was actually an easy find," he had told her. "We snare the virus with a bacterium that is, in effect, *vulnerable* to white blood cells. It is also heat sensitive and seeks to get out via feverish perspiration and urine. When it leaves, it takes the AIDS virus with it. We call it the Exodus bug."

"That has a hopeful sound."

"It does, I suppose. It could also suggest the Lord who smiteth, a God of war. Unfortunately, it isn't the reason we chose the name."

"The bad news."

"Early on, we had to deal with the white blood cells

killing individual Exodus bugs before they could complete the journey. That set the AIDS virus free—the process was worthless. We had to aggregate them—essentially, get the bugs to reproduce swiftly and cluster around each virus. White blood cells come en masse but the bacteria learned—blunt survival, of course, not thought—they learned to form layers to finish the trip to the promised land."

Niekerk had eyed the doctor. "The bad news is the tenacity of the white blood cells," she had said. "You rid the body of an immune-suppressing virus . . . but you take the body's only defenses with it."

"That's part of the bad news," Raeburn had agreed. "The white blood cells cling to their prey all the way out. Virtually any infection can kill the patient. We've simply reinvented the AIDS problem."

"Well, you didn't quite do that, did you?" Niekerk said. "In time, the white blood cells will repopulate and the patient will survive."

"Correct."

"I see. The rest of the bad news is the caveat. Each patient must live in a sterile environment for weeks . . . maybe months," Niekerk had said. She had smirked. "A single human life is beyond evaluation yet the cost per person would be unthinkable."

"I'm sorry," Raeburn had told her.

Niekerk told him what he already knew: the solution was profoundly admirable but impossible. The government already spent 15 percent of its annual budget on health care. This program would have trebled that. Raeburn asked for an extension of the project with a scaled-down staff to try and find a way to hide the Exodus bug from white blood cells.

But the money had run out. Permission was regrettably denied.

"And Gray," she had said, "you're a man with a conscience. But if you seek to go out of country with this, they *will* hang you. In time, you may find a solution."

"You know the damn thing?" he had said. "The bug loses mobility in the air rather quickly and dies without a host. Sixty minutes at the most. It can't harm the patient, then."

"Just everything else in the air," she lamented.

Enter then-Major General Tobias Krummeck.

Raeburn was surprised but not shocked to learn that ever since BWANA had been established, the intelligence officer had a team following and eavesdropping on Raeburn. In a government of widely divided loyalties, no one with access to potential war and anti-war matériel could be entirely trusted.

Krummeck had summoned Raeburn and funded a continuation of his research. When Raeburn had reasonably asked why, Krummeck had answered that if a cure were not found, not just this government but the entire system of government in South Africa might fall.

"People can be bludgeoned into giving up smoking, even narcotics, but not sex," he had said. "There is a faction in the South African Communist Party that wants to arrange 'chance' encounters with young, infected men and women with susceptible leaders to take them down. This must not be."

Raeburn was impressed with the levels of Krummeck's penetration into the SACP inner circle, and said so.

"Not how it happened," he had said. "I was a target."

Work on the Exodus bug continued for a year. Raeburn was the only researcher on the project. The results were worse than before.

"To strengthen each bacterium means they survive ejection from the body," the exhausted doctor had said at the end of it. "Inhaled, it immediately draws white blood cells to it, causing congestion that instantly collapses arterial walls."

"A formidable weapon," Krummeck had observed.

Raeburn had been instantly electrified by that remark—and the pensive, unfrightened expression that came with it. He did not know, at that moment, sitting in Krummeck's office, if that had been the real motivation for the continued research. Not a bug but a potential Exodus plague to unleash against the opposition.

"Sir," Raeburn had replied with unutterable caution, "this thing is murderous on a level we cannot even conceive. Instantly lethal *and* ungovernable. It can't survive more than an hour in the air, but think of a city. A dense population would be devastated, urban centers would suffer hundreds of thousands if not millions of casualties within hours."

"I understand, truly. You gave it a try. You're sure that further research won't—"

"Help? If by 'help' you mean finding a better way

to kill millions in a matter of days, that's what we are looking at, sir. We have to erase everything. I am going to destroy all the research."

"I see. How do you safely dispose of the bacterium itself? It seeks a cold environment, you've explained—fire, then? Immolate it?"

"That will work, in theory, but if even one germ survives it can seek a host and replicate. At that size, we cannot be sure. No, better to put it in an environment where we know it will wish to stay. A freezer, perhaps."

"No," Krummeck had said. "We do not want it where a rogue officer or agent can stumble upon it. We must treat this like radioactive waste. Dispose of it, inter it, but in cold."

Raeburn had then conceived of his plan for a secret subantarctic burial. The bacteria were encapsulated. The program was killed.

But apparently not the bugs.

Raeburn stopped remembering. He had gotten good at that over the intervening years. And the team that had accompanied him on the mission to Prince Edward had not known what they were handling.

If in fact the bug had been responsible for the felling of the commercial aircraft, Raeburn was sorry. But this was not the time to affix blame or to find explanation for the bacterium's survival.

"We have to quarantine and destroy at least the source," Krummeck said, coming out of his silence with the obvious.

"I suggest napalm," Raeburn said.

The general actually laughed. "That's a solution, of course. And with civilian authorities on the way to Marion Island, they will of course not notice a firestorm on Prince Edward."

"General, this is the Exodus *plague* we once discussed! This is not a time to consider—"

"Our careers? Prison? Try this thought, Doctor. Who but you can possibly *fix* the problem? Do you imagine that, once arrested, you will have access to a laboratory in a timely fashion?"

The general was correct about that. And it did not solve all their problems. There were still samples at 35,000 feet. The cold and thinness of the air might enable them to survive longer than an hour.

"All right," Raeburn said. "I hear that."

"Good. What about the wreck? Is there any chance of the bacteria having survived?"

"Not likely."

"Even in bodies?"

"If the flame did not destroy them, the heat, reaching about fifteen hundred degrees Fahrenheit, would have killed them."

"Then we have some time before outside medics autopsy whatever remains," Krummeck said. "We need eyes on the site. You say there's a navy helicopter on Prince Edward? Can the fuel be used to incinerate the bug?"

"Yes, but if the block is only fractionally split it can also open the vent wider."

"Christ, Raeburn. Christ. We can't have an amateur fumbling around out there. You'll have to go."

Raeburn had been circling, unhappily, that same conclusion. "Yes, sir."

"Where are you?" Krummeck asked.

"My office at Saldanha Bay."

"The training facility?"

"Yes, sir."

"Take—I don't know. Take whatever equipment you can get together."

"I'll need explosives if the pit has been exposed."

"Thermite grenades?"

"That seems the most expedient way to close it, for now."

"Very well. I'll have a helicopter there to meet them, designated as MAP-14. Special team—as last time. After that, you are not to contact me again unless it is with an all-clear alert. Is that understood?"

"Is that an order, General?"

"It is emphatically an order," Krummeck replied. "I will clear it with Environmental Management. Good luck," he added, and hung up.

Raeburn was not surprised or especially disappointed by the general's moderate, largely hands-off reaction. The South African Environmental Management people would not interfere because of the civilian crash. And it made sense for Raeburn to go to the island—even if Military Assistance Program-14 designated this as a civilian assist project, and to the wrong island.

He went to a locker and removed six hazmat masks: two for the men on Marion, two for the flight crew, one for him, one spare. They were from the same shipment he had used when he initially developed the Exodus bug. The expiration date on the seals was just a month away. That meant the vulcanized rubber was within six or seven weeks of shrinking to unreliability.

Given the size of the bacterium, that was not optimal. But that was the best they could get right now. Placing the masks in a pair of aluminum carrying cases, and getting his cold-weather gear from an adjoining locker, a tired Gray Raeburn filled two backpacks with medical supplies and grabbed his microscope case. Then, his arms awkwardly full, he headed through the corridors to the small helipad not far from the science facilities.

He was about to leave when his phone chimed.

"Shit," he said, rejecting the call and hurrying out.

CHAPTER ELEVEN

November 11, 7:02 P.M.

Nahoon Beach is a miles-long stretch of sand with spectacular waves that caught the fading light.

Cold and weary from her shoulders to her soul, Katinka watched as the silhouette of the southern bluff cut a dark, familiar shape against the twilight sky.

The beach was deserted at this hour, in this season. She swept in like a battle-worn Valkyrie, the vessel caught in a sudden wind that caused her to turn suddenly toward her left. A soft landing was out of the question. She needed to set down. She did so with a spine-jarring thump.

Though exhausted, Katinka did not linger. The police would find and wonder about the autogyro, and would contact MEASE—but not before she reached him. Tourists and tourist helicopters frequented the area and no one would bother reporting one that had landed on the beach.

The wind was strong but not as biting as it had been farther south. She lived a short walk past Beach Road, on quiet, modest suburban Plymouth Drive. She owned a small cottage in this flat landscape dotted with closely built homes and shielded from sun and wind by palm trees and sturdier oaks.

She had grown up in a mud hut with a thatched roof not far from here, raised by a single father who still worked as an automobile mechanic. His endless hours of hard work—and a certain skill for dice, which frequently cost him protection money from the local police and just as frequently wiped out his winnings—put her through school and she longed to return that love and kindness. Though she cherished her comfortable retreat it was not where she wanted to spend the rest of her life. There were mansions in Cape Town, Western Cape. Foster had a place on Val Du Lac, Franschhoek. It wasn't one of the bigger mansions but it was comfortable. That was where she yearned to be. Perhaps when he moved up, she would have earned enough to move in.

You can always hope, she thought.

Though there was a ceiling to her dreams. She sometimes fancied—usually while chopping or dissolving rock, away from any distractions—that Foster would one day realize what a bright, eager, intelligent woman she was and they could be more than boss and worker. But he had shown no interest in her or any woman, save for those models he occasionally dated. Katinka did not want to know about them. They were the enemy.

The families all knew her but the location was

about more than any of that. From here, she was able to walk to the less thunderous sections of Nahoon, near the estuary of the river, where the dinghy from the *Teri Wheel* would always meet her. She could also ride her motor scooter to the MEASE office, where she would be driven to whatever site she was to work on or else to the helipad.

There was another reason for living here. Katinka knew her way in the dark. Given the work she did, that was essential. Foster was insistent on that and on other clandestine skills, such as saying as little as possible on phone calls or in texts or e-mails.

The house consisted of a living room, a kitchen, a bedroom, and a bathroom with a shower. There was a shed out back on the small lot where she kept her scooter and garden supplies. She turned up the heater in the shed and let the water tank warm before stepping in. It held enough for five minutes of a modest stream. The woman did not want to waste a moment of warmth.

After plugging in her near-dead cell phone, Katinka took off her clothes, checked for blood spatters. There were none. Her exit had been careful. Most of the crew had DNA on file as part of their criminal records. She was a MEASE employee. If investigators came to question her, there was nothing to connect her to the boat. That done, she stood in the fine spray and considered her plan. She had told Foster that core samples were recovered. That meant either lying about the total or telling him the truth: that she was keeping one.

She would lie. If he ever found out, it would not go

well. When it came to honesty it, like loyalty, had to be absolute.

The sun was just beginning to emerge from the sea as Katinka snatched up her phone and stepped in the wood-fenced backyard. She was dressed in a warm wool coat and fur-lined boots. She had transferred the two samples to a backpack and carried the third.

She went to the large shed out back. Katinka had it built with the expectation that one day she would own a motorboat and store it here. There had not, as yet, been time for that. She blamed it on what she called "the hustle." It was a disease, and she knew it, but there was no avoiding it. Growing up, anyone who was poor and found a way out was also a victim: the fear that if you ever stopped hustling, you would slide back to poverty. And then it would be worse because there had been a path out. She kept promising herself she would get the boat "tomorrow." Yet each tomorrow was the same as every yesterday.

The hustle.

There are worse habits than working, she told herself whenever she saw this big empty space. If nothing else, the shed was a reminder that there was a reason for working so hard.

Katinka tugged the string of the bare overhead light. Her Sym Blaze 200 motor scooter had a platform on back with a case for holding rock samples. She put the two samples inside, still in the backpack to cushion them from being knocked about. She looked for a place to hide the other container.

A bag of fertilizer that she used for her small rose garden.

"From the earth you came, to the earth you return," she said as she removed the cord that bound the top of the plastic sack and gently screwed the sample down into the mulch.

She walked the scooter outside through the back door of the shed where she would have better cell phone reception. The woman had no doubt that Foster had remained at the radio all night—not just waiting to hear from someone on the boat but listening to communications of the harbormaster and the NSRI. The National Sea Rescue Institute was staffed by 980 volunteers and had a total of 32 coastal bases. If anyone had seen the fire, boats would have been dispatched.

"Katinka!" the voice burst from the phone. "Is—is that you?"

"It's me. I'm home and coming over."

"We had a distress call from—"

"I know. The boat is gone. I came ashore on the autogyro, in case anyone asks. I'll explain everything, Chief. I'll see you soon."

"But the *call*—the reason for the call!"

"It's under control." She sat on the bike and started the engine. "I'll see you soon."

She hung up. Two minutes later, having strapped on her beige cap helmet and slipped into her sunglasses, Katinka Kettle was headed down the street, rousing dogs one after the other, the morning and evening heralds, as she made her way to the coastal road and East London.

* * *

MEASE was located on the top floor of a small, modern, unassuming two-story gray office building on Old Transkei Road. Occupying the bottom floor were a car dealership and travel agency, also owned by Claude Foster. Both allowed him to move people, machinery, and cash to wherever it was needed for MEASE business.

Parking was in a small lot behind, with a chain-link fence. On the opposite side of the fence was a repair shop that handled everything from motorcycles to airplane engines. Foster owned that as well.

The forty-eight-year-old college-educated accountant and football enthusiast was savvy and confident in a way that attracted devoted employees. In a nation where racial discrimination was illegal but old biases remained, the son of a white father and black mother was extremely generous with every member of his diverse team, in all of his operations. The man himself had no political or social worldview. His older brother, Aaron, was a trade union activist in the 1980s—rare for a white man. He was shot in the spine and died two years later, a paraplegic. Foster lived in the modest Val Du Lac mansion alone, save for the occasional escort he brought for a visit. He did not believe in relationships. He could not afford a moment of weakness in which he would trust anyone.

For Foster, success was the only cause that mattered. To achieve it, there was not a day that he defied a socially unbalanced system that had replaced a racially unjust system in which mining and wealth were the only constant. And that was controlled by powerful interests that ruthlessly stamped out entrepreneurs.

The MEASE office itself was a large open area with no walls, just workstations. Foster's office was a glass cubicle. It wasn't that he did not trust any of his employees. It was that he could not afford to. Security cameras were trained on every computer and on every landline. Smartphone calls were not permitted. Everything remained logged, recorded, or stored in the office.

The glass was also bulletproof. He was dealing with mercenaries. By their very nature, they were greedy and untrustworthy. Even Dawid Aucamp, his oldest employee, could be double-dealing. There were other illegal mining concerns throughout the nation. Aucamp rarely identified sites in the Northern Cape Province. Perhaps he was selling information to them as well.

Just now, Foster was not thinking about what he might be missing. Everyone had gone home but he had remained before the incident on the *Teri Wheel*. He had remained, napping at his desk and ordering food from the café across the street. He made his own strong coffee, a lifelong habit.

The call from Katinka was like a jolt of caffeine.

Hearing her terse explanation, his first reaction was relief. The organization was safe.

"The boat is gone."

Hearing that, after Krog's frantic call, there was no self-reproach. If some act of God had brought this on, there was nothing he could have done to prevent or even anticipate it. If the destruction had been willful, then Katinka—who was smart and resourceful—had done what had to be done.

He would know very soon. At least there was nothing about the boat on the Internet. All the news was about the South African airliner that went down.

Security was always Foster's primary concern on these expeditions. Not the loss of a vehicle or even the crew. Insurance would cover one, and the others— they knew the job was dangerous. Society would not miss them. *He* would not miss them. He could always hire more. Like cockroaches they were everywhere and defied eradication.

What worried him was the investigation that would follow. The cover story he maintained—that MEASE exported only collectible rocks such as crystals, meteorites, and trilobite fossils—would not bear up under careful scrutiny. Not everyone could be bribed. Or cleanly removed.

One of the reasons Foster had bought this building was that, from this spot, he could hear the elevator mechanism or footfalls on the stairs. Security cameras had since replaced what he called his "early warning system," but he was still attuned to every sound from outside the office.

Katinka had entered the building using the keypad then walked with uncommon heaviness up the stairs. Whatever was in the backpack sagged; it no doubt added to the burden she carried inside. Plus exhaustion. The crossing from where the yacht was back to shore would not have taken long but the wind, cold, and waves would not have been pleasant.

But Katinka Kettle is tough and ambitious. Otherwise, she would not be working for me.

The main door to the office opened with a beep. Foster rose from behind his desk. He waited until the door had clicked shut behind the gemologist before emerging from his office.

He was surprised by the woman's expression. Her brown eyes were open very wide and her mouth had an exultant set that emphasized her naturally feline look. Foster noticed one thing at once. She did not swing her backpack off with a catlike dip of her shoulder, as she usually did. She removed it with deliberate care and set it on her desk.

Foster's gray eyes caught the light and seemed to glow within their deep eye sockets. His long face showed salt-and-pepper stubble. He was examining the young woman carefully, her puzzling expression.

The man eyed the contours of the bag. "Two core samples."

"That's right."

"What did you find on the island?"

"The better question is what did we unleash?"

"Krog spoke of a malady."

"Like a man receiving last rites, he finally spoke the truth," she said.

That, too, was new—God-fearing Katinka making light of death and misadventure. She was always the cautious scientist, reserved with her opinions.

"We found diamond dust, but something underneath

it was instantly deadly, communicable by air, and held safe within these samples. A microbe, I suspect, because something like uranium-235 would have killed me long before I got here. I was closer to it than anyone on the boat yet I alone survived."

"You were using filtration because of the dust."

"That's right. Consider it, Mr. Foster. The entire crew infected and dead in less than a quarter hour. I blew up the boat to sink any evidence—whatever particles remain will be corrupted or destroyed by the sea."

The lean man of medium height did consider it.

"You chose not to destroy the samples," he said.

"No." She pointed to the bag. "Whatever this is can make us rich."

He regarded the gemologist. She went to church, she believed in prayer—yet a superficial part of her had always been a bit of a carnivore, a little hungry. As much as she spoke of faith, there was something feral in the eyes.

A baptism of reality, he thought. *Greed is theoretical until suddenly wealth is attainable.*

This was a leap to something bigger. He needed to think. The man walked back to his office, returned with coffee for himself and Katinka.

"You are aware of the commercial jetliner that went down?" he said.

"Yes. Where?"

"Marion Island."

"We heard an impact—did not know until later what it was," she said. She looked at him strangely.

"I'm tired, Mr. Foster. Are you saying the drill team did that?"

"There is talk, serious talk, of bioterror. I was listening to the maritime channels, seeing if there was any news of the *Teri Wheel*. People were talking about a report from investigators in New York. It must be somewhat credible, because the aviation rescue and recovery people are gearing up accordingly. Hazmat suits, the works."

Katinka's wide eyes grew larger as she turned back to the bag. "A biological agent."

"How could something that deadly just have been lying around?" Foster asked. "Your team didn't—you *couldn't*—go very deep. Not with a hand auger."

"The acid," Katinka thought aloud. "I had to use two quarts to get through the ice, the ground, the rock. It may have gone deeper. We may have hit a primeval air pocket, a frozen bog."

"But *you're* alive."

"I was wearing my acute toxicity inhaler because of the acid. I only had the one mask so everyone else was back at the dinghy, sheltered from the wind."

Foster regarded the bag with a blend of fear and awe. "I heard Krog's descriptions. People vomiting blood, tissue—"

"That's what I saw. Here's something curious, though. If it was a microbe, it may have clung to my clothing as I made my way to the ship."

Katinka noticed Foster start.

"Don't worry, I took them off, they're back at the house," she said. "That's not the point. If something did get snared in the fibers, it was dormant or dead. This may be airborne but the germ has a narrow life span in that medium."

Foster returned to what Katinka had said earlier. He was rich but he was a big player in a very small game. Legally and with force of arms, the gem consortia kept him and others away from the large deposits. This find would allow him to leapfrog over everyone, like a lanky kid who was suddenly and to everyone's surprise the top player in Confederation Football.

Surprise and horror, he thought. This wasn't just about elevating him but crushing those diamond bastards and the bureaucrats. Under apartheid, people were kept down because of their skin color. After apartheid, they were kept down if they could not pass wads of cash under the table. The system was still rotten, only in a different way.

Katinka had perched her tired body on the edge of her desk. She stiffened, stared out the window. "I just realized something. We have to move very, very fast."

"Why?"

"The excavation point—it's still open. Investigators will see it, possibly the navy outpost on Marion. Maybe someone will die from it. We will no longer have a monopoly."

Foster smiled. "You were thinking of selling the samples for weaponization."

"Yes. Those are international waters with sophisticated vessels. Someone certainly heard Krog's broadcast."

"Even in his panic, he was vague—but you're correct. He may have been overheard. We have to act quickly. But why sell? What is wrong with black-mail?"

The woman remained sharply upright as her eyes turned to him.

"Why would anyone believe you?"

He replied, "We will show them."

Foster excused himself as he called the police to let them know his autogyro had experienced mechanical trouble and had set down on Nahoon Beach.

They did not seem overly concerned, except for the well-being of the aircraft when the tides came in.

Katinka assured him it was parked well enough in-land.

Foster was not concerned.

CHAPTER TWELVE

November 11, 9:50 P.M.

The nearly three-hour ride in the Atlas Oryx helicopter was a rich pageant of things, none of them pleasant.

It was loud. Even the headphones could only muffle, not silence the noise. If it were only the monotonous beat of the rotors, Lieutenant Colonel Gray Raeburn might have been able to treat them as white noise. But it wasn't. The wind kept up an uneven whine that rose and fell without a pattern. Sometimes it was a whisper, sometimes a scream.

It was cold. The forced air that warmed the cockpit did not do a very good job in the small, inadequately padded cargo and passenger bay. The wind made sure to remind them they were heading into the subantarctic.

It was also too bumpy, another gift of the air currents, of passing from strong westerly to strong easterly currents. The harness kept him secure in the seat but that meant he went with every jump and dip of the helicopter.

But the worst of it was not the ride. After about an hour, the tight plastic mask with its old, stiffening rubber seal had abraded his cheeks. Every knock of the wind and bounce of the chopper spread that discomfort. But he dared not shift it, even as it rubbed raw, mask-shaped contours into his flesh.

The doctor did not even try to sleep. The physical discomfort aside, the ugly unreality of what had happened and the life-changing suddenness clawed at mind and soul. He had not even contacted Commander van Tonder. What would he tell him?

Raeburn thought about returning the call of Barbara Niekerk. He did not worry about whatever message she had left in his voicemail. It would have been nothing more than an insistent *"Call me."* He wanted to, if only to tell her he was on his way to try and deal with the problem. But she would want to know more than that—such as the bug's viability in the atmosphere and how to treat it. These were things he could not know. Not until he had obtained a sample and looked for mutation.

The one window beside his plastic bucket seat was damp with condensation and smudged with filth. But the skies were relatively clear and misleadingly cheerful as Prince Edward Island appeared on the sea ahead. It did not seem as if eight years had passed since he was last here. Then, he had traveled in a helicopter not unlike this one, with a select special ops intelligence team that reported directly to Krummeck. They did not know what was being buried here. The hole had been dug and the coffin-sized casing winched down. Raeburn himself—and alone—went down on the winch and interred the canisters. Then the top was lowered and the hole was buried.

The naval outpost on Marion Island had been ordered to stand down during this operation. There were no outside witnesses.

Now there are, he thought as the helicopter swept in low over the sea. Whatever he did here, it would have to be for the first time, as it were. He could not have seen the burial chamber or what was inside.

The familiar shape of Ship Rock came into view, standing solitary over the sea with the main island behind it. Both were crusted with ice but no fresh snow. Small floes of ice had clogged the waters between the island and the rock. They would be solid enough to stand on while Raeburn investigated whatever had happened here.

He was glad they were too low to see the wreckage on the far side of Marion Island. There was no smoke; whatever fires there had been were out. They had passed the two Maule M-7-235C amphibious planes an hour earlier, as well as the refueling boat that was coming along behind them. The Maule was an adaptable aircraft with removable pontoons. One of these two, he suspected, was a flying laboratory the Civil Aviation Authority used for crashes on sea and land. The other bore a red cross: medical evac.

The navy Denel AH-2 Rooivalk was soon visible.

The sunlight bouncing from the bubble front made it impossible to see the men inside, but there would have been nowhere to go.

Raeburn was about to tell the pilot to radio the navy aircraft when the flyer contacted him.

"Doctor," he heard through the headphones, "there is someone else off the island."

Raeburn craned to see, but his side view was only to the east. He did not want to unbuckle and could see only sky through the other window.

"Any idea who it is?" the doctor asked.

"Yes, sir," the pilot replied. "It's a corvette, model 056. People's Liberation Army Navy, China."

Commander van Tonder had seen the Chinese ship when it was still dark and the vessel was far out at sea. The silhouette of the corvette was visible against the stars, and by its own lights flashing red and blue on the tower.

It was not uncommon to see Chinese, American, Russian, and Indian naval vessels in the region. With increasing aggressiveness, the Chinese and Indians were vying for control of the Indian Ocean Basin. Part of this was their inability to flex military muscle on land with the Himalaya Mountains between them. A larger part was the need for China to keep its economy growing. That required oil, which came through these sea-lanes. Increased investments in the ports of Myanmar, Bangladesh, Sri Lanka, and the Maldives gave China exponentially greater access to the waterways.

South Africa was mostly a bystander in all of this. Neither nation came to these islands, merely passed by.

Until today.

Lieutenant Mabuza was not well. He was feverish, dehydrating—the water had already run out—and rarely conscious. Van Tonder kept him covered; there was nothing else he could do.

Ensign Sisula kept the commander informed about developments regarding the crash. Except for the fact that they were on the way, there was no news from them.

"Simon says there's another heli on the way," Sisula said. "No details, but it's one of theirs."

"Medical, I hope."

Sisula had not been aware of the Chinese vessel. Until they contacted the outpost. Van Tonder listened to the communication over the radio.

"SAN Outpost Marion Island," a voice said in highly polished English. "This is Command Master Chief Petty Officer Kar-Yung Cheung of the corvette *Shangaro*. We note two explosions in your vicinity. One occurred this morning at 12:39 A.M. on Marion Island. We understand this to have been South African A330-200 Airbus flight 280. We note that assistance has not yet arrived. We stand ready to help."

"*Shangaro,* Outpost Prince Edward has received your offer and will pass that offer along. Thank you."

"The other explosion was at sea earlier this morning. Our helicopter photographed debris. Is the identity of this vessel known to you?"

"It is not, *Shangaro*. We recorded the incident at 2:59 A.M. and it was reported."

"Very good, Outpost Prince Edward. We note as well that you have an ailing officer on Prince Edward Island. As we are at the coast, may we volunteer the services of our trained medical personnel?"

Sisula was silent. Van Tonder quickly considered the matter. Without knowing whether medical help was on the way, he had to decide whether Mabuza's recovery was worth risking inviting the Chinese ashore. He believed that humanitarian rather than hostile intent would spare him from any disciplinary repercussions.

Not that it mattered. The lieutenant needed help. Military regulations allowed for SOS assistance by foreign forces—as long as national security was not compromised, or, as a poster on the mess hall at Simon cautioned: *Emergency? Shun Over Sharing.* There was also the Chinese crew to consider. They might recognize the risk.

"*Shangaro,* this is Commander Eugène van Tonder on Prince Edward," he said. "I can see your corvette from the ledge above Ship Rock. I urge you *not* to approach. There is an unknown toxin abroad."

"You are unaffected?"

"We *are*. When we approached the coast by helicopter, my pilot became ill. We immediately turned back to Point Dunkel but set down when the lieutenant became too ill to fly."

"Then exposure was limited."

"So it seems."

"We understand the risk and have consolidated our crew in sealed areas," said Cheung. "We wish to be of assistance."

Van Tonder did not believe that. But if they could help Mabuza, he was not going to argue.

"Do you have hazardous materials gear and a means of quarantine?" van Tonder asked.

"Our medic informs me we do. What are your pilot's symptoms?"

"Like the flu but much more debilitating. He's perspiring, shivering, feverish."

"Your proximity to him seems not to have affected your health. Have you touched him?"

"Not with bare skin," van Tonder said. "I'm also wearing a surgical mask, as is the pilot."

"We will send our medical officer by helicopter to your position," the Chinese officer informed him.

"Sir, I would advise you *not* to bring the ship any closer."

A new voice came on. "Commander, this is Chief Medical Officer Han. We do not detect radiation or gas. Toxins rise with the heat. We believe that, being below your point and with reasonable precautions, our shipboard crew will be safe."

"Thank you for the caution, Commander van Tonder," Cheung added.

"Thank you for your assistance," the South African commander replied.

The formality of both men disguised mutual mistrust. The conversation was by the book, no doubt recorded. The Chinese knew about the Marion Island outpost, had flown over it many times. No secrets were betrayed.

The commander told Sisula to terminate the call then removed his headset. He turned to Mabuza.

"Help is on the way," he said.

The pilot just shivered and nodded. For his part, the commander was getting cabin fever just sitting here.

How much worse can it be on the ledge than it is here, with an infected man? he wondered.

But he couldn't leave Mabuza. Just wiping the man's forehead let him know he was not alone.

Within minutes, a long, sleek patrol boat had left the starboard side of the corvette, headed toward Prince Edward Island. The sound of the engine, echoing through the cove below, made the boat sound close and immediate. As it reached a crescendo, van Tonder saw Mabuza's hands come to life.

Choking up, the commander steadied them with his own.

"It's okay, Lieutenant," van Tonder said. "That's not us. It's the rescue ship, I think."

Mabuza nodded weakly. "I—I am glad."

"Me too."

After a moment Mabuza relaxed.

Van Tonder looked out again and saw, in the distance, the corvette slicing through sparkling waters and coming closer to shore. Though the seas were dark, the lights were not. It stopped roughly a quarter mile out. The lights on its bridge tower flashing, the patrol boat continued toward the island, finally vanishing below the ledge. He knew from his many patrols that the seasonal land bridge, Ship Isthmus, would prevent them from circumnavigating Ship Rock. It appeared when ice piled high on submerged rocks, creating a tenuous link with the larger island.

He also knew that the patrol boat did not have to go around. What they wanted was on the eastern side.

Van Tonder slipped the headset back on.

"Michael?"

"Yes, sir?"

"Report to Simon that the Chinese have come to Ship Rock with what appears to be an armed military unit," he said. "Tell them I think they mean to stay."

CHAPTER THIRTEEN

November 11, 5:00 P.M.

Traveling eastward, toward night, Williams was reminded of all the jet-lag journeys he had taken, often in big, rattling C-130s, which seemed to exist in their own perpetual twilight.

The small, slick, ivory-white C-21 was not that. The passengers felt every bump and nudge of turbulence, though that did not stop Rivette from napping, Grace from reading Daoist texts or meditating, and Breen from reading about the South African health minister and everyone associated with her. One thing Williams had learned about the major was that, like any great attorney, he liked to be prepared.

Williams had been following Berry's almost continuous stream of updates and forwarded intelligence reports. The latest was that a Chinese corvette had made itself at home off Prince Edward Island and a helicopter had landed. Then there was a photo with this caption from the National Reconnaissance Office:

THE PLAN TROOPS ARE ARMED AND ALL IN HAZMAT MASKS.

Berry called a few minutes later. "Beijing's got balls, I'll say that."

"You have said it, many times."

"Yeah, but dicking around with Taiwan and Japan or even India isn't the same as planting a flag so far from their shores."

"It's not the same, but it was inevitable. Geographically, the islands in the South Indian Ocean are in the path of their westward expansion. Militarily, they want to control whatever is loose on that island."

"That can't be allowed, Chase."

"No? Anyone who approaches, other than South Africa—who will be no match for them—risks a showdown. My white papers at Pacific Command, which no one read, suggested remedies for just this kind of creeping expansion."

"What did you suggest doing about it?"

"Boosting our financial ties with the nations in that region before China could make them dependent, and quickly boosting their military capabilities."

"An arms race and investment, multi-pronged escalation," Berry said. "A recap of what we did with NATO and in Eastern Europe."

"It broke the USSR," Williams said. "Forty years

later, Russia and the republics are still near bank-ruptcy."

"True, though it's too late for us there, now," Berry pointed out.

Williams laughed. Once. "I know that tone. What's your solution?"

"I have what may be a terrible notion, but let's see how it plays out. What if you and the major were to go see this Barbara Niekerk while Rivette and Grace took a trip to Prince Edward?"

Williams's mouth twisted. He had not seen that sneak attack. In his mind, Black Wasp and Yemen was an aberration. A terrorist on the run had to be stopped. Rules did not apply. Now, as then—and with a lifetime in the military clinging stubbornly—his mind was still in the old Op-Center way of doing things. That meant relying on the Joint Special Operations Command, a small cell of special operators who were combat ready at any moment. But there was a big difference. They were seconded to Op-Center by a secret memorandum of understanding between the White House, the Department of Defense, and Op-Center. They had a command structure and rules of engagement.

Black Wasp had no restraints.

"My initial reaction?" Williams said. "It's an effective use of Black Wasp. But baked into that is the uncertainty factor of two young people who like to fight and overreach."

"They wouldn't be there otherwise," Berry said. "They'd sure surprise the hell out of the Chinese."

"Matt, I'd consider this very carefully," Williams said, then was silent for a moment. "Dammit. You *have*, haven't you? This isn't a 'notion.'"

"What the hell is Black Wasp about, if not this exact kind of scenario?"

"I'll ask another way. Do you *want* them taking out Chinese troops?"

"Do you want Beijing to create a weaponized microbe that could be exponentially more lethal than the anthrax they currently have?"

"That's a stupid question."

"To which the answer is 'no'?"

"You are talking about a military with massive resources in the region, and the will to use them—"

"We don't know that, Chase. No one's seriously challenged them yet."

"Then why not send in the *Carl Vinson* and move other naval assets into the region? Blockade the island, nothing in or out."

"Because the president is concerned, as am I, that the Chinese may not need arms to punch their way out," Berry said. "If one corvette can use a microbe to upend the U.S. Navy, the balance of power shifts globally, instantly."

"Until we get the bug. Or a cure. Or both."

"From the bodies of dead seamen on a ghost ship? No. That's a new Vietnam, a Desert One, a defeat that lasts for generations."

Williams had known it was a losing argument from the start. The way Berry had described things was the way they were going to be played. Rivette and Grace in guerrilla warfare against the People's Liberation Army Navy.

Christ.

"What's your endgame?" Williams asked. "You want this—what's your best-case scenario."

"I don't know how we stop the Chinese from obtaining whatever is out there, but we need it too."

"What, we swap electron microscope photos? Mutual assured destruction?"

"Something along those lines. We both develop warheads, we both develop cures, we wait for the arms race to go somewhere else."

"And if Black Wasp is caught?"

"They'll be in civvies," Berry said. "They'll have no ID and the Chinese have no imagination. Ideally, they'll take one of them to be local, the other as somewhat local."

"And *not* ideally?"

"It still works for us. The Chinese haven't been shy about fly-by and sail-by near collisions with every military power in the region, including us. Imagine the game changer this could be. They have a hive mentality in the military. Wasp buzzing in their military ear? That will shake them up."

"The legacy of the Midkiff administration," Williams said. "A final attempt to rattle Beijing."

"You think this is a Hail Mary? It's not. It's a tactic we've been considering for over a year, since we authorized Black Wasp. This is part of what commanders in chief are supposed to *do*. Stay ahead of an enemy. I didn't think I had to explain that to you."

"You don't. But part of *my* job is not to send troops on suicide missions."

"That's what your job *was*," Berry reminded him. "I never told you what the code name for this project was before we settled on 'Black Wasp,' did I?"

"You did not."

"'Loose Cannons,'" Berry said. "The president had grave reservations about this idea, as he should have. The *Intrepid* attack forced our hand. The election is forcing it again. How long will it take for President Wright to get up to speed? Six months? A year? In that time, China can control the Indian Ocean. To the north, Russia can reclaim more of its old empire. We need to show them what the United States is doing to define twenty-first-century counter-aggression. We've got Space Force above, Black Wasp below—maybe a whole nest of them before long—and the rest of our streamlined, armed-to-the-gills military in between."

"Sounds good in the telling."

"You know as well as I do that nothing is guaranteed," Berry said. "Except doing nothing. That's certain failure."

Williams had no rebuttal. His concern was his team—now. Back when he was combatant commander for both Pacific Command and Central Command, he made these same pronouncements, tacitly okayed dangerous special ops missions. Some other officer, who knew the faces, had to worry about their safety.

"Work it out," Williams said. "I'll tell the team."

"Thank you," Berry replied.

"Sure," Williams said. "All I have to do is figure out what advice to give them, not that they'll take it."

"How about 'don't screw up'? They will know exactly what that means."

Berry was being glib but he was right. When Williams gathered the others around and laid out the situation, he expressed deep concern about the ambiguous mission plan.

Grace was untroubled. Apart from her martial arts skills, her deeply etched belief system showed why she had been selected for the Black Wasp experiment.

"The Chinese neigong philosophy of the Five Positions offers guidance," she said. "In any situation there are only five things one can do. Progress, regress, stay, expect, and fix. If a fix is not clear, you do one of the others. If it is, you act."

Major Breen was unconvinced. "What if your fix, in that moment, *is* clear—say, surviving by killing a Chinese naval officer—but it risks a larger conflagration?"

"That risk is already present," she said.

"I saw this movie about General Patton, right?" Rivette said. "He wanted to fight Russia while he already had an army in Europe instead of having to go home and come back when the enemy was even stronger. Isn't that what happened, in Eastern Europe, in Ukraine?"

Williams chuckled. Breen was not amused by that or by the unified militancy of the younger members.

"I guess it's pointless to ask what happened to diplomacy," the major said.

"Never stopped a gang war back in L.A., ever," Rivette said. "I don't know about all this Shaolin stuff, except what I saw in the movies, but I know that if you let a street fall, then a block fall, then a neighborhood fall—you got Detroit or Watts. No, Major. You stop a bully, you *stop* a war."

Breen looked at the clean carpet with its gold and blue pattern. No grime anywhere around the bolts that held the seats to the floor. It was cleaned and maintained by the military. It was done right because there was order. Just like the laws he was sworn to preserve.

"No one can have certainty about anything," Breen said. "Maybe that's why I trust in regulations and guidelines. No knock intended, Lieutenant, but to me that means something a little less vague than 'fix.'" He shrugged. "Maybe I just don't understand the Five Positions. But I'll say this. What happened in Yemen was lawless. If we repeat that, and make a habit of repeating that, and forget what it's like to be civilized, then we haven't fixed anything."

The meeting broke up and Williams went back to think about what he and Berry had set in motion.

No one is wrong, he said. *The problem is, it also doesn't necessarily make anyone right.*

Fortunately, Williams's concerns were less subtle, less complex.

All he had to do was try and stop whatever contagion had been let loose in the world.

CHAPTER FOURTEEN

November 11, 10:09 P.M.

As his helicopter neared its destination, Dr. Raeburn was alarmed to see the sleek Chinese ship below the island's high ledge and a patrol boat moving toward the cover that was home to Ship Rock. It wasn't national sovereignty that concerned him but the contents of the pit at Ship Rock.

At least the sailors were not at the internment site. Not yet. And it was actually encouraging to see the activity inside the bridge of the corvette. The bug was either lost in the atmosphere or depleted. Perhaps there was nothing left in the pit.

He needed orders from Krummeck and he dared not communicate on the helicopter's open radio. Fortunately, he knew where he could get a secure line.

Raeburn, the pilot, and the copilot were wearing

masks, so they communicated by text through the internal silent-running system. Dr. Raeburn wrote:

```
Do not report to Simon
```

The pilot replied:

```
Civil Aviation may spot
```

Raeburn answered:

```
May not coming to Marion from NW.
Dangerous for SA pilots. Must land
tell PLAN to leave.
```

The pilot acknowledged with a nod.

All of what Raeburn had said was true. Focused on their approach to the crash site, the two amphibious planes might be coming in too low to see the corvette. The mountains of Prince Edward would block the pair of helicopters. He also did not want South African Air Force pilots racing down in response. That was not just for their own safety. Raeburn and Krummeck still were at risk of being exposed. He did not want additional eyes on the microbial burial ground until he could seal it.

The question was what to do first. He had to get in there to see what conditions were. Of course, the Chinese would follow.

If they knew where to look they would be doing it,

he thought. *But if they take the AH-2 crew aboard, they'll have it anyway in throat swabs.*

It suddenly occurred to Raeburn that there was something worse than both of those possibilities.

If I land, they will have me.

The doctor had to get instructions from Krummeck. He texted his pilot.

```
Do not land. Go to Point Dunkel.
```

The pilot responded with a thumbs-up and swung the Atlas Oryx back out to sea and headed southwest. As he looked out the window, Raeburn could see a medical officer stop walking toward the AH-2, look up, shield his eyes, and watch the helicopter depart.

Terns were everywhere, dangling fish, and the scavenging black-billed sheathbills flew below them to pick up pieces that fell away. The helicopter rose to avoid them all. As they neared the blackened earth where the plane had come down, Raeburn was horrified to see that the sheathbills and other small birds were flocked across the wreckage. The doctor turned away. The pilot dipped inland to avoid not just the birds but their ugly feast. Within a few minutes the helicopter set down on the pad usually occupied by the AH-2.

There were lights on inside the outpost.

"I think we're okay to take these off," Raeburn said after removing his mask.

The pilot and copilot did the same.

"Wait here," the doctor said. "I want to tell my superior we've arrived and get instructions about the Chinese."

The two members of the flight crew acknowledged. Zipping his coat and pulling on the hood, the doctor stepped outside. His boots crunched on the frozen ground, which was hidden in the shadow of the high, domed President Swart Peak. His face stung from the cold and he paid attention to his nasal passages and throat as he hurried to the building. The door opened as he neared.

A Chinese seaman stepped out, his QSW06 Wéishēng Shǒuqiāng pistol pointed at the doctor. He was wearing an olive green Sherpa-style trench coat and matching hat with the ear flaps tied over the top. The seaman waved the gun, indicating that the lieutenant colonel should come inside. His stern, set expression indicated that the young man would not hesitate to fire it.

As Raeburn entered, seven other naval officers filed out. All were armed and the doctor could hear their heavy boots scraping the hard earth. The lieutenant colonel just now noticed the young South African ensign. He was seated on a swivel chair, pushed well back from the communications center in the far corner of the room.

Except for the hum of a generator out back and the wind that was sweeping loudly through the open door, everything was silent. A minute or so later, Raeburn once again heard the sound of the boots stepping hard and fast. The sailors ushered the two-man helicopter crew back into the small living room and shut the door.

No one had raised their hands, nor had they been asked to. When everyone was gathered, the South Africans were in a circle comprised of Chinese—just like the AH-2.

Beijing and its institutional simplicity, Raeburn thought.

Back at Simon, the navy held regular briefings about the evolving tactics and technology of other militaries sailing the Indian Ocean. Russia had its crude, often reckless muscle. India was governed by a strict, inherently cautious hierarchy. China had its policy of "engulfment." They identified strategic targets and then isolated them from their allies. In effect, the Chinese surrounded and consumed the weakest or key links.

It was then that Raeburn noticed only five of the Chinese had returned. The other two came back moments later. Each was carrying a crate containing six thermite grenades each.

The man who had initially been standing guard went to the radio set and raised the corvette. The room was hot and while Raeburn removed his gloves and unzipped his parka—under the twitchy scrutiny of his Chinese captors—the man spoke briefly with someone, then indicated for Raeburn to come over. The ensign gave him his chair. The doctor wheeled it close to the radio.

"I am Command Master Chief Petty Officer Kar-Yung Cheung of the corvette *Shangaro,*" said a crisp voice on the other end. "With whom am I speaking?"

"Lieutenant Colonel Gray Raeburn, medical officer in the South African Navy."

"What is your reason for coming to the Prince Edward Islands?" Officer Cheung inquired.

"To treat one of our seamen, and may I point out that you are delaying—"

"Was it your intention to cure your pilot with thermite explosives, Lieutenant Colonel Raeburn?"

"We departed in a hurry. Those happened to be onboard."

"What did you intend to do with the hand grenades?"

"Nothing. As I told you—"

"Then you will leave them where you are," Officer Cheung informed him. "As for your comrades on Prince Edward, we will collect them."

"You mustn't do that," Raeburn blurted. And immediately regretted it.

"Why not?"

"I cannot say," Raeburn told him.

"Lieutenant Colonel Raeburn, you know more about this than you are telling. Explain quickly, please. We believe this is an infection and that it will become dormant, or nearly so, in a cold environment. That is why the helicopter heaters were not active."

These people were not unobservant. Raeburn quickly weighed his too-few options. The Chinese had apparently suspected that the doctor was not randomly selected for this mission. He had just stupidly confirmed it. Whether at the outpost or on the corvette, they intended to hold him for now.

"Your silence seems to confirm our suspicions," Officer Cheung stated. "You will be brought aboard."

"And create an international incident?"

"While investigating a possible case of bioterror?" Officer Cheung said. "I do not believe that will happen."

Encircled by the Chinese, with those circles closing tighter, Raeburn thought. He could not afford to be taken by these people. *The truth must not come out.* At the same time, the pit needed to be sealed. That was the priority.

"I have an alternate suggestion," Lieutenant Colonel Raeburn said. "Let these men take me to the place I need to go, to the source of the contagion. Let me destroy what's causing this."

"They will take you but only to recover, not to destroy," Officer Cheung replied.

"I will not do that."

"Then you will do neither, Lieutenant Colonel, and we shall find it eventually."

The doctor was about to warn them about reckless misadventure when there was muted conversation from the other end of the transmission.

The mood in the outpost was tense as the men waited to hear what had happened. Raeburn's fear was that the crew of the corvette was not as safe as had been presumed.

"Doctor, how were my comrades?" Sisula asked suddenly.

"I did not get to see them," Raeburn told him. "You heard the transmissions?"

"Yes."

"The fact that your pilot is still alive is a sign that his exposure was extremely limited."

"I thank God," Sisula said.

After nearly a minute, the Chinese officer returned. His voice was still composed as he said, "It appears, Doctor, that you may have a larger concern than *Shangaro*."

CHAPTER FIFTEEN

November 11, 10:50 P.M.

For his entire life—as much of it as he could remember—Claude Foster had not made decisions.

"It is an essential step," as one of his teachers had once told his mother, "that the young man defiantly skips."

The seven-year-old was punished with a switch for that ignorant, conformity-soaked review. Even then, the boy did not hate his mother. Miriam Foster had had to pretend she was raped by his white father since interracial marriage was not legal. He did not even blame his teacher. The woman ran a small school from a shed in Mdantsane, southwest of East London. There were nine students, two of whom were her children, one of whom was a girl Foster fancied. He liked touching her. She did not like being touched. He did not care.

But that was not what drove the teacher, Miss Ntombela, to visit Miriam Foster. It was over a football the boy had stolen. His father was rarely around and never played with him, there were no boys black or white who would play with him, so he stole the ball from a group of blacks in a dirt lot. After all, they had another and they were using it. This was a spare.

With the name of one of the boys, Danny, written on it.

Foster got a beating from them and then another from his mother. The only thing that changed was Foster was proud of himself for having taken action in a matter that urgently required it. He did not, thereafter, mope around weighing crime against punishment. He took action, took precautions not to be caught, and discovered that bold strokes in fact befuddled the law. He leapt while they crawled. Either they lost his trail or were distracted by warmer, easier trails left by others in the meantime. They might suspect he was lawless but they could never prove it. When men and women sometimes died—until the *Teri Wheel* there had been seven, killed by dogs or guards or cave-ins—there was a sense of "they got what they deserved," and the law had better things to do than investigate MEASE.

Up in the mansion on the hill, Foster's brother urged him to go legitimate, warned him that his good luck would end. Aaron did not understand. He did not understand when his brother tracked the football kids to their shanties, waited till night, and stabbed Danny when he came outside to urinate. Not to kill him;

in the leg, the thigh, cutting a muscle to make him scream. While the family was at the doctor, Foster went inside the hut and stabbed the ball dead. Neither the boy nor the ball was able to take the field again.

Foster had not thought about any of it. He just did it.

After Katinka left to go home, to sleep, Foster did not think about the yacht or insurance or an investigation. The authorities had a bigger concern: the downed jetliner.

There was, now, in Foster's chest, a rising envy and rage. His deep-set eyes locked on the backpack that sat on a wooden chair in his office. It sat there, unassuming and still—

Like a sleeping lion, he thought. Then he corrected himself. It was more like a church icon, Christ on His Cross, latent with greater power than a pack of hungry cats.

The crash was a blank tablet. No one had claimed responsibility, because Katinka had apparently released this thing. It was new and he not only had a chance to own it, he had a chance to stab another football. Not a few diamonds but an entire society that had made him an outcast. He did not consider the aftermath, because the result would be chaos. He was accustomed to improvisation; South Africa was not. He did not contemplate failure, because everyone's eyes were on the skies, not the ground. He did not worry about capture, because he had at least two doses of mass extermination—possibly more. He did not know how many deadly bugs were in each canister.

Though he sat in his office serenely—part of which was exhaustion from the long night—he was giddy inside with possibilities and power. Real power, for the first time in his life. Not in the dark or under the radar.

He did not bother thinking. He had all the equipment he needed in the storage lockers in an adjoining room. Decided, he went to the bathroom—thinking, as he always did, of stabbing Danny before he went so he would wet himself—then went about executing what had emerged fully formed and fully decided in his brain.

Foster slept at his desk for two hours, then made his preparations, then went to one of twenty burner phones he kept in a locker. He called the South Africa Police Services on 3 Fleet Street and located two and a half miles to the south. Arriving for the 8:00 A.M. shift, the men and women in uniform would be having their morning coffee or tea and rusks in sight of the Buffalo River.

This would wake them.

He used his burner phone to call the twenty-four-hour Crime Stop Tip-Off Line. He chose this, instead of the emergency 10111 line, because he wanted to generate excitement at the station, not with a dispatcher whose job was to take down addresses and send patrol cars here and there.

A man answered promptly.

"This is Warrant Officer Berkley. To whom am I speaking?"

"You are speaking to a man who is about to offer the authorities their second puzzle of the day."

"Your name, sir?"

"Call me God of War," Foster said. "I am about to mass murder again."

His chest light, big, joyous, powerful, he killed the call then left to kill a system he despised.

Traffic on the NE Expressway over the Nahoon River was heavy, especially at Batting Bridge. It was always a bottleneck, regardless of the time of day. Tourists to East London were swept up in the nighttime lights on the water and the nocturnal sounds of the Nahoon Estuary Nature Reserve. They slowed to take pictures or to deposit passengers on the walkway that ran alongside the two-lane roadway. Punching the horn did not hurry visitors along. At times, the wind was so strong that they could barely hear. After a long, heavy rain, locals—many of whom did not have smartphones or weather apps—came up to see whether the boats or barges on which they worked were in jeopardy.

No one thought much about the old Toyota Hilux pickup truck heading toward the bridge from the west, from Old Transkei Road to Batting Road. The back was covered with a flapping white canvas, loosely tied. The windshield and windows were dark—a custom job. The license was forged.

The driver had a hazmat mask on the seat in the back of the truck.

A quarter mile from the crossing, Foster pulled over and went about tightening the tarp on the back of his truck. While he was there, cars buzzed by and he confirmed that no security cameras were in any of the streetlamps or traffic lights—a fact he knew from previous canvassing of routes to and from his office. Satisfied, and with a final look around to determine there were no police cars in view—some had new video surveillance systems—Foster put on the mask, opened the canister containing the core sample, and placed it back beneath the tightened tarp with the open end facing behind. Then he hurried to the cab and drove on, trailing the microscopic contents in his wake.

The mask covered his ears and he continually checked his rearview mirror to see if anything was happening. As he reached Batting Bridge, he looked back and smiled.

The only thing Jane Chun liked about South Africa was the chance to study animals.

The South Korean veterinarian had come here with her husband, a diplomat who was stationed at the embassy in Pretoria. She did not like the racial tension here, the decaying infrastructure, or the poverty. But she liked the opportunity to study animals in the wild and work with rescue efforts such as the Hillside Animal Outreach.

In the back of her station wagon, Jane had six poodle puppies running free behind a chicken-wire divider. The barking, growling, and sounds of play were music.

She was distracted as the old Chevy Commodore neared Batting Bridge. An elderly woman who was just stepping onto the walkway suddenly dropped her camera and selfie-stick, turned toward the water, and threw herself against the waist-high railing. Her hands gripping the metal, she coughed out blood.

Jane pushed on her flashing lights and pulled up beside her. As she braked, the Korean woman coughed into her hand. Her eyes were on the woman as she opened the door, still coughing, and walked toward her—

The older woman heaved again, hard, blood pouring from her mouth onto the concrete and railing. Jane stopped, considered going back to get rubber gloves from the wagon.

She never made it. A Camry plowed into the Chevy from behind, pushing it onto the walkway and into the veterinarian. The impact broke her right leg and she fell. The Camry did not decelerate. The left rear of the wagon continued forward, the dogs yelping wildly. The Chevy crushed Jane into the pavement, rolling over her before slamming into the other woman. The rear-door impact splintered her spine as it smashed into the steel tube railing.

The Camry continued moving, the driver having died with his foot on the gas, his shoe and the pedal coated with gore. The two cars scraped along the railing, causing pedestrians who were farther up to run—and then stagger as they began to cough and spit blood and fall.

Cars farther west were beginning to swerve or stop, some bumping into others or into the railing, their headlights scouring the bridge or the river like spotlights. Other vehicles were just stopping as drivers tried to figure out what was going on ahead. None of those cars moved again, the drivers dying in their seats or leaning out the windows. A mother took her young child from their minivan, which was stuck near the entrance to the overpass. They took a few steps before dropping, both of them spitting up blood and tissue.

As all movement on the bridge stopped west of the halfway point—the direction in which the wind was blowing—a Bell 206B helicopter following the Nahoon River on electricity pylon checks began a graceful spiral toward the water, its lights winking like the eyes of a wounded sparrow. The cockpit was over the bridge, then over the water, then over the bridge—and it was finally the tail structure that struck the span. The slender red skin of the helicopter ripped away, the internal supports snapped, and the fuel tanks at the joint opened up. The cabin hit the river with a dull splash, the oil pouring over the water and catching fire as the electric circuits shorted.

A riot of flames shot up, several licking Batting Bridge. They found a car whose tank had ruptured, causing it to explode and triggering a chain reaction of blasts that went all the way back to the main road. Each detonation sent vehicles and their dead occupants roaring into the sky in burning pieces. They tumbled down to the river, to the homes on either shore, and to the bridge. The heat of the fire caused the roadway of the bridge to melt, split, and drop whatever remained into the river.

The charred skeleton that remained was a fitting memorial to the East Londoners who had perished there. No motorists and no one from law enforcement approached by water, land, or air. The only sounds were the rush of the river, the creak of the metal supports on the bridge, and the poodles in the back of Jane Chun's wagon—which had avoided the conflagration because it was off to the side.

And then, in a final act of surrender, the center of the bridge twisted toward the north, carrying the rest of the structure with it and diving into the water. The waves overwhelmed boats and backyards and the bodies of the few residents who had come out to see what was happening.

CHAPTER SIXTEEN

November 11, 4:01 P.M.

"How is that possible?" Harward asked.

The national security advisor, President Midkiff, Matt Berry, and Angie Brunner had listened to the recording of the call to the East London police station. There was an advisory that followed by exactly seven minutes, stating that triangulation of the call, pinpointing the number, and identifying the owner had proven fruitless.

The call was being analyzed by every intelligence agency to which the material had been sent. That was Europe and the United States to start, followed by Russia, China, and the rest of Asia.

"It is possible," Berry said, "if you buy a prepaid phone, purchase minutes using another phone, and activate them. That buys you thirty days till they expire."

"But activation leaves a trail, doesn't it?" the president asked.

"To nowhere," Berry replied. "You call a number, usually somewhere in India, and provide the IMEI number from the burner phone. You also give the operator your name."

"Your actual name," the president asked.

"The name on the existing account," Berry replied. "That one is fake. The account is typically paid for with stolen credit card information. That data is hacked moments before the transfer is done. Hacks like that are done in time zones where people are likely asleep. By the time it's discovered, the minutes have already been transferred to the unknown burner."

"How the hell did we keep inventing technology without built-in safeguards?" Midkiff wondered.

"Mr. President," Harward said, returning to the reason they had gathered, "what about this Chinese presence our ships and satellites are watching?"

"They went right to Prince Edward, not to Marion Island where the plane came down," Berry said.

Midkiff regarded him. "Beijing may have had the same intelligence you did."

"Did I miss something?" Harward asked.

"My gemologist talked about light being emitted from a point on the island," Berry reminded him.

"Something no one else reported," Harward said.

"When you're looking for and at navies, you may miss geologic phenomena, Trevor."

"And the Chinese did see it? With what satellites?

What ships? They had no eyes on that tactically insignificant nature sanctuary."

Before the conversation could continue, Dr. Rajini jumped into the meeting by phone.

"What have you got?" the president asked.

"Two things," she said. "The South African Navy dispatched a medical team to Marion Island, which just arrived. A patrol helicopter set down earlier when the pilot became ill near a location called Ship Rock on Prince Edward Island."

Harward looked at his map. "Northern coast. Where there's been recent sea traffic."

Dr. Rajini did not have security clearance to let her know about the Chinese ship.

"Ill but still alive?" Berry asked.

"We believe so, along with a passenger who was apparently uninfected. Wind currents and proximity may have blunted the impact—we do not have enough information to say."

"What's the other news?" Midkiff asked.

"The helicopter that came down in East London was feeding video to the Department of Energy," the science advisor said. "The camera missed whatever 'vehicle zero' might have been but the incidents definitely spread west along the bridge while rising: cars not yet on the bridge were not affected but the helicopter was."

"Lifted by thermal currents," Harward said.

"It would seem so. The government immediately ordered the skyways cleared along the path the air currents were moving. But what we are trying to ascertain is whether this contagion has an expiration date once released."

"Which you'll only know if someone accidentally gets in the way," the president said.

"There's nothing but mountains for some two hundred miles heading west," she said. "Radios, TV, and social media are warning people to stay indoors, close windows, turn off any air conditioners or fans, and cover their mouths with anything they have. The military is dispatching helicopters with protected pilots to get up there and warn residents—and assess casualties, if any."

"Is there a shelf life for these things in general?" Harward asked.

"That's a good question and I've had my staff focusing on it," she replied. "Bacteria that we sneeze or cough out won't last an hour. Outside the body. The consensus is that this strain—and we still don't know exactly what it is, bacteria or virus or still, possibly, chemical—we hope it wasn't somehow bioengineered to have a longer life span."

"Though we can't rule that out," the president said.

The men did not mention what their shared looks told them. If the Chinese ship was anchored offshore, it suggested the crew was safe, that the disease did not in fact live for very long in the atmosphere.

"Anything from the surgeon general?" the president asked.

"Dr. Young and the Centers for Disease Control and

Prevention are in contact with their counterparts at the South African CDC to try and find out whether this microbe is natural or came from a lab."

"Dr. Rajini, do you still think there's a possibility that this is a natural phenomenon tied to the geology down there?" the president asked.

"It cannot be ruled out," she said.

"Why?" Midkiff asked.

Harward answered, "Because the virulence and speed and cruelty of what it does has the stink of a military bioweapon program."

"The South Africans are not known to have conducted bioweapon research," Berry pointed out.

"With respect, Matt, we are looking into the apartheid era," Dr. Rajini said, adding gravely, "There were rumors of using disease for domestic intervention."

Midkiff thanked her and terminated the call.

"The old Pretoria-created-AIDS canard," Berry scoffed.

"True or not, there is apparently a South African who isn't afraid to use this thing," Midkiff pointed out.

"Which brings up the obvious question," Harward said. "Why wasn't there a warning before the attack on the jetliner?"

"The two incidents may not be related," Berry suggested.

The others considered this.

"Separate perpetrators?" Midkiff asked. "Multiple specimens out there?"

"That or someone, somehow, got a sample from the jetliner and is exploiting the damn thing."

"The caller didn't ask for anything," Midkiff pointed out.

"Yet. Unless he's a complete sociopath—which we cannot rule out—there is more to come."

"Getting back to the Chinese," the president said, "they may not know what to look for, or where, but there are South African naval officers on the islands who do. Beijing will find it before long."

Berry rose. "I'm going to my office to make some calls, see what I can find out. There's nothing I can add about China—they're doing what China does."

"We should do one better," Harward said.

"What's that?" the president asked.

"Blast Prince Edward with a sea-whiz barrage from the *Carl Vinson*. Let the Chinese know that the South African government has requested our assistance."

The Phalanx CIWS was a radar-guided 20mm Vulcan cannon used primarily against antiship projectiles.

"Do you disagree?" the president asked Berry. After eight years with the man, he already knew the answer.

"Apart from the provocative nature of that action, I'm all for letting Beijing take the risks with something this deadly. If they get something, we'll know it."

"You don't care if they control the source, the spigot?" Harward asked.

"Not if we can figure out what this is and find a way to lick it."

Both the president and Berry knew there was another reason.

Angie Brunner, who had been silent the entire time, seemed to catch the look the men shared.

The deputy national security advisor left to go to his small office down the hall. There was no reason for Harward to know that Op-Center had something hopefully more effective than a Chinese landing party on route. He wanted to brief Williams about that and also tell him to lean hard on this Barbara Niekerk.

He had a feeling, an instinct that she knew something more about this, given that she suggested a "time frame" in her call to Australia. If that referred to potency rather than air currents, she *definitely* knew what this was.

As he walked past his secretary's cubicle and opened the office door, a text to the men at the meeting arrived from Dr. Rajini:

```
Medical chopper overdue PE Is. SAN
checking.
```

"Matt, the president wants to see you for a minute," his secretary said as he was shutting the door.

Berry turned back and passed Harward in the corridor. The men did not speak. There was nothing to say. Angie was with him, though she was busy texting—probably President-elect Wright, wanting to brief him.

The president's executive secretary shooed Berry in. The president was behind his desk. He motioned for the deputy national security advisor to shut the door.

"The NRO just informed us the SAN helicopter landed at Marion," Midkiff said. "There's also a Chinese launch moored there."

"That would explain the silence," Berry said.

"Matt, I'm not inclined to disagree with Trevor on this sea-whiz approach. We can't let them land and stay where and however long they wish. But I don't want to do that if Op-Center can do it cleaner and quieter."

"We've still got at least eight hours till boots are on the ground."

"Which worries me," Midkiff admitted. "I don't get the impression that even South African Command knows what's going on out there. If the Chinese are the only ones who figure this out, that's a lot of catch-up for us to do. And a lot of damage they can do—with clean hands."

"Mr. President, we don't know that. The Chinese may have been *behind* this, using the islands as a staging area. They've been pushing the territorial envelope there."

"Naval intelligence considered that," Midkiff said. "Communications suggest they were as surprised as everyone else."

"Good cover, if they pull that off."

"C'mon, Matt. The Chinese are some of the worst bluffers on the planet. If the Indian Ocean were a poker table, they'd have been busted before I was elected. No," the president went on, "I don't think it's them and I don't think it's the Russians. We know all their bio-weapons programs."

"Who's got eyes on the islands?"

"NRO, NASA, DNI—the fleet is listening. But now that everyone's deep in the game, no one's going to say anything of value. Which is the problem and why I'm back at the sea-whiz scenario. The Chinese may have a clear path to success here."

"Unless Op-Center can stop them."

"I prefer 'until,'" Midkiff said. "If we see some sign of the Chinese moving in on that northern location, I'm going to give the attack order."

"If that's the mission, sir, the sea-whiz is not the best weapon for that job—"

"I'm aware of that. Can't put planes in that area until we know more about the toxin," Midkiff replied. "And I can't risk the Chinese taking a shot at one, because then we're in a shooting war."

"Mr. President, I just want to point out that we don't even know if that will work. It could make things worse, blasting particles of whatever-this-is into the ocean."

"It's lethal where it is, and we cannot risk any more of it getting out. The Chinese must not have it."

Berry did not pursue the discussion further. He told the president he would emphasize all of this to Chase Williams and advise him of any developments on that end.

There was just one thing that concerned him beyond the deadline the president had just set. Unlike during their mission in Yemen, the Black Wasp unit was being sent into the eye of an ongoing storm with scrutiny from every nation in the region.

In light of that, there were three things he prayed: that the team was successful, that they got out safely . . . and that they got out unseen.

CHAPTER SEVENTEEN

MARION ISLAND, SOUTH AFRICA

November 11, 11:20 P.M.

The Chinese had waited for the early moon to settle into the darkness before moving. They knew the Americans and the Russians would be watching from space. They did not need to make the job easy for them by operating in any kind of light.

A few minutes earlier, they patched the outpost radio through to a live broadcast from East London. Lieutenant Colonel Raeburn had listened to the report from Batting Bridge with rising anger and nausea.

You did this, he said over and over to himself.

His motives did not matter. His reasons for putting the Exodus bug here did not matter. Only that he had been responsible for hundreds of deaths in just a few hours.

But the idea that someone had taken the microbe from here and used it strengthened his resolve to see that the Chinese did not get it, that no one did.

Whatever had been taken was not an unlimited supply. Save for the germs that had been incinerated in the plane crash, the bacteria that had already killed would return to the air. In a quarantine area, they were unlikely to find another host and would perish. At the very least they would weaken in the air, as they had apparently done in the case of Lieutenant Mabuza.

When the report was finished, and with the leader of the landing party still holding his pistol on Raeburn, Command Master Chief Petty Officer Kar-Yung Cheung, onboard the *Shangaro*, addressed the South African again.

"I am authorized to make an alternate suggestion," the seaman said.

"Mr. Cheung, this thing has to be stopped! How can you even discuss 'suggestions' after what you just heard?"

"That makes it easy. You and I are agreed on the need to find a cure. That is why it would be better for us all, I think—for humanity as a whole—if you were to cooperate. But you will come with us, in any case."

Raeburn did not expect that, nor did he believe it. The Exodus bug would no doubt be weaponized. But the prospect of being free to openly seek a remedy would go a long way toward satisfying his conscience. That was something he would not be able to do in South Africa, at least not from prison if his part in this became known.

Prison or worse, he thought, if Krummeck were at risk of being implicated.

"I presume you have appropriate gear for this expedition?" Raeburn said.

"The full hazmat suits are onboard the patrol boat."

"For the crew of the boat as well?"

"Of course."

"You left port with them," Raeburn said. "Before all of this."

"We do a good deal of spray painting. The antarctic and subantarctic weather is hard on our hull."

There was that, Raeburn admitted. There was also the sinister reality that the Chinese handled biotoxins onboard as a matter of course.

"Officer Cheung, I will take your team to the source of this contagion," Raeburn said. He was surprised at the strength of his voice given the weakness he felt from his ankles to his gut.

"I will tell them to follow your directions," the Chinese seaman said. "Be certain you work directly and honestly."

"I want this stopped."

"I'm glad to hear this. Your three comrades will remain at the outpost with four armed guards. Show any sign of treachery or delay and they will be sent one by one into the sea."

"One thing," Raeburn said. "The civilian investigators will be arriving off these shores in a very short while. They may radio or come to the outpost."

"Your man will warn them that it is infected," Cheung said. "I will be listening."

Raeburn looked at Sisula. "Best to do it, Ensign," the lieutenant colonel said quietly. "That's an order."

"Thank you, Doctor—sir."

Having been told to do it would go a long way to absolving the man of any complicity. Coming from a medical officer in a health crisis, the command would naturally carry even more weight.

Raeburn zipped his parka and pulled his gloves on. He regarded the man with the gun.

"Officer Cheung, if the civilian investigators see your ships and radio South Africa—"

"Your outpost will be grateful for our offer of assistance," Cheung said.

Sisula looked beaten. Raeburn forced a smile. The prodding was ineffectual as the ensign, shamed, looked away. The doctor understood. The man had no doubt grown up hearing tales of the struggle to radically alter South Africa, to achieve racial parity. Others had sacrificed so much so that his could be the first generation to hold the new torch.

He clearly felt he was dropping it.

They left the building and headed east along the rocky ledge, away from the direction of the helipad. The gravel path began some fifty feet above the sea and terminated at a natural cover of large boulders that sheltered both the waters and the complex of bird nests. The smell of dung was overpowering when they were low enough for the rocks to block the wind.

It was worse than he had remembered over on Prince Edward Island. But then, everything was.

The crew of the aluminum patrol boat had remained onboard. Two men came on deck from the bridge, both armed with raised 5.8mm assault rifles.

The vessel was smaller than the Houbei-class missile boats, but Raeburn did not recognize the design. Despite being in the navy he was impartial to the sea. He had grown up in Simon's Town and the navy afforded him the chance to be close to his family.

The men kept their cold-weather wear on as they donned their oversized yellow hazmat suits, the gloves included. Their protection consisted of fully sealed coveralls, shoe covers that zipped to the cuffs to create a seal, and gloves that did the same with the sleeves. There was a full-face respirator with a large, clear visor that afforded peripheral vision.

The uniforms did not have a spot of paint upon them, a natural hazard of at-sea touchups in oceanic wind.

The twin gasoline engines pushed them along at twenty-five knots. Standing in the enclosed bridge, Raeburn heard the tarp fluttering in the elongated stern. He turned and caught a glimpse of the rails used for mine laying. They were empty.

Because they were used, or idle? he wondered.

He began to feel that this was not just another example of the slow-burn Chinese expansionism. Perhaps the opportunity was so great that the methodical Chinese nature was shoved aside.

That's how wars start, he thought. *With the impulse or impatience of just one man. . . .*

The trip to the northern coast of Prince Edward Island took the better part of an hour due to contrary currents and the need to go wide of land to keep from being slapped back against it. They were actually about a half mile north of the corvette by the time they reached it. Once there, the lieutenant colonel directed them to Ship Rock.

The large, narrow, high slab of land resembled a schooner coming to anchor in the natural cove. At its closest approach to the island, Ship Rock was just under one hundred feet from shore. The top of the elongated mass was flat and mossy green, the walls sheer and craggy. Only the "rudder" section of the islet was truly accessible.

That was where Raeburn had buried the virus, deep in the ancient bedrock. The day did not seem so remote to him as they came at the island from the very angle he had those many years ago.

The same large, lumpy rocks sat at the northeastern waterline. Raeburn remembered from his reading, at the time, that the islands were built over tens of millions of years from piled-up silt, gravel, and the remains of dead sea creatures. It was compacted, but not in a way that would crack and fissure like granite or basalt. That made it ideal for burying the concrete container. It would become part of the earth, just as the root of a tree becomes part of a walk.

Just before Raeburn reached Ship Rock, he saw the two amphibious planes coming in low across the sea. He could see their lights and the reflection off the sea. They vanished behind the promontories of Prince Edward, their shadows dragging behind. It was dark, and since they would be looking ahead at the wreckage, he did not know if they would have noticed the patrol boat or the corvette.

The lieutenant colonel turned his eyes back toward their destination. They were on the moonless side of the cliff and Raeburn indicated for the pilot to turn on spotlights. The twin lamps snapped on, throwing a figure eight on the rock. The visor had a slight polarization for bright-light situations and gave the view a barely perceptible red tinge. What he saw caused his brain to hiccup for just a moment: What the *hell* was he looking at?

The materials had been buried diagonally in the cliff behind an edge-worn pyramid of a boulder some seven feet high. The rock butted up against the wall, providing concealment and shelter from the elements. Around it were smaller rocks that had served as a platform for the doctor and his team to work.

At Raeburn's direction the boat had cut its engines and circled to the south of the rock. That outcropping was the same but the once-stubbled but uniformly surfaced cliff behind it was scarred to the point of grotesqueness. The excavation he had made, not far from the waterline, had been eroded shut by the elements, as he had expected. But there was new damage.

Three small holes had been drilled in the selfsame spot he had selected. They were aligned, each about a foot apart. The site could have been selected purposely—but more likely it was practical, the best place to stand. The holes themselves were small, the size of a handheld tool. Raeburn's conclusion would have been that a geologist or climatologist had been here collecting samples. But the holes were not all there was. They were simply a way in, like construction engineers used to plant dynamite in rock.

But TNT had not been employed here. The driller had used a powerful acid.

And not with a glass pipette. It had been poured in, burning away rock, so a core sample could be gathered in a stainless steel tube.

The rock below the holes was scarred, marked with deep rivulets, rotted. There were meandering cuts like a river seen from space—a microcosm of the macro-world, strangely fractal. The doctor counted seven in all. In some spots the fissures were so deep that their depths were lost in shadow.

And the smooth rills went down, to and below the waterline. The sea fingered its way in, water cascading in each of the narrow channels. The fact that the water was not filling the cavities suggested they went deep. Perhaps the acid had connected with air pockets below the surface, deep in the base of the rock.

That could have released gases that would have helped the bug to rise, Raeburn thought.

What a maddening scenario: something presumably safe had been the ideal medium to release the bacteria from captivity.

The Chinese were speaking but the lieutenant colonel had no idea what they were saying. He continued to look ahead, watching the interaction between the water and the rock, considering what the saline content in the sea would have done to the bacteria. The organism was not a halophile. As engineered, it did not bond with sodium in the human body. Otherwise, it would have become stuck on arterial walls. The rush of salt water would have been another impetus for the bacteria to leave the breached containment area. That, plus the fact that the sea temperature was warmer than the rock.

How did I fail to consider all of this? he reprimanded himself. Though he knew the answer. Because he and Krummeck were in a rush to dispose of the thing.

As they neared, depending on the angle, Raeburn could swear he saw tortured expressions and figures in the etched stone. They moved when the light did, reaching, twisting, elongating—

The man with the gun used his free hand to tap the doctor on the side of his visor. The Chinese made a shrugging motion.

"What do we do?" Raeburn said in his hollow, filtered voice. He pointed to himself and then at the hellish carving. "I go out."

The man slapped his chest. He was going too.

The pilot remotely angled the spotlight to the waterline and the Chinese officer who was to accompany Raeburn was helped into a backpack. The two men went on deck. The railing consisted of two tubes, knee- and waist-high. They held the higher rail as they moved forward across the slippery deck. The rubberized deck and aluminum hull were thick with spray, some from waves but most of it kicked up by the wind; the large, semicircular cove created something of an accelerator, spinning the air toward the pebbled surface of Ship Rock. The engines were practically idling, used only to steer as the current moved them forward. The pilot skillfully maneuvered them so the prow was facing away from the stone. It wasn't going to be possible for them to work from the deck; they would have to get a foothold somewhere on the low rocks, which were greasy with moss.

The cowl of the outfit created a hollow, constant drone in Raeburn's ears, a combination of wind and sloshing surf. Moving was awkward due to the multiple layers of clothing, and it was cold. Their perspiration turned icy and chilled them unremittingly. It took effort to focus. Reaching the prow, the Chinese seaman opened a gate in the rail, reluctantly but finally putting his gun in a deep pants pocket.

Where the hell am I going to run to? Raeburn thought as he studied the roughly twenty square feet of erosion-flattened rocks that lay below the scarred rocks and alternately above and below the swirling tide. It struck Raeburn as strange, these many years later, but one of the things he remembered from the long-ago visit here was the strength of the tides. They were at their peak now. Coming at night, hiding from van Tonder's patrol, encroachers would have had room to move, to crouch, to push themselves into stony nooks.

The seaman descended first. He gripped the lowest rung of the ladder, which was chest-high, even as he stood on the rocks. He let go only when the unpredictable rocking of the vessel threatened to yank him from his perch. He nearly skidded on the dark brown surface but managed to reach the ledge right beside the excavation. He planted his back against the surface and motioned Raeburn over.

The South African hesitated. If he went over, the waves would carry him off before his escort could even push off the wall. The impatient sailor motioned him again, more insistently.

Turning, the lieutenant colonel backed down the ladder. The salt water already made the rungs an uncertain footing and he held the sides of the ladder tightly. Reaching the rocks was actually a blessing: at least they were steady. He pushed off from the boat and half walked, half slid to where his companion was waiting. The man grabbed him by the sleeve, Raeburn turning his face toward the man and showing him an alarmed expression.

The South African shook his head. "Don't pull my goddamn suit! There's a deadly bug here, ass!"

The Chinese could not understand the words but he received the message. He carefully released his grip. Raeburn put his palms against the rock wall to steady himself then used it for support as he shimmied toward the eerie and abstract carving.

The three holes were shoulder high. Someone about his height had put a bit in there and leaned into it to turn—by hand. There was none of the external smoothness that would suggest a rapidly, evenly boring drill. He looked down at the open channels. He looked down in the widest one, as deep as his bulging face plate would permit.

The seaman tapped him and turned, presenting his backpack. Raeburn understood. He unzipped the side, angled the contents into the light, and removed a flashlight. He shined it into the opening.

The view, as far as he could see, was of a foreign, surreal landscape. The acid had indeed cut a path to the excavation they had made. The slime-covered concrete bunker was in there, about four feet below the waterline. Its top had holes created by dripping acid, ten in all, each no wider than a few inches. But the penetration had been sufficient to expose the sealed containers of bacteria to the acid.

Raeburn looked at the other man. He wanted to tell him there was nothing there, but the Chinese would not believe him—and there was also the matter of finding a way to destroy the thing. Reluctantly, the lieutenant colonel nodded.

The seaman took the flashlight and shined it on the surface of the water. He knelt, looking at the wall of compacted rock. He picked up a tiny stone and scratched at it, like some primitive man trying to start a fire. Where he struck he left a deep white scar.

Satisfied, he rose and dropped the rock and motioned Raeburn back to the boat. There was, for the first time, no urgency in the man's movements. The meaning was clear. The Chinese obviously knew the local tides as well. They would wait until the late-evening ebb and then they would go in through the ledge itself to extract the contents.

CHAPTER EIGHTEEN

November 11, 10:30 P.M.

It was dark outside the windows of the giant aircraft, and both Williams and Breen were asleep in their seats.

Grace and Rivette were not. They were sitting together, studying maps of the two islands where they were bound, and checking stats about temperatures—both air and water—winds, and poisonous flora and fauna. Grace downloaded the digital images and data into her smartwatch. Yemen had been an on-the-fly operation against loosely organized bands. Prince Edward was a mission against the Chinese military. She wanted to be thoroughly prepared.

With some regularity, they would receive updates from the Defense Logistics Agency, no sender ID, but very little that pertained directly to their assignment. They were mostly interested in up-to-the-minute weather reports and temperatures, since both martial arts and marksmanship were not well served by ice or other slippery substances.

"Couple of unoccupied sheds on the tiny island, military outpost on Marion," Rivette said.

"We should reconnoiter the outpost first," she suggested. "It would have communications the Chinese would have to control."

"Agreed. What kind of landing party would they use?"

"A large one, which is why we should approach with caution. They're not making a secret of their presence so they'll probably have lookouts."

"In those temperatures? That wind?"

"They'll fight for the privilege," Grace said. "Manhood, nationalism—they'll want to show 'face.'"

"Like a goddamn gang back in L.A.," Rivette said. "Well, at least we'll get to see the countryside," he joked.

"Have you ever been to South Africa?"

"Not even ancestrally, far as I know. Pretty small percent of Cajuns have that. We're from North Africa via France, I've been told. You been there?"

Grace shook her head. "Nor the subantarctic."

"You did cold-weather training, though."

"Alaska," she said.

"Same here. Probably not the same as what they got down south."

"Wondering how they plan to get us over," Grace said.

"Way we barged into Trinidad, I don't think they'll want to chute us in."

Grace smiled. "I liked that, though."

"You hit the deck butt-kicking," Rivette pointed out. "A big-ass island, that's something different. They'd see us coming."

"My guess is they'll put us in with the civilians working on the wreck. If anything else is happening on that island, the perps will want to avoid the investigators."

"True. We also have the toxin to worry about," Rivette went on. "Working with gas masks is a pain."

"And it'll be dark," Grace said. "Most of the glass in those things is tinted. We'll probably fall into the sea."

"I swam with seals at the San Diego Zoo once, so I'm good with that," Rivette joked.

Grace looked at him. "Was that something you were supposed to do?"

"Nah. Good training for this though, right?"

He had a point. Grace had never played by rules other than her own. Growing up in New York's Chinatown, she used a devastating roundhouse kick to make her way into the male-centric world of kung fu. As a girl she would insert herself into the pick-up-style competitions in Columbus Park, getting thrown and leopard-punched—and learning, from that, how to fall. Then she figured out how to use her smaller size and speed to avoid being hit. Then she studied the techniques of using her core energy and technique to overpower anyone who relied on muscle.

When she finally enrolled in classes at age ten, in

a Mulberry Street walkup, she was known as Big Yin—a tribute to her strong female center.

An update from Matt Berry reached the devices of all the Black Wasp members. It showed images of a Chinese presence on both Prince Edward and Marion Islands.

"Shit. You speak Chinese?" Rivette asked.

"Mandarin."

"A dialect?"

"The official language of China," she replied. "As opposed to Cantonese, which is regional."

"So you'll be able to talk to anybody we run into," he said. "Make like I'm your prisoner or something in case we're caught."

Grace marveled at the way their age difference and upbringing gave them radically different views on life. Lance Corporal Jaz Rivette confronted the world as if it were a movie. Everything was a scene or an act or a con.

"Do you think you'll have trouble fighting them?" Rivette asked.

"Chinese? No. I don't see faces, I feel the negativity from the *dontian,* the 'cauldron.' Mindless aggression. It's difficult to explain."

"I don't understand what you just said, but I dig that you're in close—I'm not. And I think about that sometimes. Daylight, night vision, telescopic—I see them. Unless they're an active shooter, I wonder if I would hesitate to put them down."

"I hope so, but not for that reason. They may have

intel. Anyway," Grace went on, "with the hazmat masks I won't be looking into anybody's eyes. I'll be trying to maneuver them so the sun is smack on the visor."

The conversation was interrupted by another message from Berry. This was one thing that Grace loved about Black Wasp. Williams had age on them, Breen had rank, but everyone got the same updates for their own tactical evaluation and application.

Both young members read it. It was about the attack on Batting Bridge and an estimate of the numbers of dead. And something more:

```
SA Navy Sp Op being dispatched,
details to follow.
Aggressive status anticipated vs.
China.
```

"My concerns just became real," Rivette said.

"I was just thinking that."

"No, I mean really real," Rivette said. "I was reading about the African leaders during lunch. Rear Admiral Mary-Anne Pheto came up during apartheid, did her share of subterfuge when she was ten. We get caught in the middle, we better think about who we're willing to take out."

Grace saw the weapons she had tucked into the backseat in front of her: the two hilted knives, one serrated; the hip packet of throwing stars; the short escrima sticks she used as batons.

"I can dole out 'unconscious' if I want," the lieutenant said. "Anything you do spills blood."

"Hey, I asked for tranquilizer darts but you know what I was told? Just what you said. 'That's James Bond.' They offered me a .40-caliber poison-dart air gun if I wanted to make less noise. Point missed."

"By who?" Grace asked. "You render an enemy unconscious, you've got to transport them or wait till they come around to interrogate and then kill them. You can't leave them behind to talk."

"Padre Hill, back at Pendleton, told me my intentions were good. That I had the heart of a missionary." Rivette looked at his own arsenal, which sat in a leather gym bag at his feet. "I wonder if there was ever a killer missionary?"

"On the way home, read up on the Poor Fellow-Soldiers of Christ and of the Temple of Solomon," Grace said. "The Knights Templar. You'd've fit in, sort of."

"A knight?"

"Sort of," Grace repeated. She turned back to her tablet. "I want to read up on the SAN—see what kind of tactics the DOD has on video."

"Probably SOP," Rivette said.

"Wouldn't bet my life on them being standard," she said. "I met a *sifu* who invented a style called kung fu zu. He was from Harlem, had learned Zulu fighting and dancing techniques in Africa and merged them with his own Shaolin style. Alternately solid and flowing. If these guys have had even a smattering of that, I want to know it."

Rivette snorted. "Maybe there's something to be said for point-and-shoot after all."

The two continued their studies in silence, though each quietly marveled at two things. First, how she and the lance corporal were a perfect balance of aggressive male yang and subtler female yin. Second, the uncommon wisdom and courage the military had shown by putting them together. They were the perfect balance of the forces of the universe.

They were, she believed more than ever, the future of perfect, proficient, minimalist combat.

CHAPTER NINETEEN

November 11, 11:56 P.M.

The generously sized office with its views of the compound and the sea beyond was adorned with memorabilia—pieces of history that Rear Admiral Mary-Anne Pheto had witnessed, even brushed against, but not created.

There were framed photographs of a younger Pheto with Nelson Mandela and Winnie Mandela, and a large framed flag inscribed to her by both. She had a signed photograph of Lieutenant General Gilbert Lebeko Ramano, former chief of the army, who had been a mentor.

There was a cross that had been given to her by Desmond Tutu, Nobel Peace Prize–winning Anglican cleric who had courageously spoken out against apartheid.

The woman had joined the maritime service in 1980 as a volunteer cadet and rose to full-time sailor within a year. She served onboard SAS *Galeshewe* then SAS *Shaka* before beginning an officer's course at the SA Naval College in Gordon's Bay. She obtained her National Diploma in Tactics and Strategy and was assigned to SAS *Adam Kok* in 2007. A stint at the Joint Senior Command and Staff Programme at the SA National War College and the Security and Defence Studies Programme landed her a deputy directorship at the Department of Maritime Warfare. It was considered a "shelf" position because there was no maritime warfare. But at least the SAN could crow about having promoted an African woman to a top spot.

Close, always so close to greatness but never quite achieving it herself.

That was the epitaph the fifty-five-year-old rear admiral imagined would adorn her tombstone—in fittingly small letters, so it would all fit. Attaining greatness in her chosen field was not for lack of desire but for lack of opportunity and, until now, lack of support for her outspoken views on absolute, even militant sovereignty.

That stagnation had changed within the past hour. Changed by a gift from a man who had not been on her radar before this morning. Triggered by his call, she had set in motion a military mobilization unprecedented in her tenure. There had never been a mission so swiftly mounted, nor one so fraught with purpose, as that which she was overseeing now.

If Pheto were not so busy, perhaps she would be the one crowing right now.

The existence of Prince Edward as a possible cause

of the contagion, and the interest of the Chinese, had been called to her immediate attention directly by no less a figure than General Tobias Krummeck, chief intelligence officer of the South African National Defence Force. He had folded her into his intelligence because, as he had put it, "You have made no secret of your desire to keep the Chinese contained."

Krummeck did not have the authority to tell her what to do. He did not have to. Nor was it likely that anyone from on high would interfere. However it went, if this action failed, her career would be over. If it succeeded—both militarily and in terms of popular support—high command would take the credit.

That was fine with her. Anything that allowed her to rewrite that albatross of an epitaph was fine.

She was sending the frigate SAS *Isandlwana* to Prince Edward, along with two Saab JAS 39 Gripen fighters. Flying at Mach 2, the jets would arrive within an hour of taking off. Each was equipped with a 27mm Mauser BK-27 revolver cannon with 120 rounds, four 13.5cm rockets, six AIM-9 Sidewinders, and both laser-guided and cluster bombs. The frigate would take much longer to reach the islands but its armaments did not rely on proximity. These included an Oerlikon 20 mm cannon, eight four-cell launchers, and two eight-cell vertical launchers. The commander of SAS *Isandlwana* had complete operational discretion. The rear admiral had granted this authority because if anything—and if it were possible—Captain Leon Jordaan disliked Chinese expansionism even more than she.

"Hostile action toward your vessel or our aircraft, or refusal to honor the sovereignty of our lands, will be perceived as aggression and responded to as permitted by international and national rules of engagement."

Both sets of law stated, explicitly, that unit commanders have the right to defend their troops, vessels, and aircraft from actions by other nations, including attack or imminent attack. South Africa maritime law further qualified such action as not just a right but an obligation.

Pheto and Jordaan had carefully considered the relative strength of the frigate and the Chinese corvette. They had ascertained that the South African vessel would dominate such an encounter, especially with the aid of the fighter jets. They believed the Chinese would back down.

The question of a possible bacteriological agent somehow attached to the region was not something the rear admiral took lightly. And she was surprised that Krummeck had not made mention of it, other than as a potential risk to the mission. It had been a topic around the command center all day, not as a possible bioweapon but as a frightening curiosity.

Perhaps Krummeck was exploring it with other departments and did not want to confuse the matter at hand. Or perhaps he was just being a professional intelligence officer: speaking, by habit, of nothing that did not need to be discussed. In any case, she assured him that the forward team, the pilots, were equipped with hazmat masks and would be flying low so that upper-atmosphere toxins might not be a risk. If the experience of the outpost crew of the Denel AH-2 Rooivalk helicopter and then at Batting Bridge had taught them anything, it was that this microbe seemed to lose potency rather quickly.

Though there were not enough masks to go around on the frigate, gas masks were standard issue. Pheto would trust them to protect the crews. Jordaan would have to use his own on-site discretion where that was concerned.

She doubted he would be backward about moving forward.

The arrangements made, Pheto rose from behind her desk to join her colleagues in the situation room down the hall, watching live video feeds and digital maps on eight wall-mounted monitors. There would be cautions from the director of maritime diplomacy and strategy, who preferred talk to action; the chief of fleet staff and director of fleet force preparation would also be present to offer advice and caution.

But, encouraged by Krummeck, the chief of navy had given this to her, the chance she had wanted her entire life. There was no way she was going to let China cow her. Though there was one thing that puzzled her in Chief Roodt's verbally delivered orders: she was to ignore the Advanced Hawk training jets that would be flying in the region. They were under direct orders from him and would not be armed.

"They are tasked with observation and reconnaissance," he assured her.

That was fine. They were supersonic but not as fast as the Gripen fighters. Her jets would get there first.

Pheto fit her hat upon her head and rose, exhaling to calm herself, and left the sunny office for the artificial lights of SR1.

CHAPTER TWENTY

November 11, 11:09 P.M.

The deal was simple and only four people knew about it: the president, Matt Berry—who crafted it—South Africa's Chief of Navy Stefan Roodt, and now Chase Williams.

No one stands to lose anything, except the team in the field, Williams thought as he listened to Berry explain it.

The deputy national security advisor had woken Williams up with the news. Not that he minded. As much as he liked to stockpile rest before a long haul, there were a great many details still to plan—such as finding an approach to Barbara Niekerk.

At least the operational parameters for Grace and Rivette were falling into place. In exchange for real-time intelligence from the National Reconnaissance Office on Chinese activity on Prince Edward and

Marion Islands, Roodt had agreed to allow the presence of two American operatives working undercover on the islands. After the C-21 landed at joint services base Thaba Tshwane in Pretoria, Grace and Rivette would be flown to Marion Island for a quick drop-off at a spot officially named Flat Cuff, but dubbed, by pilots who had used it, as "Flat Enough."

The ground had been leveled for an airstrip in the days of prop planes, but the environmentalists would not permit the work to be completed. Because of the hills to the north and south, and the constant winds to the south at this time of year, the approach would be "silent enough," as Berry put it.

Before leaving the aircraft, the Black Wasps would swap out their onboard oxygen supply for gas masks—though the risk of infection was deemed to be virtually nonexistent at that low altitude and given the prevailing winds.

Before finishing with Berry and briefing the others, Williams went over the latest China update, which he was just reading for the first time.

"The jetliner crash gives them cover," Berry said. "They can always say they were there to help figure this thing out."

"Wouldn't be a lie, as far as it goes."

"The woman in charge of South Africa's response hates the poker-faced bastards," Berry said. "Wasp has got to step carefully. Especially Grace. SAN rank and file won't be getting the memo about our participation."

Grace's ancestry had not even occurred to Williams.

People were just people until someone else made them categories.

"Apart from being obliged to fall on our swords, what's your stand on us being forced to take someone down?" Williams asked.

"You mean what works for me?"

"Yeah."

"The bug," Berry said. "Especially with China there and Russia watching. As far as we can tell, they haven't fielded a unit. They've got enough going on in Eastern Europe to worry about stepping on Chinese claims. Whatever the price, Chase, stop it, get it— either of those."

Even if it comes back inside a cold, dead, infected but quarantined member of Wasp, Williams thought. Even so, he could not really blame Berry. If an enemy were to obtain the microbe, there was no limit to the scale and scope of blackmail and extortion they could enact.

Williams went up a few rows to talk to Grace and Rivette. Breen was awake and joined them. He stood beside Williams in the aisle. Throughout the briefing, the major seemed unusually distracted. He would check his phone, look out a window at the darkness, and seemed generally restless.

When Williams finished, he asked the officer for his reaction.

"None of that is surprising," he said.

"But?"

"While you were asleep and they were studying," he said, indicating the younger members, "I read a long e-mail from Becka Young in the TS/SCI-cleared folder. There was no tickler to us, I just decided to have a look."

The blanket-cleared Top Secret/Sensitive Compartmented Information folder was for all intelligence and defense agency personnel who qualified. The program was instituted post–9/11 to encourage the sharing of intel.

"The surgeon general was looking into this matter of what is still a theoretical microbe being unable to survive in the air for very long."

"Looking into—how?"

"Running simulations on known bacteria and viruses that adhere to this kind of pattern. Active inside a welcoming, nutritious environment—the body—and perishing without that. She took thirteen known specimens, ran computer simulations in the two known 'attacks,' if you will, and felt strongly enough to write it up. There's a problem with all this."

Williams found himself growing increasingly concerned as Breen spoke. The major was nothing if not a calm, logical, reasonable man. The man standing before him was not that. Fittingly, given the topic, the mood itself was contagious. Even Rivette, who was prone to interjections, had been tempered by the man's obvious concern.

"What problem?" Rivette finally spoke.

"Four of the sampled microbes did not die," he said. "They simply became dormant. In the given situation, she wrote, the germs would be lifted to the upper atmosphere, where they would disburse and represent an infinitesimal danger. There would be no way for them to get back down or intersect with human activity. But," he emphasized, "that ascension process depended on thermal currents providing more lift than crosscurrents blowing them sideways."

"Meaning they might stay close to Earth," Williams said.

"But dead, still, so what's the big whoop?" Rivette asked.

Breen looked at him. "Not dead. Four of the samples she ran were just dormant. If they found a host, they came back. Fast."

"So a germ that was released at Batting Bridge could float to—anywhere if the winds were with it," Grace said. "It could cross an ocean."

"Yes, especially in an area where thermals are either seasonally short-lived or nonexistent."

"East or west, back home's in the crosshairs," Rivette said, thinking it through. "It's like a damn sleeper cell. It can go undercover and wait till it's ready to blow your ass off."

"All right, everything about this is still speculative," Williams said.

"Except for the fact that it kills, quickly," Grace said.

"You could be walking the dog and drop dead," Rivette agreed.

"Both true, but we do not understand the mechanism by which this happens," Williams went on. "Our mission is to collect intel from a person or persons in South Africa and to try and stop the Chinese from securing a sample. Dr. Young, the CDC—those people are more highly qualified to do the worrying."

That came out a little more like a unit commander than Williams had intended, but nothing was gained by having the team slip into a "what if" scenario over which they had no control. Non-hierarchal as Black Wasp was, each member still had to be focused on the task before them.

There was, in fact, only one thing Chase Williams knew for certain. By any means necessary, at whatever price, they needed to obtain a sample.

CHAPTER TWENTY-ONE

PRINCE EDWARD ISLAND, SOUTH AFRICA

November 12, 4:30 A.M.

Lieutenant Colonel Raeburn actually welcomed the nighttime hours he spent in the cabin of the Chinese patrol boat.

He was seated on the galvanized floor, surrounded by the sailors who remained standing, studying their instruments, watching the sea, and receiving instructions from the corvette. He barely heard their chatter over the sound of his own breathing in the mask. Staying comfortable and trying to sleep, just a little, gave him something to do other than to think about the Exodus bug. Added to that was nausea from the constant rocking. He did not dare throw up, however. He could not risk removing the mask.

When ebb tide arrived it was time to move out. Raeburn's eyes were shut; his only signal was the toe of a boot and the gesturing of the pistol.

The doctor's knees were bent and it took effort to move. When he finally got up on his painfully straightened legs, he stood for a last moment savoring the heat of the cabin. The instant the door opened, the icy wind gusted in, making the yellow suit flutter. His parka would only retain heat for so long, though the airtight hazmat attire would hold it in a little longer.

He and the man with the pistol made their slow, cautious way back to the unnatural excavation in the seawall. The sailor was followed by a man with a small hatchet that had a ball-peen knob on the other end. Raeburn presumed it was onboard for chopping caked deck ice if the corvette went farther south.

The spotlights were on again, their white light on the black stone making the vista seem like a Doré etching, something from *Rime of the Ancient Mariner*—agonized faces cut into ice and rock or briefly formed by full-bodied, high-crested breakers. Because of the curvature of the rock wall, the sea smashed every which way and rebounded, arching backward, often higher than when it came in.

Tiny chunks of ice floated on the waves, worn smooth and occasionally cracking as they were heaved skyward.

The man with the ax removed a vinyl covering from a coiled rope hanging on a hook at the top of the rail. It was attached to a life preserver that hung beside it. He undid that end and, tucking the hatchet under his arm, tied the rope around the waist of each man. Raeburn wasn't sure whether this was to keep them from drowning or him from trying to escape. There was nowhere to go, but the Chinese were cover-your-ass efficient that way.

With the sea spray, Raeburn realized those knots would tighten and solidify very quickly. The fate of one was the fate of all.

The man with the hatchet descended to the stones first, followed by the South African and then the sailor with the gun. The man put the pistol in a zippered pocket on the right leg, obviously realizing it was extraneous here. He removed a waterproof flashlight.

The men got their footing, the first man slowly putting his fingers around one of the wider cuts in the rock, careful not to tear his suit. He eased forward and used the ball-peen hammer to lightly tap away the edges of the opening from the inside out. Chips fell at their feet and plunked into the sea. When the hole had been sufficiently enlarged, the seaman swapped with his superior, the hatchet for the flashlight, and shined it down into the artificial fissure. There was enough play in the rope and room on the rocks for Raeburn to half walk, half slide his way around the man to peer down.

If Raeburn thought he had been sick before, he was wrong. What he saw made bile, shame, and tears rise in equal measure. Below, its heavy lid eaten like ratty cheese, was the concrete container with the canisters of the Exodus bug. It was set in the well-like tomb they had cut in the natural rock. Most of the large container was submerged in pooled water left over from high tide.

Raeburn took the sailor's wrist and adjusted the

flashlight so he could see inside. The acid had eaten through two of the six containers.

The people who had been here would not have seen that. Obviously and illegally looking for evidence of gem deposits, they had hand-drilled three holes in the roof of the well. He could see, in the light—as they surely did—faint traces of what looked like diamond dust. The person or persons had used acid to eat away the rock below them simply so they could fit their tools to drill up. They did not realize what they were releasing as the acid continued to burn down.

These were not careful geologists, Raeburn thought bitterly. *They were poachers in a hurry.*

Tragically, the recent visitors had drilled here for the same reason Raeburn had buried the bug here. The rocks afforded footing and the environment made it unlikely that anyone would come nosing around.

He did not know who was more reprehensible: himself or the pirates who had done this.

Accessing the containers from here would be difficult, especially in the time they had before the tides returned. They were going to have to chop through the rock near the waterline.

He indicated as much to the man standing beside him. The leader was watching and shook his head. He ordered the others back to the patrol boat. Raeburn hesitated as he looked up on deck, shielding his eyes from the bright spotlights. He saw two seamen on deck, each with a CQ 5.56 assault rifle.

They were going to shoot the wall away.

"No!" Raeburn shouted into his face mask. "You

may damage one of the other containers, release more—"

"*Tíngzhǐ!*"

Raeburn heard the leader's muted shout, saw his arm sweep angrily toward the patrol boat. He did not have to know the meaning to recognize he was being told to go back. To make the point, the leader withdrew his pistol.

The lieutenant colonel steadied himself on the wall to turn around, and did as he had been ordered. The man with the hatchet followed and the leader came after. When they were all back on deck, the two armed men listened to shouted directions from the man who had looked into the opening with Raeburn. He pointed and they nodded.

With the three men standing behind them, still tied, the sailors opened fire on the stone wall. Bullets and shards of stone pinged and ricocheted in all directions, sparks lighting the sky beyond the rocking cones of light. Raeburn watched carefully as the rock was picked apart, chewed up around the edges of the area with the container. As they continued firing, larger pieces of wall fell away. More and more of the concrete case was revealed; the way the lights were rolling with the flow of the ocean, the shifting shadows made the container seem to be breathing . . . alive.

Suddenly, the fusillade came to an abrupt stop as one of the lights went out. In the moment of silence, a single shot broke from above and shattered the other light.

The five men on deck stood very still in darkness that had suddenly become their enemy.

Commander Eugène van Tonder had not been able to reach anyone by radio for several hours. He did not expect to be able to talk to Simon but he had heard nothing from the outpost, either. Nor were they answering.

Equally puzzling, what was apparently the helicopter from the mainland had flown directly over—then continued on to Marion, without stopping. There was no way they could have missed the downed helicopter. Despite the drain on the batteries, he had kept the navigation lights on so the AH-2 would be seen.

It was perplexing and van Tonder wondered if Simon knew more than he did about the toxicity of whatever was out here. Perhaps Sisula had been evacuated. The commander would not necessarily have seen or heard the helicopter if it refueled and took off from the eastern side of Marion.

There was nothing to do but sit there with the mask on as Lieutenant Mabuza slept. An explanation would come—eventually. One of the many things van Tonder had learned in the navy was that it took its own time doing things, a pace that left no seaman content.

Van Tonder was forced to run the heater from time to time, and managed to sleep a little between. Waking up from the cold, he happened to notice the faintest glow from somewhere below the northern ledge. It was not long after midnight and the lights were only there a short while, but he had bundled himself as tight as possible against the wind—which included stuffing his gloves against his chest and shoving his hands in his deep pockets—and had gone out to investigate. He knew the terrain well enough from twice-daily patrols to know where the cliff ended.

Reaching the ledge, he looked down and saw what resembled a ship anchored and sloshing nearby. The lights were off, and he couldn't be sure. Nor did he study it for very long. Off to the east, maybe a mile and a half, he saw lights that seemed to describe a shape he had studied and knew well, the silhouette of Chinese corvette.

Van Tonder was patriotically indignant and personally vengeful. These people had endangered the life of his comrade. The commander understood why the helicopter had not landed—and, most likely, why the outpost had gone silent.

He went back to the helicopter to wait for daylight. There was nothing else to do, except to make sure his firearms were in good working order.

When he heard the shots droning below, he got out again—this time with the clunky but powerful machine gun. That was the spot where he and Mabuza had been headed. He understood too, now, exactly what the Chinese were doing down there. They were trying to get at whatever this was.

That wasn't going to happen.

The men were some two hundred feet below. He did not aim the M1919 Browning at the men but at their lights. The lamps exploded in turn and he dropped flat on his belly, his head back from the ledge. He expected the men to return fire.

They did not.

Either the Chinese Navy is suddenly afraid of the SAN or they are close to their goal and don't want to be distracted, he thought. The latter, almost certainly.

He edged forward and looked down.

Working by flashlight now—which was protected by the back of one of the men so van Tonder could not shoot at it—three men were kneeling and huddled close around the gunned-out section of the wall of Ship Rock. One man appeared to be reaching into the wall while another was standing by the ladder of the rocking boat. He was handed what looked like a cooler, the kind used for organ transplants. Van Tonder could not be sure in the dull light.

He considered the situation carefully.

They are military trespassers. Are they invaders? *What happens if I cut them down? Does the corvette open fire?*

Still lying flat on the cold rock, he trained his gun on the rear of the vessel, where the fuel tanks were located. If he could perforate those, the patrol boat would not be going anywhere.

He fired again.

He saw the distant sparks of the bullets as they met the hull. It was impossible to tell what damage he might have caused. He would only know by the reactions of the crew.

This time the Chinese on deck fired—lower than

the ledge, not at him. They drove him back, which was apparently all they wanted.

He wished he could offload Mabuza and drive the damn helicopter over the cliff onto the stern to stop them from leaving.

Van Tonder heard shouting from below. Something had happened but he could not be sure whether it was his doing or something at the wall. He edged ahead even slower than before.

The shouts were from the wall. The light was playing every which way and it was like trying to see terrain by flashes of lightning. But what he saw—what he thought he saw—was a nightmare made real.

CHAPTER TWENTY-TWO

November 12, 5:05 A.M.

Katinka Kettle overslept.

She did not feel rested as the sun crawled over the sill and caused her to stir. It had not only been an exhausting night but a tiring week. She was not accustomed to such long sea voyages, nor the savagely cold, unwelcoming shores of Prince Edward.

Unrested or not, it was time to get up, time to get back to MEASE and figure out what they should do with her find. She turned on her fully charged phone and washed her face. She regretted that there wasn't time to do her hair; it would take more than one washing to get the smell and fluff of seawater and the clinging odor of the burning *Teri Wheel* out of it.

Returning to her nightstand, she ignored her phone inbox, noted that there were eleven calls from Foster, which she would look at as soon as she checked the news. She wanted to see if there was any mention of the explosion of the yacht. If not, she would dig a little deeper on the Web site of the South African Navy Maritime Forces—

"What?"

The headline grabbed her eyes and throat in equal measure. The news—the only news—was about a mysterious attack on Batting Bridge and the possible relationship it might have with the downing of the South African jetliner.

It took a moment for her to find her voice again.

"How could it have *randomly* showed up there?"

That word did not sit well. It made no *sense*. Had the pathogen floated in from the *Teri Wheel*, made its way up the Nahoon, skipped all the homes and businesses on the riverbanks, and then happened to run into Batting Bridge?

It was flatly not possible. Not as possible as—

"Someone releasing it," she said quietly. She tried to dismiss the thought with a shake of her head. "No. God Almighty and Jesus—tell me he's not desperate enough."

But the idea clung.

Breathing hard and wishing she had not given up smoking, Katinka braced herself as she read the full story on the South African news service. There had been an anonymous phone call placed with the East London police, warning of an attack. She jumped to News24 and then to the BBC. They all had the same information, the same call transcript along with a few fuzzy security camera photos of crashed cars, the descending helicopter, and then the destroyed bridge.

There were also shots of teams in hazmat suits making their way through the ruins piled jaggedly, haphazardly on the water. A pool reporter had provided the latter images since access was restricted.

Katinka's mouth was dry and her eyes were damp.

"Yes," she said. She had been intending to find a way to monetize the bug.

"But by selling it, not by *releasing* it!"

She sat heavily on the bed, her hands limp on her lap, the phone plopping to the carpet. Katinka knew Foster to be greedy, and after all these years she knew, or thought she knew, his demons. He hated the diamond cartel. He hated the authorities who enabled the monopolies. But, God, he did not hate people. Did he put those two on a scale and have innocent South Africans come up short?

"That has to be it. It *has* to."

She wept. She had not foreseen anything like *this*! She hoped there was another, a less personally horrendous explanation. Another player, someone who found the toxin in the wreckage of the plane.

"Megalomaniacal," she muttered, sensing the truth. Foster could be that. "God forgive me, what power did I *hand* to him?"

She considered, for the briefest moment, that someone else at MEASE may have taken the sample and released it. Another employee, perhaps. Eavesdropping. A mistress, of which Foster had several, hiding when Katinka arrived unexpectedly.

"What does that matter?" she asked. This was done and she'd made it possible. She had to figure out what to do next. Because Foster—or whoever—still had another sample.

She wondered if she should go to the authorities with hers, give them a chance to study it?

"No, they'll have samples aplenty when they pull bodies from the river," she said. "But if they ever figure out that I'm part of this, and I'm arrested—cooperation may save me."

Or doom her. How many times had she seen members of Foster's wide circle of mercenaries and associates arrested on minor charges and given maximum sentences to serve as an object lesson.

And then something terribly urgent occurred to her. He might send someone to keep her from doing just what she was thinking.

"No," she thought aloud. "It will take time. His most efficient mercenaries died on the *Teri Wheel*."

But there were other men and women, arms dealers who also hired those soldiers-for-hire. They would have more, especially Nicus Dumisa in Swaziland. He recruited from the African tribal death squads where there was an endless supply of killers.

She might be able to get away, to think. She would take the sample. There was no choice: if Foster did come by at some point and find the canister, he would know she had her own scheme in mind. That was as good as a death warrant.

Maybe she could disappear, find a way to sell it in a way that did not get back to Foster.

"Go," she told herself. "Now."

Katinka dressed quickly, in a sweatshirt and slacks.

Then she grabbed a few items and threw them in a bag. Foster would know that she had run, but he would—no, *might*—presume it was out of fear of being attached to this monstrous act.

As she stood at the foot of the bed amidst a riot of clothes, personal devices, and an empty canvas grip to put them in, the doorbell rang. Katinka shot from the bed and stood there. The woman did not socialize with many people and her neighbors not at all. They never came by.

The bell was followed by a firm knock.

She collected herself, looked around for her phone, saw it beside her old Adidas. She picked it up, unplugged it, and walked numbly, stupidly from the bedroom.

"Coming!" she said.

Katinka paused by a window that overlooked the front walk. She did not draw back the sheer polyester curtain but leaned near to the wall and peeked under it.

She felt sick all over again.

It was the police.

CHAPTER TWENTY-THREE

November 12, 5:20 A.M.

With the sea roaring in his head and the engine of the boat making strange, ripping sounds like metal on metal, Lieutenant Colonel Gray Raeburn worked on in the near-darkness. There was nothing else to do. The tone of the Chinese leader had been urgent, insistent. That, and the other man had redoubled his efforts to get through the lower section of wall.

Raeburn had been helping to pull chunks of rock from the opening. He had just dropped a two-handed chunk into the sea, a greedy mass that seemed to anger the sea. Simultaneously, the wall beneath that slab crumbled inward and the sea rose up in seeming disapproval. There was a moment when the risen sea and the collapsing wall seemed frozen. Then the water smashed high and mighty and the wall collapsed and the hatchet seaman fell with it. The man fell forward and down, his mask smashing against the concrete.

His lifeline pulled both the doctor and the other Chinese sailor forward. The two men slammed against the edges of the opening, both hoping the sides did not give way. Even as they struck and were pulled toward the gaping chasm, they were grasping for knobs of rock, for handholds. At least the weight of the man was not a drag: the lifeline went a little slack after the man hit the lid.

Somehow, the leader had retained the flashlight as he skidded forward. Upon regaining his footing and pushing from the wall as far as the rope would allow him, he shined it into the opening.

His comrade was in the process of dying. Raeburn knew it and the leader apparently did as well; he made no effort to pull the man up by the rope. The leader seemed afraid to move lest he disturb the wall and end up beside the other man.

So they watched.

It was a grotesque thing, this death. The man pushed up and then his back began to jerk. He remained in that position for a moment, his body quivering and finally giving out, dropping him back to his chest. His back continued to rattle.

The coughing, Raeburn thought with awful certainty.

Then the man's left knee pulled up as though his bowels were in agony.

They are. They're coming apart.

A few moments later and the seaman was flopping like a fish, his head jerking this way and that, his fingers digging frantically at the concrete below him. Then there was blood, fat wedges of it pouring from the mask before mingling into a thick pool and spreading. Some of it oozed over the sides of the container, some found the acid-drilled holes and seeped down.

The Exodus bug has its blood.

There were twitches and jerks as the body surrendered the bulk of its liquefying organs. The scientist in Raeburn was fascinated even as the man himself was aghast. This bacterium had not only survived these many years but the action was inexplicably fast. As the father of these things, he wanted to know why.

You need to know why if you're going to find a way to stop them.

When the seaman stopped moving, Raeburn was willing to bet there was more of his nonskeletal mass on the outside than there was in the deflated husk that remained.

He was soon to find out. When the dead man was still, when pockets of organs were no longer erupting, the Chinese leader turned to the others and shouted something. The men were just dark shadows against the slowly reddening sky. They had been watching the cliff, guns raised, and could not see into the opening in any case. Now the crew left to do whatever the leader had bidden.

Holding the flashlight in one hand, the Chinese sailor gingerly stepped away from the wall to the extent that the taut rope permitted. He jerked the flashlight to and fro, at the wall, away from the wall. Raeburn understood. He, too, stepped back to the length of the rope.

The seaman gripped the brittle, half-frozen rope with his free hand, shined the light on himself, indicating for Raeburn to do the same.

Of course, the doctor thought.

The poor bastard below had made this easy.

Flexing his knees allowed Raeburn to put more weight directly on his feet. That gave him some purchase on the slime below his rubber soles. The leader did the same, then nodded once. They did not pull the man up. Slowly, arduously, carefully, they stepped back. The rope scraped the lower lip of the opening precipitously but there was no way around that. Pieces fell off but the rope continued to be withdrawn. In a minute the body came into view.

It was a hideous sight, as Raeburn had expected. The front of the suit was still sealed but it sloshed with the viscera and blood of the dead man. The doctor wondered if the seaman would open a zipper and let it bleed out into the sea.

He did not, probably due to caution rather than a loathing for the grotesque: he did not know in what part of the man the bacteria would reside.

When the body was on the rocks, the crew of the patrol boat came down with a body bag. Raeburn was alarmed but not entirely surprised that they had one on the patrol boat. The Chinese were known to shoot pirates on sight. Those dead were placed in bags lined with lead so they sank.

The ropes binding the three men were cut, and once

the corpse was sealed it was hoisted onto the patrol boat. There were urgent, uttered words and pointing. The engine was still growling unhappily.

Raeburn gathered that the gunfire from above had damaged it.

Good for the shooter, he thought—which was no doubt Commander van Tonder, doing his job.

The leader waved the concerns away and ordered the body stowed. He would call the corvette and apprise them of the situation. They had secured what they had come for. One way or another, they would get the cargo aboard.

Above them, van Tonder watched with revulsion as the breaking light revealed the ghoulish activities of the Chinese team. He saw the dings he had put in the engine casing. The engine had a rasp, like sandpaper, but that might not be enough to stop the boat from departing.

The last time the Boers had fought a war, over a century ago, the British had won and forced the humiliating Peace of Vereeniging upon them. Van Tonder had viscerally wanted for history not to repeat itself with these invaders.

It took quite some time for the Chinese to maneuver in the shadow of dawn with their fragile, dangerous bundle. When they finally had him inside, van Tonder watched, pleased that he had been able to inflict damage, at this distance, with the M1919 Browning.

He waited anxiously as the helmsman, dimly lit by dawn, took his place.

The patrol boat engine rasped, then clanked. It was throttled down. It came to life again more slowly—and banged again. The helmsman throttled down. There was no third effort.

That actually sounded like the propeller hitting the bottom of the boat, van Tonder thought. He had not hit what he thought he had but it didn't matter. The boat was not going anywhere. Most likely they would have to radio for help from the corvette.

Content, for now, he returned to the helicopter.

CHAPTER TWENTY-FOUR

EAST LONDON, SOUTH AFRICA

November 12, 5:21 A.M.

The two tall, older South African Police Service officers stood shoulder to shoulder at her door, their expressions distressed and impatient. Clearly, they—and their department—had had an unforgiving night.

She only saw one car at the curb and the men were not trying to look past her. This might not be what she feared.

One man touched the brim of his hat. "We understand from Mr. Claude Foster that you were the pilot of the autogyro that we found unlawfully parked on Nahoon Beach."

Katinka unfroze when she heard that. She laughed. It was partly relief but also the idiocy of the priorities of local authorities.

"I will remove it," she assured them.

"Mr. Foster has additional instructions," the officer said.

So that was how it was. Foster had often mentioned a "flag" system of security. If his name came up in an investigation, officers knew that a month's pay awaited anyone who made the situation go away. These men had broken from a national emergency for pay.

"I'm listening," Katinka said.

"He has reserved a lot at the Vandermeer Car Rental at the airport," the officer replied. "He said you know the place?"

"Yes, we . . . provide them with automobiles."

"Very good. There will be cones with red flags at either end. May we take you there so we may report it was done?"

Katinka did not want to go. What she wanted was more time to think.

"I will go myself so that—"

"Ma'am, that was not a request," the officer interrupted. "We do have other, rather urgent duties today, as you might understand."

"Of course," was her only response. "I'm sorry. I was not thinking."

There would be no packing, getting the core sample, and then flying north. What's more, she had a very good idea that Foster would be waiting for her. This may have been part of his plan all along. She was the only one who could report him to the authorities.

Katinka snatched her keys from a table beside the door and followed the men to their patrol car. A man walking his dog had stopped to watch. Police escorting a resident from her home was not a common occurrence on this quiet street.

Five minutes later, Katinka was on the beach.

"We have been told that it is safe to fly west and then north, at a ceiling of five hundred feet," the officer said as he walked her to the autogyro.

"How was that calculated, based on what data?" she asked.

He looked at her. "Ma'am, if you have a question I am able to answer—?"

"No, Officer. None. Thank you and be safe."

"Our appreciation," he replied.

Two minutes later, Katinka was airborne. Only then did the police car pull away.

"I do not want to be a prisoner of Foster but I cannot leave without my core sample," she thought aloud.

There was a third option, she suddenly realized. So direct it had not occurred to her.

"That's how long you've spent being devious," she admonished herself.

To this point, she had done anything.

"Not done much," she corrected herself. She drilled illegally at Prince Edward Island and blew up a boat—though she could cover that somehow. "You knew about the toxin but you kept it safe. You meant to turn it over to the proper authorities, right?"

Her phone vibrated in her pocket. She looked at it. "Shit."

It was Foster.

"Okay," she said. "Either you're ignoring him and

going to the authorities or confronting him and land-ing."

She opted to answer the call. It was better to know where she stood.

"You didn't return my calls," he said. "That was in-considerate."

"I'm in the autogyro," she answered flatly.

"I know," Foster said. "Officer Cronje informed me."

"What do you want?" she asked.

"You know, I had intended for you to be a part of this. A part of the plan I've created."

"I don't want it. None of it. Is there anything else?"

"Yes," Foster said. "The officer put the canister I used in the storage space behind you. You cannot reach it while flying, nor have you the time to try. It is rigged with a detonator cap that will crack it in—let's see, seven minutes and thirty-three seconds, unless you have set down, as instructed. I will be there to disarm it. And if you somehow manage to reach the sample and toss it—well, perhaps you can outrun the toxin, perhaps not. But many will die and the authori-ties will know who is responsible."

Katinka felt as though the bottom had dropped from the autogyro and she was falling. Yet some cor-ner of her brain managed to stay on point and con-tinue flying.

"Why did you do this?" she asked. "How did I never see?"

"I'd concentrate on landing, not antisocial resolu-tion, yes?"

Katinka angrily killed the call and looked at the time.

"Less than seven minutes," she said as she peered from the phone out at the landscape two hundred feet below. Over the rooftops of the homes and low-lying industrial structures she saw the airport and, south of it, the rental car parking lot. She would not have to cross any air lanes to land.

"He planned that too."

She would be landing in less than four minutes. She understood, now, another reason Foster had selected that lot. If she set down and tried to run, if he allowed the canister to open, most likely she along with untold numbers of travelers and airport workers would die.

As she approached, she saw Foster's van. He was propped against the hood, arms folded, relaxed.

What he had done was monstrous, and his betrayal of her after so many years and exploits was unfathomable. As the autogyro set down between the cones, she found her desire for wealth replaced by something stronger.

Guilt so strong that she intended to destroy him and whatever he was planning.

CHAPTER TWENTY-FIVE

November 12, 6:19 A.M.

"For a waterfront kid, I'm in the air a lot now."

Rivette was not quite complaining as he crossed the airfield from one plane to another. He didn't mind flying, but the confinement that went with these long trips made him want to claw at the seat back. That changed once he and Grace left the C-21 behind them and he was airborne in the Advanced Hawk.

Snuggled carefree in the canopied back seat it was not just the flight in a screaming-fast nearly Mach 1 jet that delighted him from his big eyes to toes that instinctively if uselessly gripped the bottom of his boots. The low passage along the Indian Ocean, which seemed to amplify their speed, was thrilling. Grace had taken off after him and he did not know if her characteristically stoic expression had cracked. He doubted it. But he was ear-to-ear happy.

The good-byes to Williams and Breen had been

quick and on the fly. That was fine too. Instructions and briefings generally bored him. The lance corporal was a survivalist at heart. He wanted to get to where he could be free and useful.

You are definitely getting there, he thought as he watched the dark expanse of water slip by.

He had not even spoken with his pilot, except to listen to the brief cockpit-to-tower conversation in his clean white helmet. The gear had its own oxygen supply so they would, in theory, be safe passing through the area that had taken down the jetliner. Still, flying low, he assumed, was a nod to the idea that this microbe rose.

Or maybe Chinese radar can't see us this low over the water. If they were buzzing San Pedro, he could have done a layup shot into the cockpit.

As Rivette looked left and right, he did not see any military ships and few commercial freighters. Maybe they were flying a course designed to avoid the Chinese and Russians. He did not understand why. The Chinese at the island would see and hear them when the jets blasted overhead.

And they sure as hell should, he thought. *It's the South Africans' damn island.*

He wondered if the Chinese would pack up and leave when that happened. He hoped not. Unlike Yemen, where Black Wasp had been constantly buzzing and weaving, he liked the idea of being where they had permission to hunt bad guys.

After the low, lulling hum of the C-21, the furnace-roar of the fighter jet was an adrenaline rush. It lasted from takeoff to landing, which was the part of the flight Rivette liked least. They flew wide of the corvette and came in from the east, not to avoid being seen—radar would have failed to notice—but to come in at the right angle to land on Flat Cuff.

The pilot lined up with the target ledge. The slope of the cockpit gave Rivette a slightly elevated view above the pilot. He watched as the island came at them so fast Rivette was certain it was the last thing he would see. He turned to his right. Icy blue water was off to both sides, followed by a flash of pebbled beach that was covered with what looked like seals, and then they were replaced by terrain that moved by so fast the browns, greens, and grays appeared a soupy blur. The lance corporal instinctively pressed his arms to the sides, bracing them against the narrow metal panel to which the canopy hinges were bolted.

Hills rose swiftly on either side, not so near and not moving as fast. The sound of the engines bounced back up at them, the canopy vibrated, and then there was a bump under his seat that felt like a kickoff— only he didn't go as far as a football, the harness saw to that. The force went up his back and jolted the base of his skull. The engines howled and the jet immediately slowed. Small stones pelted the undercarriage like flak, adding a staccato din.

And then they stopped with a suddenness that threw Rivette forward against the straps and gave his neck another jolt. There wasn't time to recover. Rivette swapped out his helmet and oxygen for the breathing mask. When he was done, the cockpit hummed open and the pilot raised his left arm, pointing to the wing on that side. The lance corporal unbuckled himself and climbed unsteadily onto the wing. One of the two air intakes for the single, rear-positioned turbofan whooshed loudly and caused the wing to tremble as he removed his gun case from the cockpit. Particles of grit and grass literally vibrated off the metal.

Rivette sat on the wing and slid off the back, avoiding the suction. Then he grabbed his two grips and hurried away. The cockpit closed. He had not exchanged a word with the pilot at any time.

The lance corporal had dressed on the C-21 and took some time getting used to the tight, warm winter gear. He was wearing a thermal jumpsuit and cotton coveralls. He wore a slender black thermal parka with an insulated hood. He was impressed with the gripping capacity of waterproof lace-up boots with cleated outsoles. His lined tactical gloves would allow him to shoot without freezing. According to the instructions that came with the extreme-weather breathing mask, the edges might become a little stiff and possibly abrasive in temperatures below freezing. He hoped he would be able to take it off.

In any case, Rivette was psyched and ready for this mission.

There was nothing to take shelter behind on the flat plain so he kept on jogging to the south. The wind wanted him to go east but he resisted. He squatted to remove his guns and holsters then covered the case with rocks so it wouldn't shine for enemy patrols, if any. He checked his phone for messages

from Williams or Washington. There were no updates. He did not look back but he heard the engine
rev again, blast across the terrain, and then he could
hear it rise. The bellowing was over land this time,
not water, and it echoed off the hills, sending flocks
of hidden birds into the air.

Rivette had felt more at home in the burning, sandy
expanses and harbor warehouses of Yemen. It wasn't
that much different from Los Angeles. This place felt
rugged and remote, like there should be dinosaurs,
Bronze Age forges, or both.

Almost as soon as the Hawk was gone, its engine
receding, it was replaced by the jet carrying Lieutenant Lee. The lance corporal simply stood where he
was, on a slope that looked like a slate walk someone
had hammered to pieces. The Hawk followed the same
path as his plane, spinning off a cloud of grassy dust
as it touched down. The plane was briefly enveloped
when it stopped. Rivette watched as Grace emerged,
not bothering to sit on the wing but jumping down.
She did not carry a bag or backpack. Everything she
needed was strapped to her body.

She must have spotted Rivette as they were coming
in, as she ran directly toward him. The jet was gone
before she reached him. It left behind a primordial
calm of wind, distant surf, and highly vocal birds.

The woman checked the compass function of her
smartwatch, then looked at the local map. During the
flight, they had agreed to use standard military visual
signaling rather than shout through their masks.

Slowing but not stopping, she circled her arm for

them to move out and pointed sharply with a ridge
hand to the southwest. She ran on, Rivette following.

I guess she's psyched too, Rivette thought. *And in
command.*

The two made their way from the valley, slowed
only by the difficulty of running and breathing in the
mask. Following the compass, she decided to go up
and over a hill that was some five hundred feet in ele-
vation. Hiking was another thing Rivette had not done
a lot of growing up, and except for survivalist training in the Rockies, this was relatively new. He was leg-
weary even before they reached the coast where the
outpost lay.

Just as the structure came into view, silhouetted
by rising sunlight falling on the waters beyond, both
Black Wasps felt their phones vibrate.

Grace's arm flew straight back, palm open. Rivette
stopped as she did so they could check the text message. It was another anonymous update from the Defense Logistics Agency:

```
Chinese   activity   location   Ship
Rock  site  of  original  contagion.
Possible regional reinfection.
```

Nuts to that, Rivette thought. Even though it was on
the other island, the mask would have to stay on.

When they started up again, Grace indicated for
Rivette to stay low. She pointed to her eyes, then out
to the sea.

What did you see besides birds? he wondered.

Instead of going around the hill they made for a higher vantage point. She stopped them again. Grace had binoculars on her hip but they were useless due to the angle and the rising sun and the visor. Despite the glare and distance, however, Rivette was able to make out what she had noticed. The new sun was bouncing from a South African helicopter parked beside the single-story outpost. The target was roughly a half mile away.

Grace looked back and nodded. He nodded back. They were agreed that transportation would be damned useful to have.

Resuming their passage toward the building, the two were no longer moving in to reconnoiter. If there was a pilot, they wanted him.

Presuming they would hear an approach from the air, the Chinese had stationed a man at the sea cliff. Lying flat at the base of the mound they had climbed, Grace saw the sailor in profile. He was not wearing a mask. The men had likely not been told about the contagion. The Chinese were using them as guinea pigs, a kind of proximity test.

However, he did have the thick, lined hood of his parka on and buttoned tight. If he had heard the two Hawks come in, he had long since lost interest. The sides of the hood would also block the man's peripheral vision slightly. He would have to turn and look at something fully to see it. The Chinese obviously were not expecting an attack from behind.

Rivette was slightly behind her and to the left. He texted her a picture of the QBZ-95 assault rifle the man was carrying, along with a note:

```
1200' pt
```

She showed an okay sign. The sentry could hit a point target precisely at that range.

She texted: `I'll take him. You follow, cover.`

Now Rivette formed an okay sign.

My God, I love this, he thought, his life proceeding from moment to moment with adrenaline and purpose. Just like when he was a kid in Los Angeles, he could afford to miss *nothing.*

They rose. The sun was climbing to their right and gave them some cover in the shadow of the hill. They stayed within it, walking low. Several times Grace had been tempted to remove the mask. She did not like the fact that she could hear her own breathing in her ears. But the winds had shifted several times in just the half hour since they had arrived. It was not worth the risk.

Rivette was carrying his Colt 9mm submachine gun. Grace knew it had an effective range of roughly one-quarter the Chinese weapon. That meant he could stop about 350 feet away and still cover her. She held up her hand to stop, pointed to a satellite dish that was at least thirty years old. Judging from the dung coating the latticed surface, the technology was only active as a bird refuge. The white dish sat on a fat metal cylinder.

Hunkered low on his feet, Rivette made for it. As he ran, he kept his weapon pointed at the sentry who was looking out to sea. If the man turned, the last thing he would see was the American.

Then we'll be in a firefight, he knew—but at least the Chinese would not know about Grace. He could keep them busy while she made her way to the outpost. No one was better at a stealth approach than Grace.

None of that happened. Rivette reached the spot unseen, and by the time he looked back Grace was already in motion. She was running toward the back of the outpost. The eastern side blocked her from the sentry's view. He would only see her when she reached the front. From there, she had to cover about thirty feet of open terrain.

She never made it.

The shift changed at 7:00 A.M. and the replacement walked out as Grace had just started her snake-low approach to the sentry.

The Chinese seaman hesitated from surprise. Grace did not. She doubled him over with a right side kick. When that foot came down she was right in front of the man. Her left knee came up into his bowed, open jaw.

She ignored the sentry and, as the man she'd hit fell back, literally ran over him. Bullets splatted behind her; they were Rivette's, chewing up the terrain between his partner and the sentry and driving the man back toward the cliff. He fell onto his belly and aimed at the young marine. By that time, Grace was pressed to the wall just outside the door. She threw back her hood so she could hear. The wall behind her was cinderblock. The Chinese would not be firing through it to try and get her.

The sentry's replacement stirred and she kicked him in the ear with a snap-kick from the toe of her boot. There was an audible crack and he flopped back down.

Off to the southeast, Rivette was moving forward, driving the sentry back toward the sea cliff, making sure he did not have time or a sight-line to shoot her. The lance corporal's shots were not random but precise and shifting; endless, droning fire would have given the guard a chance to get ahead of the bullets. Also, before long, Rivette's supply would have run out.

The men inside were shouting. Grace listened.

"Send the pilot out to reconnoiter!" someone shouted.

Smart, but stupid, Grace thought.

"What are you bloody doing?" a man said in English. "Stop pushing—"

"Get out there!" a Chinese seaman barked.

She could not afford to allow this man to become a moving hostage, either for his sake or her own. Grace listened to the cold floorboards creak as she watched the door. She removed her right-hand glove, held it in her teeth, and wriggled her fingers in a spider maneuver so they'd be flexible. There was warmth coming through the door; whatever he was wearing, the fabric would not be stiff. His arms were apparently raised, because the first thing she saw move slowly through the door was an ivory-white sweater—

Grace's right hand shot across the doorway, palm facing the inside. She slapped on the garment, her palm hitting first and her fingers immediately curling around the wool like talons—an eagle grab. She did not use muscle to pull him out. That would have taken time and effort. She took a wide step to her left and dragged him with her. Surprised and off-balance, he literally fell to his left, following her.

Gunshots cracked and missed him, though a circling albatross exploded in red and dropped beak-first.

Grace immediately dropped to her knees, the man falling face-first with her. She kept her palm on the back of the man's neck—not forcefully, but enough to communicate that he should stay down. He nodded into the dirt. She tapped him on the shoulder. He looked up. She motioned him to move from the wall slightly. He quickly obliged, scuttling two feet to the south. In case the sentry at the sea managed to fire a round in their direction, the rolling terrain offered the man protection.

But that was not why she had moved him.

Grace pressed herself back to the wall. The men inside were quiet but Grace heard the footsteps. Two pair. One pair was moving toward the window to her left. The shades had been drawn, probably by the Chinese, looking to conceal themselves.

Dumb, she thought. The sun's glare would have done that if they had been thinking. *The Chinese and their tactical rulebooks.* If they didn't have a billion-plus people to throw at the world, few would take their aggression seriously.

Leaving the South African, and still squatting, Grace made her way to the window. It was just over five feet away. Hanging just to the side, her back to the wall, and pulling her glove back on, she watched as the shade was drawn from the nine-pane window. She did not see a face.

"There's one man firing at Lung Chen," a man whispered.

"Who is *here*?"

That would require the observer to move. The face moved cautiously toward the middle pane on her side. The glass would be strong but not strong enough.

Once again, Grace flexed her now-gloved right hand. She formed a leopard fist—all five fingers tightly bent and held firm against her palm. The knuckles were pointed up, the palm toward the window. She saw the face and was already in motion as the face saw her. She rolled her back off the wall, an upward corkscrew move, and at the same time propelled her palm into the pane. The glass exploded inward, causing the seaman to gasp and jump back.

The other man fired in that direction, bullets destroying the other panes.

The men inside were only distracted for a few moments, but in that time Grace had turned and run back to the open door.

The man with the gun was momentarily paralyzed by her arrival. She front-kicked his automatic up and out of his hand. Then she drove her left hand, a leopard paw, into his throat. Even as he gagged and stumbled back she turned toward the man at the window.

The African radio operator was already in motion, bear-hugging the man around the chest and driving him into a desk. The furniture moved back and both men fell sprawling, but the seaman still had his gun.

Grace ran over and stomped on his wrist. The man's fingers reflexively flew open and he released the semiautomatic. She picked it up and turned to the other man as the radio operator rose and punched down hard at the seaman's face.

Grace swore.

She had heard the other man hacking and gagging, trying to recover from the neck-strike, but he had not been immobile. Grabbing a backpack, he had run to the window that faced west and was just jamming it through. Then he dropped to the floor and Grace realized why. She ripped off her mask.

"Get down and cover your ears!" she yelled to the radio operator as she dove to the opposite side of the room, landing flat behind the desk. A moment later, the bag exploded.

A red-yellow blew through the shattered window, taking out the remainder of the frame. Shards of glass and wood splinters traced wide, dizzying courses through the room, followed by the smoke. Grace smelled thermite.

"Stay down!" she cried as a second, much larger

blast rocked the outpost. The ground itself shook, the walls and ceiling rattled, and the entire room went red as the helicopter exploded. The outside wall was pelted with metal, followed by a rain of debris on the roof.

Rivette had used the distraction of the explosion to rush his prisoner. If his training had taught him anything, it was to focus on only that which was an immediate danger. Even if Grace had just gone up in smoky particles, there was nothing he could do about it. But there was something he could do about the sentry.

The seaman had watched the blast and was not aware of the lance corporal swinging in from the opposite direction and putting a warm gun barrel to the back of his collar. The seaman surrendered and stood, arms raised. The two walked toward the burning tableau, the helicopter in formless, melted ruin and the outpost intact but half-concealed in blowing smoke.

The man in the white sweater had risen when two Chinese appeared in the doorway, their arms raised, followed by Grace and an African. The latter had the only gun among them.

Rivette removed his mask. "All clear?"

"No one else," Grace said.

"Thermite?" Rivette said, sniffing as they arrived.

"I didn't even think about it," Grace said angrily.

"It came with Raeburn," the pilot said. "I'm Captain Velts, by the way. You are?"

"Where is Raeburn?" Grace asked, shaking her head firmly in answer to his question.

"He left with a Chinese patrol, by boat," said Sisula.

"Left?"

"Was forced to go," Sisula said. "He's a doctor, name of Raeburn. He came to help Commander van Tonder and Lieutenant Mabuza, who took our helicopter to Prince Edward."

"I wondered about your own transportation," Grace said.

"Now we're stranded here," Sisula said.

Grace thought for a moment. "No," she announced as she returned to the partially shattered outpost. "We are not."

CHAPTER TWENTY-SIX

The attack on Batting Bridge had been tracked into the mountains to the west, where three people fell ill but did not die. Williams received this information from the woman who met their C-21, Deputy Chief of Navy Caroline Swane. Williams said he was encouraged by the quick degradation of the disease germ.

"Not half so much as we," the forty-nine-year-old naval officer replied. Her large eyes were heavy-lidded, as though she had not slept for some time. Her brown uniform was crisp but spotted with perspiration. Williams was sure the already eighty-degree temperature and unobstructed sun were only partly responsible.

The trio saw Grace Lee and Jaz Rivette off and had been shown to a spacious—and subtly armored—van for the ride from the Thaba Tshwane facility to their next destination. The men placed their gear in back, declining the driver's efforts to do so. Williams followed Breen inside, where he learned that they were not going to see Minister Barbara Niekerk. He had spent the better part of an hour reading up on her background.

"We are headed a short distance to Defence Ministry Headquarters," she told Williams, who was beside her, and Breen, who was sitting across from her. "There are new developments."

Breen's expression said he was alert for a hustle. Having no choice for now but to cooperate, Williams remained hopeful.

The woman said, "Minister Niekerk was at one point—around 2009—involved in a research project with Dr. Gray Raeburn, who was serving then, as now, with the navy's Military Health Service. They were working on a cure to the AIDS virus and made, I'm told, admirable progress. Until the cure proved as potentially deadly as the disease."

"Let me guess," Williams said. "What they came up with got loose."

Perhaps because she was exhausted, the woman smiled and said, "Thank you, Commander Williams, for whipping 'round to the finish line. Your reputation for clarity and grasp was not overstated."

"I wasn't aware I had one," he said. "A reputation."

"The man we are going to see knows of your work. General Tobias Krummeck, our chief intelligence officer."

"I've met him," Williams said. "I don't imagine he

was involved with Minister Niekerk's original project."

"That, Commander, I do not know. When we had Dr. Raeburn's name, we sought him out and learned that he had been sent to Prince Edward this morning. The flight was logged as a fact-finding mission authorized by General Krummeck. It remains unclear why a communicable diseases specialist went directly to the intelligence chief, but he did."

"Did the men have a social relationship?" Williams asked.

"That does not appear to be the case," the woman said. "And your inference bears exploring, Commander. The general was not unaware of the research project."

They pulled up in front of a columned white mansion at the corner of Nossob and Boeing Streets. The deputy chief of navy motioned for them to remain.

"The general seemed disinterested in cooperating until I informed him that neither the doctor nor his pilot had been heard from since their departure," the woman said. She regarded Williams. "I do not know why, but he agreed to talk only to you." She nodded toward the guard standing at the door. "You're expected."

Breen's cautioning look returned.

"I will remain here with Major Breen," the South African officer added. "There are considerations I wish to discuss with him."

"It's okay," Breen told Williams. "The general obviously knows more about you than I do."

Williams did not miss the subtext. The criminologist missed nothing. Breen was on a mission with a man that the woman had called "Commander." That was something the major had not known. That Williams had been in intelligence had probably been inferred—but the general knew it for a fact, more than the other Black Wasps did.

"I'll address that later, Major," Williams assured him as he slid the van door back.

Major Breen was too professional to let outsider status affect the mission. He was also too smart to waste by keeping him in the dark. Matt Berry's orders be damned, it was time for the two men to have a talk.

Williams went up the wide stairs, was checked through, and was directed to room 309.

He took the ornate staircase to a third-floor warren of offices. Though the building belonged to a bygone era, it reminded him of Op-Center's old headquarters—but up instead of down. People were moving through quiet halls, acknowledging those they knew and worked with, but not stopping to chat.

An efficient adjutant was standing behind her desk when Williams arrived. The woman showed him directly to the spacious office in back, with bay windows that overlooked an old section of the city. General Krummeck rose. He came around his desk, hand extended, as the office door closed heavily.

The general was a big man with the body of a bear but the face of a tiger. Strong, carnivorous qualities were what you needed to survive in this business.

Krummeck was fortunate to possess them outwardly; it saved time.

"It is good to see you again," the officer said with apparent sincerity.

"The same. I was thinking—the International Security Conference, 2016, wasn't it?"

"In Copenhagen, yes. But it took me some doing to find out exactly what a supposedly retired military officer with no known intelligence affiliation was doing there. Well, that was the key, wasn't it? You were not affiliated with a very public organization."

"That is true."

"I had heard of your National Crisis Management Center when it was run by Mr. Paul Hood. We . . . learned that you two had met several times, so it was a natural deduction."

"It's one of the great flaws in espionage that one never imagines allies spying on them," Williams remarked. The statement flirted with being an accusation.

"In our case, it was not for information but to justify a budget. You understand."

"Use the money or lose it."

Krummeck smiled benignly. "Coffee? Tea? Something else?" the general asked as he indicated a pair of facing armchairs.

"Thanks, no. Deputy Swane said you wanted to talk to me."

"Yes. I was very happy to hear from Chief of Navy Roodt that you and a team were being fielded. We need trusted help on this."

"May I ask, General—the country . . . or you?"

The men sat and Krummeck smiled, with teeth. "Both, Commander. You have people bound for Marion Island. They will need to go from there to Prince Edward. As you probably know, that is where this problem originated."

"Something you put there?"

"That's right."

"A confidence you trust I will not break," Williams said.

"Unlike my enemies here, you have nothing to gain by my downfall. And you might benefit from a relationship that provides eyes-on intelligence regarding the Chinese in the South Indian Ocean."

Despite the indecency of using South African lives as leverage, dealings of this kind were to be expected.

"I'll keep your confidence, of course," Williams assured him.

Krummeck thanked him. Either the intelligence chief was trusting or, more likely, he was canny. If his participation in this "Exodus bug" were to become known—and at last, finally, there was confirmation that this *was* an engineered toxin—powerful international allies would help give him job security. Especially in the face of Chinese aggression.

"Deputy Swane has briefed you, yes?" the general asked.

"A little."

"That's all she knows . . . a 'little.' Years ago, Dr. Raeburn was working with Minister Niekerk on an

AIDS cure. The cure cured the disease but disabled the immune system, hardly a gain. I financed Dr. Raeburn's continued efforts."

"Why?"

"The Communist Party wanted to use the disease to eliminate enemies, is the short answer. We needed a cure. The Exodus bug was to be it. Unfortunately, all the lieutenant colonel's efforts succeeded in doing was making an even more potent disease, an airborne plague germ with the capacity to kill millions. To have destroyed it or stored it would have required additional personnel—the possibility of either an intelligence or physical leak was of great concern."

"So you buried the samples deep in a place you thought would never be found," Williams said. "A cleaner solution than trying to destroy the thing. The cold kept them inert?"

"Very good understanding," Krummeck said.

"I can't take credit," Williams said. "A geologist suggested it."

Krummeck continued. "Between the constantly frigid climate and the environmental protections put in place, it *should* never have been found. But it was—by whom, we do not yet know. And it has been again—by the Chinese."

"You're sure of this?"

"The Marion outpost has been silent for quite some time. We believe it may have been commandeered by personnel from the corvette at anchor off Prince Edward."

"My team is—well, it's an independent team, not

really mine, and I will hear from them only when they feel the need to communicate," Williams said.

"I see. They are good?"

"They are very good. But you have a more immediate concern than the Chinese. You have an active killer here in South Africa."

"We believe that whoever made their way to Prince Edward returned with samples of the bug," Krummeck agreed.

"You trust Raeburn? Might he have sold the information to anyone?"

"I don't believe so, but that was the first thing I checked," Krummeck replied. "As soon as he left I had his residence searched, his accounts examined, his phone records studied. Nothing surfaced."

"But he is missing, now. He could have left to give himself an alibi."

"A thought that is concerning, actions that are suspicious—but I have watched him since we worked on this for expressly that reason. I do not think he is responsible."

"And no one else had access to his data, the burial location."

"Two men went with him to Prince Edward. One was a pilot, killed subsequently in a plane crash. The other is the deputy minister of planning, monitoring, and evaluation, with an eye on the presidency. I vouch for all three men."

"Do you have any leads?"

Krummeck smiled thinly. "If I did, you and I should not have met again. I can give you the precise location of the site where we put the toxins. I am hoping you have access to reconnaissance that might cover the hours before the passenger jet went down."

"General, I have looked at two days' worth of reconnaissance in that area from a variety of sources. There was nothing suspicious. What would someone have needed to reach the microbe, either by accident or design?"

"Apparently not much, if it was done this clandestinely."

"That radio intercept from a vessel seemed to suggest that," Williams said. "The men on the call were careful not to say very much, other than that the caller was terrified."

"But they may not have been the precipitating cause," Krummeck said. "Just in the wrong place."

"Possibly," Williams said. He thought back. The men had talked about a boat and a dinghy. There were boats in some of the surveillance photos. He might not have noticed a landing party in the dark.

"Would any environmentalists have had reason to take samples from the island?" Williams asked.

"Those are openly sanctioned by the Department of Environmental Affairs. No one with a legitimate research project need sneak ashore."

"What would constitute an illegitimate research project?"

"Poaching. Poisoning."

"Poisoning what?"

"Mice," Krummeck said. "They came with early explorers and were adaptable enough to survive and multiply. There are tens of thousands of them and they eat albatross chicks—bird fanciers have been after the government to eradicate the pests. Perhaps someone was secretly testing bait. But that would not have required digging."

"I assume you buried the bug deeper than mice could dig."

"We actually considered that when we picked the site, so yes."

Williams thought back to his research that morning. He held up his phone. "General, is there an office I can borrow?"

"Use mine," Krummeck said, rising. "Ten minutes?"

"No more than that," Williams said.

Obligingly, the general rose and left. If this were Washington, time would have been wasted summoning an aide and finding a place to relocate him. When the door clicked shut, he texted Berry.

```
With SANDF. Analysis of Prince Ed
boat pics from yest?
```

Williams waited. The original call, the one the navy had intercepted, had come from a boat. They had a position, north of Prince Edward. General Krummeck had certainly heard the call too and hadn't been able to piece anything together from it. He was not looking to shift blame. He was trying to solve the problem and at the same time build a relationship to prevent this sort of thing from happening again.

The phone pinged. Berry's image grabs were returned with notations:

```
Filtered by proximity to PE and
anchor/delay in region:
```

- ✓Australian meteorological vessel *Wanderer*
- ✓Philippine fishing ship, logged engine repair
- ✓Private cruise ship Cape Town—*Antarctica*
- ✗Private yacht, no ID
- ✓Indian bulk freighter *Pooja Rana*
- ✓New Zealand doc film crew vessel *1221-F*

The checkmark meant that every ship had been verified with its port of origin, had returned, and there were no open questions about known crewmembers or the purpose of the passage.

Williams looked at the enhanced image of the yacht. *It reeks of up-to-no-good,* he thought.

If there was a name at the stern, it was artfully covered with flapping canvas so it could not be seen by satellite. There was an autogyro without obvious markings. It had to be IDed in some fashion. As a flying craft, that meant underneath. It could be seen from the ground, or by bending and looking once it landed. Not from above.

There was also no indication about where it had originated or ended up.

Krummeck returned while Williams was examining the photograph. He stood and showed it to the general.

"Recognize this?"

The general withdrew reading glasses from inside his uniform jacket and bent low over the photograph.

"No. Where was this taken?"

"About two miles north of Prince Edward not quite two days before the jet went down."

"Did it stay in those waters?"

"It did not, and—yes—other planes would have passed overhead between the time this photograph was taken and the Airbus crashed."

"It's not likely they deposited a party of some kind," Krummeck said. "Difficult to hide there, and we patrol by air, low helicopter flights, twice daily."

"That leads to the next possibility, that there may have been a corrosive process at work." Williams shut the phone. "On the day of the accident there was a glow rising from the area. In previous images, it was not present. If not for the attack on the bridge, I would have said it might have been natural erosion that released the bug. But someone was there. Someone harvested it."

"Which means finding out about that unidentified boat," Krummeck said. "Of course, it may not have been one of ours. There's Crozet and the other French islands to the east, Madagascar, Mauritius—"

"The bridge was here. The attacker wanted to get *your* attention."

"He has more," Krummeck said, resigned to a reality he had already deduced.

"We have to assume so."

"You know he called the East London police."

Williams nodded. "But not since the attack?"

"No. And that location may have been a feint, a ruse. He used an untraceable phone."

"Sophisticated, then," Williams said. "Accustomed to covering tracks."

"My conclusion, which suggests a human trafficker, drug- or gun-running, or clandestine surveillance for a foreign power."

"But someone who had a reason to go to Prince Edward and dig," Williams pointed out.

"Possibly to bury contraband for later recovery," Krummeck said. "In which case the seawall would be a perfect location. Quickly accessible from the sea, not easily observed by the island patrol."

"Who among the list you just gave me is also a sociopath willing to unleash a weapon of mass destruction?" Williams asked.

The leonine smile was long gone. "That's just it. Our known enemies, those who dodge justice, are known, their whereabouts tracked. This one is either new or off the radar."

"Or about some business you haven't looked at," Williams said. "That original radio call we intercepted. The man talked about other trips they had taken.

"Regardless, he has to be found, and in a backdoor fashion that won't cause him to release it again."

Williams's admonition and clarity sent Krummeck moving quickly to his desk. "Commander, if
I may have that photograph—I'd like to send it to
someone."

"Who?"

"The man who knows our coast and its shipping
better than anyone," he answered.

CHAPTER TWENTY-SEVEN

November 12, 8:08 A.M.

Katinka was afraid as she opened the door of the autogyro. Foster's expression was untroubled. He seemed rested and had probably slept after his long vigil waiting for her—and attacking Batting Bridge.

"Get the container and press the green button," he instructed as he unfolded his arms and opened the door of the van. There did not appear to be anyone inside, as far as she could penetrate the shadows.

She leaned into the small cargo area and, with trembling fingers, did as she was told. Katinka felt vulnerable, afraid even to be showing him her back. She looked out the window on the other side of the autogyro. A pair of parking lot employees were hurrying over, carrying a tarp. Even though they were in public, she did not know but that Foster intended to kill her anyway.

Katinka held the large canister to her bosom—her

foul progeny, something she should have left behind in its rockbound cradle. She sat and Foster slammed the door, shrouding her in darkness behind the charcoal-black windows. He got in and drove on as the autogyro was covered.

He drove away, peering at her in the rearview mirror.

"What was your plan?" Foster asked.

"To get away," she said.

"To run to obscurity or the authorities?" he asked.

"Away. Home."

"How uncommonly familial, Katinka. So, to hide. From what? You know that if I am found out, you are not far behind."

"I had no part in what you did," she said. "I would never have."

Foster chuckled as his eyes returned to the road, filled with much less traffic than usual. "A wounded bird. Again, uncharacteristic. Do you know what I'm doing right now, Katinka? How often were we afraid because of their stupid laws, their self-serving restrictions? How many times did our people run, or get shot on sight for trespassing? Just for *being* on someone else's land? Attempting to work for just a little of what they already had in abundance?"

"You know how I feel about the diamond industry and the government," she said. "That did not justify murdering innocents."

"Many of whom were profiting by this old monopoly! We tossed off corrupt, racial bonds, but money—but money . . . ah, money stayed where it was. Out of reach except for widespread and dangerous efforts to collect scraps."

"Not everyone you killed was guilty."

"Should I have gone to a bank? A diamond mine, assuming I could have gotten near enough? Would no one innocent have died? Let me tell you, Katinka, do you know what I feel right now? For the first time in my life I feel like I'm free to walk in the sun, to operate without looking behind me, worrying about surveillance or hacking, just for engaging in a legal enterprise! I am savoring their fear!" His eyes snapped back to the mirror. "And you—this haughty indignation does not suit you. You brought this to me for a reason."

"To threaten, not slaughter!"

He looked back out the windshield, smiling and shaking his head. "Did you not think that would become inevitable? That the authorities would simply hand over the combination to a bank vault and let us walk in? No, Katinka. Don't be righteous on top of being naïve. And hypocritical, I might add. *You* realized this contagion, not I."

"By accident," she said, her voice contrite. She set the container on the seat, newly ashamed.

"Pandora did no less, unwittingly releasing the ills of the world. I'm sure the families of the airline passengers would be consoled by your clean hands."

"I don't accept that blame," she said.

"So innocent," he said. "You know nothing about the guards or law enforcement we sometimes—*remove*? Of course you do. Yet you persist. And did you check everyone on the boat before you blew it up?"

"That was to destroy a disease."

"One that you yourself wanted to exploit! How did you plan to do that, without a demonstration?"

She had no answer for that.

"And what am *I* doing, Katinka? I'm destroying a disease. The world around us has been changed, an old regime overthrown. That hasn't benefited you and me and a restricted financial class."

"You're an activist now?" she asked.

"I am damn well not, and you can stuff your sarcasm. I am sick of having to feel ashamed of the way we live our lives. Your core samples were not just a revelation, they were a gift. A means to break our own bonds. Back down? That I will not do, nor allow anyone else around me to do so." He glanced at her again. "Tell me, Katinka. Are you for me or are you against me? There is no other choice."

The woman looked at the canister. "Would this have really detonated?"

"It would." He thought for a moment then looked back at the road. "Why do you fight me? We are on the same side. You have so much of life ahead—how do you want to live it?"

"With an unblemished conscience," she responded. "I want to be able to sleep."

His sneer was instant. "No one—not the men who established apartheid or those who overthrew it—can claim *that*! Nothing in this land is clean. You want to sleep? Open the goddamn container. I won't stop you."

Katinka sat very still. She was numb and her mind

was empty of further arguments. Foster was right about this much. There were not very many paths for her to take.

And what had been done was done. She could not change that. But staying close to him, she might be able to affect what happened next. And also to survive.

"All right," she said contritely. "I am with you."

Foster did not smile. He simply nodded, as if she'd said "present" at a roll call.

"Discuss this with no one at the office," he said.

"No. Of course not."

As they rode in silence, she was overcome by a familiar—*clutching* was the word that came to mind. An insistent part of her wanted to be near Foster and let his confidence, his certainty steady her as she moved through unknown territory.

But for the first time there was something else—a growing sense of loathing, not just for what Foster had done but with herself for having depended on him for so long. She thought this discovery would let her get away from him, a windfall and she was free.

Instead, you're bound to him more than ever, she told herself.

And not in the way she had wished.

CHAPTER TWENTY-EIGHT

November 12, 8:15 A.M.

The Chinese seamen were lying facedown on the floor of the outpost, bound hand and leg with heavy manila rope used to tie down the helicopter, the composting canopy, and other outdoor items during strong winds. They had covered them with a quilt to keep them from freezing as cold air blew through the broken window.

The men had defied Grace's efforts to question them, and she did not have time to "pain" it out of them, as she called it. For that she would employ a series of manual wrist and elbow locks that worked joint against joint to cause unbearable agony. The locks left no scars, caused no permanent damage, and Grace never understood why interrogators did not employ them as a matter of course.

Ensign Sisula and the helicopter pilot, Ryan Bruwer, had pulled on their cold-weather outer garments.

Sisula was seated at the radio, Bruwer and Grace behind him.

"We gotta think this through," Rivette cautioned as he stood over their four prisoners. "We do this, the enemy will know."

"If we don't do this, the enemy wins," Grace said.

"They've got big guns," Rivette pointed out. "We would have none."

"They won't use them," Grace said. "It would trigger retaliation, bring in other warships in the region."

The lance corporal shook his head. "People got guns, they usually fire them."

"There is no one else around," the small, wiry Bruwer remarked. "Nothing else was allowed to fly to the island, of course."

"Can you call in the military?" Grace asked.

"I can request aid but that will take time. Our mission was very low-profile."

"Yeah, we know something about that tune," Rivette said.

"I believe we should call my commander," Sisula suggested. "This is, after all, his outpost."

Grace shook her head. "Both of those options, SAN and the commander, give the Chinese a heads-up and window to finish what they're doing. We're wasting time *now*. Ensign, your commander may be ill, like your pilot. Put in a call to the civilians, please."

"The Civil Aviation—"

"Yes," she said. "Quickly."

Sisula had not considered that. He pulled on his headset and adjusted the radio to the civil band. He put the audio on "speaker." The Chinese would most likely be monitoring those communications. He had to keep this humanitarian. And not give away the fact that the Chinese had been taken prisoner.

"This is Ensign Michael Sisula at Marion Outpost calling Civil Aviation Authority aircraft," he said. "Come in, over."

The wind was the only thing that moved in the room. It brought wisps of gray smoke and white ash, as well as the faint, noxious smell of melted plastic—all that remained of the exploded helicopter. It reminded Rivette of junkyard fires. He chuckled inside, thinking how much training and distance had gone into putting him right back where he started.

Sisula repeated the message.

"Chinese corvette is probably going a little crazy right now, not hearing their squad," Rivette remarked. He smiled openly. "Gotta admit, I *like* that."

The answer came through muffled, pushed through a mask, Sisula presumed.

"We heard an explosion!" said a woman's voice.

"That was a medical helicopter, destroyed by an accident."

"What kind of accident?"

"Inexperienced pilot," he said with an apologetic look at Bruwer. "Our commander and his pilot from Prince Edward. They are stranded, ailing after a long night. They may have been exposed to a toxic agent. We need to evacuate them."

"We?"

"Members of the SAN," he fudged. "Can you carry us over? We can come back with the helicopter."

"We are civilians," the woman replied.

"You're the only help around," Sisula said. "We only need a ride from our outpost a mile east of you to the west coast of the island. You don't even have to wait. We have a helicopter there."

"We saw it coming in," the woman said. "This is highly unorthodox, sir."

"Please."

"Wait a moment."

The radio operator heard muted conversation on the other end. The woman had not sounded unsympathetic. Of course, Sisula also had not mentioned that Mabuza was ill with the toxin and that he did not even know if they were alive. Or that the soldiers intended, somehow, to repel the Chinese invaders.

"The pilot says he can land you near your man's position on Prince Edward," the woman said. "You will hear us coming. It is not a quiet aircraft we have."

"Thank you," Sisula said, and terminated the call. He switched back to the military wavelength. Free of the Chinese, he wanted to ascertain the commander's status.

Behind him, Rivette gravely fist-pumped. Grace remained thoughtful.

"They're gonna suspect you're not SAN," Rivette mentioned to Grace.

"Masks go back on, so maybe they'll hesitate," she said.

Rivette nodded then looked down at the prisoners. "We just leave these guys?"

"For now," Grace said. "The target has to be the Chinese who were at ground zero."

"That may be easier than you think," a voice said over the radio.

Sisula's expression brightened. "Caller, we are receiving."

"Ensign, this is van Tonder," a voice said. "I shot the hell out of their screws. The patrol boat is still there and it isn't going anywhere. Corvette personnel arrived on dinghies, working for two hours. And if you're listening, you goddamned Beijing pirates—get the hell off my island!"

CHAPTER TWENTY-NINE

PORT ELIZABETH, SOUTH AFRICA

November 12, 8:34 A.M.

National Sea Rescue Institute Station No. 6 in Port Elizabeth was not fancy, but it was his. Fifty-seven-year-old Station Commander David Hughes sat alone in the second-floor office of the teal blue wooden building. Around him were old, sun-faded prints of ancient sailing ships and shiny framed photographs of his own boats. Hughes had worked for the all-volunteer service most of his adult life. He was a boat designer professionally and wrote songs on the side, and he drew inspiration for both from the sea.

David, his wife, and their daughter, hydro-engineer son-in-law, and granddaughter lived close to the sea. Rarely a waking hour went by where the man's sun-bronzed face was not turned toward it. He knew its moods, its moves, and the vessels that called it home.

He was on the job today, early, because the bridge that had fallen into the Nahoon River had created logistical ripples that rose the levels of traffic. Engineering and rescue boats were moving in—carefully, given the nature of the attack—and medical vessels were waiting to be admitted when the air was deemed safe.

Hughes was not surprised when the call came from General Tobias Krummeck. The intelligence officer often consulted him on matters pertaining to the movement of suspected smugglers and foreign vessels. The station commander was only too happy to help. His love for his homeland was the last star in the trinity that included family and sea.

"A photograph?" Hughes said in response to Krummeck's question. "Yes, I'll look at it."

Hughes considered for a moment how to put the smartphone on speaker while he accessed a text. His son-in-law had showed him how; he wrote it down to remember the process, but he wrote it on his phone Notes app and was afraid he'd cut Krummeck off. After a few stabs, literally, he accessed his messages without losing the general.

"Let me just magnify a little," he said, saving the image and expanding the boat. "That's the *Teri Wheel,* General."

"Who runs her?"

"MEASE," Hughes replied. "Mineral Exploration and Acquisition Survey Enterprises out of East London."

"When did you see the vessel last?"

"A week or so. They passed here on the way to

Mossel Bay. Station there reported them asking for an update on the currents to the south."

"Where south?"

"Prince Edward. General, has this anything to do with—"

"Thank you, Station Commander," Krummeck said. "Very much."

"Any time, General," the man replied.

But the intelligence officer had already terminated the call. Hoping he had contributed something to the current investigation, and wondering what involvement MEASE might have, Hughes looked out at the sea.

"What do you know about all this?" he wondered aloud. "If only we could understand your language," he added—then went to the closet where he kept his guitar and began playing so he could expand on the line. . . .

"Claude Foster," Krummeck said as he set the phone on his desk. "Illegal gem prospector, dealer. The diamond conglomerates have pressured the government, and the government has pressured us. But we've never been able to pin him to anything, not directly."

"How does he operate? Drills? Blasting? Something that could have opened your buried chest?"

"He would not have blasted where the outpost might have heard," Krummeck said. "But . . . drills, yes. He uses drills and acid."

Williams thought back to his conversation with

Dr. Goodman. It was not a natural gas glowing in the light. It was an acid.

"General, was that Foster's voice on the ship-to-shore radio call?"

"It might have been. He's never been in open court. The call to the East London police has a lot of noise." Krummeck reached for his landline. "I'll ask my people to see if there are old wiretaps and have the SAN look for the *Teri Wheel* at the last known position. I'm going to—"

"If you're thinking of having him brought in, remember—he might have the biological agent."

"Which he would release suicidally?"

"He may have given it to someone else. Or there may be more than one."

Krummeck picked up the receiver but stopped. "If this is his doing, and we leave him at liberty, he will be free to hold us hostage, and on *his* timetable. We cannot afford to give him more time."

"I don't disagree, but you said yourself he's slippery. He may know you, your people, your methods. He does not know me or Major Breen."

The general hesitated then replaced the receiver.

"Do you have a file on Foster?" Williams asked.

"Names, dates, activities—no profile. We have not really needed that, you know. Everything is still so much about a man's heritage."

"Is any of that digital?"

Krummeck shook his head.

"All right. Anyone approaching him would not necessarily know those things anyway," Williams reasoned.

"How will you approach him?"

"The major knows criminals, knows them well. He'll have better ideas."

"Legal ones?"

"General, he'll have the kind we need right now, ones that can come together while we travel from here to there."

Krummeck appreciated the tactic and respected the hubris but was still undecided. Williams leaned on the desk.

"General, a man like you described—he's not a sociopath or a terrorist, he's a savvy son of a bitch who does this for the profit but also for the fun. I'll bet my life on that. He may not have gotten back in touch because he's savoring this, maybe waiting to see what we do next so he can slap us again."

"That's a fair assessment," Krummeck admitted.

"Okay, then. That means our side has to take charge of this or we'll be playing catch-up until one of two things happen. Either we get lucky, or he wins. Let us go down there, make sure this is even the guy we want."

Krummeck was not a man who liked to share his jurisdiction or his resources. He had given in to Raeburn's request for transportation to Prince Edward because they had to know if their old operation had been compromised. Raeburn was MIA.

"This is beyond what it was," the general said vaguely, more to himself than to Williams.

"Sorry?"

Krummeck's tired eyes locked on Williams. "I've got a pair of men I need to find. It will take ninety minutes to ferry you down. I will have a man meet you, an undercover driver. Whether we have any additional communication or not, you have this for at least a few hours after that. Is that acceptable?"

"Very, and thank you," Williams said. "Do you have other men in East London?"

"Informants, watchers—noncombatants."

Williams grinned, barely perceptibly. He and Breen would be the only soldiers on the ground. Not South African. Someone to blame if things went wrong.

"My adjutant will get you a flight. Do you have money?"

"About two thousand rand," Williams told him.

"More than enough for whatever you need. Hazmat?"

Williams nodded and turned.

"Good luck," Krummeck said to his back as he left the office.

Williams knew the man was sincere. Krummeck wore the uniform of a nation under a toxic cloud. It was a small thought in the big picture, but Williams hoped that he had never been as plainly territorial when he was running the previous Op-Center organization.

When Williams emerged, the adjutant was already on the phone, listening.

"Yes, sir," she said. Without acknowledging Williams standing before her, she called a number. "The airfield, section three," she said, then hung up.

She finally looked at the American. It was the same look of bulletproof reserve that he had come to expect, and dislike, at the DNI.

"Deputy Chief Swane will take you to Pretoria Central Heliport," she said. "She will also provide the name of your contact in East London."

"Thank you," Williams said as he hurried toward the staircase.

The adjutant did not wish him good luck.

CHAPTER THIRTY

EAST LONDON, SOUTH AFRICA

November 12, 8:49 A.M.

The door to the office was closed. Seated behind his desk, rocking slightly in his office chair, Foster sipped coffee and turned to Katinka.

The young woman sat stiffly in the corner of a leather couch to his right. There were hazmat masks in a plastic bin that usually held mail. She wanted to be numb, feeling nothing, but she had gotten a good rest and could not stop *thinking*. And that made her alternately scared, sick, and depressed to the point of tears. She did not let Foster see her weep, artfully turning her face and finding some way to sweep them away.

Perhaps he knew. Perhaps he did not.

Employees were arriving for work. They chatted as they did, no doubt discussing the Terror at Batting Bridge, as the headlines called it. No one bothered the boss when his door was shut, though the eight office workers all looked at him now and then as if taking a cue from his expression as to what they should feel.

Apparently, nothing. His face was expressionless and still.

"I have been staring at the phone, thinking," Foster said after a long silence. "I may not want to sell this to our government."

"Sell protection, you mean," she said. It was not an accusation but a clarification.

"That's right. What would Pretoria do with a weaponized core sample? Force whites to give up the seventy percent of farmable land we own?"

Now Katinka looked at him accusingly. "Is that what's behind this?"

"Is what behind this, Katinka?"

"You know damn well."

"A reactionary attack on a system that has gone from being lopsided one way to aslant another way? You mistake me for my brother. Have I ever seemed political to you?"

"No, but that comment—"

"Is fact. It's about the deep stupidity of our people, isn't it? In the name of equality, they would be, *are,* eager to kill skilled farmers because of their color and replace them with unqualified farmers because of *their* color." He set his mug down hard and swiveled to her. "But you are right as far as this goes. I would do a great deal to keep the idiots from interfering in my life and my work any further. They have forced me, you, us to work in secret with their idiotic regulations and payoffs from monopolies. Frankly, I don't care if things fall apart, again, and have to be rebuilt. The man or woman or group that controls something to force true equality, not retribution—he or she or they would be great patriots!"

Foster turned back to his desk.

"What I wanted to do with my first call, I did. I let the world know that someone controls this extraordinary power. Now we must decide what to do with it. Do we justly enrich ourselves by terrorizing a venal system, or justly enrich ourselves by offering that power to someone else?" He shook his head. "I'm unable to decide that, Katinka. Do you still think we should sell it to an arms dealer or a foreign military?"

"When I realized what we had, I thought—that. Selling it. Negotiating. But nothing more."

"Surely you realized that a buyer would have tried it."

She shook her head.

"Really, Katinka. How did you expect this would go? Beijing or Tehran were just going to take your word that what you had brought down the plane? You don't think they would have tried it on prisoners? Some remote village somewhere?"

"I realize now . . . I didn't think," she admitted.

"Of course. I have always been here to do that. And I'm not criticizing you. That was my function, just as digging and analyzing was yours. And so here we are." He pursed his lips and nodded. "To hell with Pretoria. Let's take it somewhere else. I will contact Nicus Dumisa. He has connections in every world capital. Then I'll call Mila to get us out of here."

The names alone made Katinka feel sicker than she already did—especially Mila Merch, who offered impoverished young women "positions" in the homes of well-to-do men. They compounded the self-rebuke going on in her brain, her idiotic idea that their relationship could be more than her being just an educated laborer.

God, how stupid you've been.

But a sudden self-epiphany did not change the fact that Foster was right. She was *in* this now. Even if Katinka had turned him in she would not have gotten away free. She'd broken numerous laws, not the least of which was abetting mass murder, and she would have had to tell authorities where she had been digging. Others would go there.

They would get a sample, carry it off, repeat. Just as Foster had said.

There was only one way through this, and that was ahead. Like it or not, she was still attached to the man who was even now placing a call to Swaziland.

He did not get to finish that call as unexpected visitors came to the front door.

Nearly a dozen of them.

CHAPTER THIRTY-ONE

November 12, 9:00 A.M.

The Robinson R66 Turbine helicopter was comfortable and quiet, a welcome break from the noise of Pretoria—and the first after the long journey that had preceded Black Wasp's arrival in South Africa.

With their gear in the third and fourth passenger seats behind them, Williams and Breen had just taken off when they received a text from Matt Berry:

```
FBI says 99% certainty voice 2 re-
cordings is same.
```

Major Breen was not surprised. He had not been idle while waiting for Williams. He had been reviewing data from the National Reconnaissance Office. The signal strength recorded in the report from the East London police and the radio intercept from the

USS *Carl Vinson* had triangulated to roughly the same location.

"So how do we approach him?" Williams asked over their dedicated headsets. The men could communicate with the pilot and he could cut in with instructions but not eavesdrop.

"By understanding his endgame, which is twofold. First, to make as much money as possible and as fast as possible. Second, to get out of South Africa as quickly as possible. Pretoria is going to want to put him on trial for mass murder. He has to get to someplace safe."

"Such as?"

"While I was waiting, I also looked up the countries that have no extradition agreements with South Africa. He can go to China, for one. Also Pakistan, Venezuela, Ethiopia—"

"He probably has a jet fueled and waiting."

"No doubt, which is why I suggest we approach him with as little artifice as possible," Breen said. "We should be what we are and, moreover, expect that we might not be the only ones quickly zeroing in on this guy. The Chinese may be running a two-prong operation: dig for the bug and offer him sanctuary. That way, they corner the market. The other consideration is that Foster will certainly have an accomplice, maybe additional stores off-site to sell to additional bidders—"

"No sudden moves."

"Exactly."

Williams shook his head. "We're on a fact-finding mission? That's it?"

"It's stronger than that," Breen said. "We go in and make a preemptive bid, tell him the DoD wants everything. And it's not like we don't have leverage. We can let him know that potential bidders are descending on Prince Edward. If he doesn't sell now, he'll be left with extortion. That has a pretty low high-end, given South Africa's divided feelings about its own population. We have to make sure he understands that Pretoria will pay considerably less and give our offer a short shelf life."

"And if he agrees?"

"You tell me. Because I'm wondering how bad our military might, in fact, *want* this bug."

"You think we should actually buy it?"

"That's the goal, right? To get it away from Foster, keep him or anyone but us from killing more people?"

The tenor of that last remark was pure courtroom: by inflection, not words, Breen had just condemned the idea that even his side should possess another weapon of mass destruction.

"I can't say I like it, but I understand," Williams said.

"It's like defending a murderer I know is guilty," Breen said. "Had that with a home-grown terrorist. He told me how he was radicalized and why. It made me sick. He took the leg off a child, blinded another, driving a van into a school bus. I had to defend the monster. I have to do my best whatever my personal feelings. You're doing the same—about winging this, I mean."

Williams laughed. "You noticed?"

"Once a commander . . ."

"Yeah," Williams said. "I wish to hell we had Grace and Rivette reporting in. Current intel about what's going on down there so we could drop that on Foster."

"Black Wasp wasn't designed to work like that," Breen said.

"Which puzzles the hell out of me."

The criminologist said nothing further. Breen wasn't just quiet, he had suddenly shut up.

Williams regarded him. "What are you not telling me?"

"Nothing you probably haven't figured out," Breen replied. "The calculation. It became obvious as soon as we started drilling. Black Wasp isn't just a test of surgical-strike special ops. It's a rethinking of the entire command structure, the design and execution of national military missions."

"I think you just said 'guinea pigs' in bureaucratese."

Breen snickered. "Complete with gene splicing. Grace said it herself. She and Jaz were yin and yang—opposites that, together, formed a perfect whole. *They* didn't need me to execute various training scenarios. My job was to watch situations and offer evolving analysis. Your job, I suspect, was to plug us into the mainframe. In this case, the White House, I presume. The military itself doesn't need more military. The West Wing does. They gave you the ability to feed the team without controlling it."

"Eliminate all fat, a huge STF minus the command structure, the overhead, by using disposable loose cannons," Williams said.

"Right. Something the military would never agree to unless ordered, since there goes the trillion-dollar budgets. And this new setup is modular. We lose Jaz and Grace, we get two others. They lose us, the same." Breen reflected briefly. "You want the pullback, Chase? What I think we're seeing here?"

"Very much."

"The notion of an experimental 'situational command' is a feint. I believe that two very different ideas, Black Wasp and Space Force, are being groomed as the new faces of the U.S. military. The unseen—one small and mobile, like the germs we're chasing. The other high and godlike, able to rain hell on nations, borders, hypersonic nuclear missiles, submarines, nuclear silos and bunkers—we can kill all targets of all sizes in all places all the time. Every military force in the middle becomes extraneous."

Williams immediately grasped that big picture. "Not just the U.S. military but every other military on Earth becomes big and ineffective."

"Exactly. And what Space Force can't obliterate, Black Wasp can behead."

Williams should have been pleased by Breen's assessment. If it were true, far fewer troops would be in harm's way or far from their families.

Except for the ones in orbit or on the moon, he thought.

He should also have been excited or at least grateful to be on the ground floor of a quick, seismic shift in a process that was typically glacial. But it was slow for a reason. Safeguards were built in—not just command structure but decision-making protocols from the top on down. With a computer determining defense readiness condition levels, wasn't it possible that one of their own Black Wasp teams would be misread and targeted?

Once a commander . . .

Williams sighed and looked at the countryside rushing by. There were communities like you'd find in Middle America with lawns and pools and cars. And they were butting against pockets of jungle and rivers and brilliant colors that looked like a romantic's idea of Africa.

It was a land both as familiar and then as abruptly alien as the life he was now leading.

It's also not your big problem, Williams reminded himself. He had this small, key part of it. He had to focus on getting that right, giving the think tanks data to ponder before sending more Black Wasps into the world.

He was pulled from the view by a text. He was the only recipient. It was from General Krummeck. Williams read it and swore. There was a case of his worst

Black Wasp fear. Of all the damn luck, an elite force had hit the right place for the wrong reason:

Wreckage of Teri found. Special Task Force at East L Target. Chaos.

CHAPTER THIRTY-TWO

MARION ISLAND, SOUTH AFRICA

November 12, 9:00 A.M.

The Maule M-7-235C amphibious aircraft had the option of taking off on water or land, thanks to tiny wheels beneath its floats. Grace would be happy if, after this, all her takeoffs and landings could be on water.

The lieutenant borrowed a radio from Sisula and said she would contact him if they needed to talk to van Tonder.

"Just in case we're delayed for some reason," she said.

Rivette knew what she meant. At least, he hoped he did.

After that, Grace, Rivette, and Ryan Bruwer went to the sea ledge and made their way to the rocky beach of Crawford Bay to await the plane. Rivette was the only person of color among the three, and decided it would be best to keep his face fully exposed. The civilian pilot would be expecting an African, not an Asian or a white Boer. The rocks were largely clear of dung due to the ebbing tides though the large, round stones were slippery with seaweed and clinging foam.

"Out there is friggin' Antarctica," Rivette kept saying as he stood looking across the sea. The Southern California native was wriggling and moving every way he could think of to stay warm. "That's awesome *and* cold."

"She's out there, yeah, but about two thousand miles," Bruwer said.

"I used to stand on Santa Monica Beach and look out at the sunset and think, 'Japan's right out there.'" He shrugged. "Same thing. It's a road, y'know? And a road means you can get there."

The hum of the aircraft sent the birds scattering and the three passengers ducking. Marine mammals of various size plunked into the sea farther to the west and came slapping through the water to unbothered ground. Grace noticed that the elephant seals and varieties of fur seals mingled freely, the way the many varieties of bird had done. It took civilization to manufacture differences.

She noted that only the killer whales were shunned, with rapid right-angle twists and dives. With good reason. Seeing their sleek black-and-white skins aglow with sun and seawater, and their large, sensual dorsal fin, she was reminded of the black-and-white silk Wudang Daoist attire of her own deadly arts.

The plane cleared the bay of its indigenous life, landing with a splash as it fought the local winds.

The pilot swung the aircraft around so the passengers could board.

"You're a lifesaver, thanks," Rivette said to the pilot as he opened the door of the passenger compartment.

The man was masked, and pointed that he could not hear through the headphones. That was just as well, Grace thought. Jaz did not sound remotely African. Sometimes he was just too exuberant.

The others boarded with their faces averted. They donned their masks and were airborne in less than a minute.

As they flew low over the mountains and rugged terrain of the island, Grace turned her eyes to smaller Prince Edward to the north. She knew the Chinese would not mistake them for South African. They had no markings or insignia to identify them as such. For all the squatters knew, they could be Russian or American.

In which case this will get messy, she thought.

The only hope to avoid a showdown lay with Commander van Tonder. She hoped he had a backbone to match that little speech he gave.

The flight took just under fifteen minutes. Grace and Rivette used the trip to try and pinpoint the Chinese positions. They saw the corvette anchored offshore but, from their position, they did not have a good view of the microbial ground zero.

The M-7 headed toward a flat plain about a half mile east of the helicopter. After making a pass, the pilot shook his head hard and pointed ahead.

He was going to have to land on the water.

He pointed toward a sloping ridge that went from the coast to the ledge where the helicopter was parked. Rivette looked at Grace, then nodded. The water landing would actually bring them closer to the target. Bruwer could make his own way up to the South African officers.

The plane passed over the eastern promontory. As it angled toward the water, Grace caught a quick glimpse of the patrol boat and Ship Rock. Moments later the plane ducked below the ridgeline and skidded to a loud, wet landing. He came as close to the coast as he was able, about twenty feet away. The compartment where the inflatable rafts would have been stored was empty; the emergency workers had already used them to reach the crashed jetliner. The three passengers were going to have to slosh to shore in the frigid, waist-high surf.

Rivette and Grace stood in the open doorway of the aircraft, pitching from side to side and back and forth as it rocked in the eddies. Grace heard him swearing behind his mask—loud enough so that she could make out the words.

She turned to him and leaned close. "I saw a Chinese patrol boat at ground zero! Have to get there!"

"How? *Swim?* In this cold, these currents?"

"No! I have a better idea! Remember van Tonder's message?"

"What about it?"

Grace waved the question away. "When I move, shut the door and follow me!"

Rivette gave a thumbs-up.

Grace motioned Bruwer to stay where he was. Then she turned back into the cabin, leaned over the seat, close to the pilot, and slapped a firm, powerful hand on his mask.

"Idle the engine."

The pilot stiffened.

"Listen to me," Grace said. "You're not going anywhere. Throttle down or I yank it off!"

"Don't!" he cried, pushing in a black knob to the right of the steering column. The engine quieted.

"Do you have a raft in storage?" She cocked her head toward the area behind the back seat.

"No room—we brought medical supplies."

"All right, then. Send an open SOS," she ordered. "Say you're being hijacked!"

"By who? Who *are* you?"

"The last person you'll see if you don't do as you're told!" she said, firmly twisting his face around so he was looking up into her eyes. "Get on the radio and tell them the Chinese have taken your aircraft."

Without looking away, the pilot fumbled for the dial on his instrument panel. The digital numbers shifted from the emergency frequency to a wider bandwidth.

"This is CAA Alpha-Seven-Five-Zero-Zed," he said. "Chinese passengers have commandeered aircraft!"

"Tell them you're sitting offshore of Voolkop, roughly a half mile southwest of Ship Rock, tending to their wounded!"

The pilot repeated the words and was instructed to

sign off. He obliged. With one hand still on the mask, she indicated for him to shut the radio. Then she motioned for him to rise.

"Bend over the back of the seat, belly down, arms down."

He did as he was told. He saw Rivette and was openly puzzled.

"I'm a traitor, dude!" the lance corporal said. "Sold out to the enemy."

"All right," Grace said, picking up on that. "I'm your translator."

"At least something's true," Rivette said.

"Tie him here," the woman went on, impressed by the improvisation. There was something to be said for street smarts.

Grace sliced off the shoulder harness from the passenger's side and passed the straps to Rivette. He used one strap to bind the man's wrists together then the other to tie them to the base frame of the seat. There was not enough room on top for the man to climb over.

"Don't worry," Grace said to the frightened man. "Unless you become aggressive, you will survive."

"He can shout through the mask," Rivette pointed out.

"They won't hear him with the wind, surf, and propeller."

The lieutenant moved around Rivette as he tested the man's bonds. She went to the door and looked out. The end of the island was about a quarter mile to the northeast. There was no way the crew of the patrol boat could fail to investigate the call. Unable to contact anyone at the outpost, and probably hearing van Tonder's broadcast, they would assume their men had been forced to vacate, perhaps with wounded, and hijacked a plane to get away.

Even if they suspect it's a lie, they have to come, Grace thought.

The sway and bob of the boat was a chance for the woman to practice centering, balance as she waited. Rivette went over to Bruwer.

"I think the plan is to not let them see you or the pilot," Rivette said. "You got a pocketknife?"

The man pulled a switchblade from his hip pocket.

"Not standard SAN issue, I'm guessing?" Rivette grinned.

"Volatile land, still," he said. "Sometimes you have to surprise your own people."

The American looked around, saw a life preserver. "So how about I tie you to a seat and you cut free when we're gone?"

"Sounds good, though that doesn't give me much to do."

"You got comrades up the cliff," Rivette said. "When this is over, however it goes, maybe you can help them."

"I like that." Bruwer offered his hand. "Thank you and *totsiens,* as my ancestors used to say."

"Is that good-bye?"

"More accurately, farewell," Bruwer told him.

"How would I say hello in something from here?"

"In isiZulu?"

"That works."

"Sawubona," Bruwer told him.

The helicopter pilot returned to his seat and let Rivette tie him with a cord from a life preserver that was still attached.

"Dude may get shot or frozen, but at least he won't drown!" Rivette said when he reached Grace's side.

The warm air of the cabin was a comfort and Grace let it soak in. Hopefully, they would not be enjoying it for very long.

She was right.

"Damn!" Rivette said as he saw what she saw. "My partner is a magician!"

Ahead, churning ahead on a sea of bright-white waters, was a dinghy with an armed complement of four seamen.

"What's the plan?" he asked.

"That depends on them!" Grace replied. "Just follow my lead!"

CHAPTER THIRTY-THREE

November 12, 9:11 A.M.

"You're with me or you're dead."

Foster's quiet words struck Katinka's ears like a church bell. She shook hearing them enter the office with their bodies armored and weapons raised.

"What are you going to do?" Katinka asked as the STF team took their time to move through the desks, surrounding and covering everyone in the office.

"One of them is Sea Rescue. They had to have found the boat, bodies, God knows. If we go with them, they find out the rest."

Foster swiveled around. Ducking low behind the desk, his back to the room, he pulled on the gas mask and reached for the canister. Though the office glass was bulletproof, the door was not airtight.

"God, no," Katinka said.

"The mask," he said thickly as he twisted the lid. *"Do it!"*

Sobbing, Katinka did as he instructed, even as two officers closed on the office.

"Hold where you are!" the head officer shouted. She was an African woman, her Vektor SP1 semiautomatic aimed at Foster through the glass.

"Don't," she told Foster.

He stepped away lest she lunge at him, and removed the lid.

"Get out!" Katinka screamed at the room.

The officers stopped moving. In a gut-kick flash, they realized who and what they had stumbled onto.

"Everyone *go,* workers *go!*" the squad leader cried, whipping her gun toward the door.

Desks nudged and chairs flew. Within moments the door was clogged with panicked MEASE employees, followed by STF officers who were crowding after them, pushing them through.

Holding her breath, the leader backed away with a look so venal that Katinka wished she had remained onboard the *Teri Wheel*. The room cleared quickly and all Katinka heard was her own labored breath.

The two waited in the office, Foster listening. After nearly a minute, he smiled under the mask.

"It's safe to go," he said. "Do you hear?"

Katinka wasn't listening. She shook her head forlornly.

"They're on the steps," he said.

"Waiting? *Why?*"

"Coughing," he replied flatly.

"Sweet God—"

Foster put the canister in a backpack with the other container then took a compact Ruger SP101 pistol and a burner phone from a desk drawer.

"Come on," he said.

He unlocked the door and led the way, listening as he moved through the disarray of chairs and desks. He ignored Katinka's tears and stumbling progress. He was too busy calculating his next move. There was no rush; the longer they took, the safer they would be.

The door was open and he looked out.

The two Special Task Force officers who had approached his office were sprawled on the staircase. The leader was lying with her head facing down, convulsions causing her to hop like a frog. Her companion was below her, facedown on the tiles. He was hacking hard and trying to get his arms under him to push up. He failed.

"Help him," Katinka blurted.

"With what, a bullet? He's already dead, you know that," Foster replied.

Foster eased around the leader as blood began to run from her mouth, spewed with each cough. They were careful to avoid the spray lest the bacteria get on their clothes.

Reaching the front door, Foster looked into the street. It was already empty as the surviving STF members ordered people to leave. Most seemed all right; a few were coughing. He felt bad for the people in the car dealership. They had probably been overlooked in the quick retreat. That was where Foster was headed.

Katinka grabbed his windbreaker and pulled her face close.

"Shut it!" she implored.

"Not until we're away! People have to fall or they will come after us!"

"No!"

Katinka pulled at him and Foster spun with impatience. He thrust the gun to her cheek. "Stay if you want but do *not* interfere!"

By the time Foster looked back at the street, a few officers and pedestrians were already on their knees, some doubled over. His van was out front but he did not want to go outside where police could gun him down. A basement connected the two businesses and was used for storing spare parts and shared office supplies. Foster unlocked the keypad-controlled door and went down the concrete stairs, Katinka trailing.

"Let me go up and warn them to leave," she pleaded.

"All right," he said. "Hurry!"

Katinka crossed the small area and ran up the opposite stairs. She stopped halfway up; a moment later, two salesmen stumbled down, blood on their hands and mouths.

Foster ran forward and pulled them down the stairs, one after the other, then pushed Katinka ahead.

"The van in back, move!" he shouted.

It was a vehicle Foster kept in readiness for an escape. He always imagined he'd be fleeing one of his clients, not a ham-fisted STF team, but that did not matter now. The van was out back behind the showroom. Katinka was there, standing too late beside the manager. He was still at his desk, wearing a look of puzzlement, his bloodshot eyes staring. There was blood coursing over his chin and down his neat tie. Then he simply fell forward across his desk.

"Come on!" Foster yelled.

Katinka moved like a somnambulist. She followed Foster out the back door. The rows of cars offered them cover from any police who might be hiding in the distance.

Foster slid the door back hard, placed the backpack inside, and ordered Katinka to go to the passenger's side. She was droning about closing the sample but Foster had no intention of doing that until they were away. South Africa had always suffered under clouds of death in the streets.

"This isn't happening!" she moaned.

Foster did not bother to tell her to shut up. She was too young and too inexperienced, too unworldly to understand.

This was just one more blow to the naïve notion that a wall of any skin color could bring peace to this socially and financially corrupt nation.

He turned on the police scanner and drove slowly through the rows of vehicles. The STF team had obviously not thought to bring hazmat masks. There were no police, no one at all in the car-filled area.

Except for a boy who had been kicking a football against the dumpster in the back. He was faceup and dead. The ball was beside him, adhering to the blood in which he lay.

Foster was sorry for that, and as he drove off he

closed the container before passing into the residential area through which they would be driving. His move had a core of compassion but it was also practical. He had no idea how this germ *worked*. He did not know how much of it he had left. A payoff to stop killing had a top limit. The sale of a potential bioweapon did not.

That done, and Katinka weeping like some Greek figure of tragedy behind her mask, Foster turned his mind to where he would go to make a deal . . . and warn the police about the price they would pay for any further interference.

"We are ordered to set down wherever we can!"

The pilot's update was not even a mild surprise. Breen already had a feeling something was wrong. Five minutes from the helipad at the East London Airport he had noticed red and blue police lights, all moving toward them. But they were not converging on a spot behind them. They appeared to be blocking traffic into a sector.

According to the map on his open tablet, it was one that encompassed their destination.

"You been watching—" Williams began.

"They're quarantining the target," Breen interrupted. "No air traffic. He's released the bug."

The helicopter set down in a small park just south of the Nahoon River. "Gents, we're about a half mile due east of where you needed to be."

"Thank you," Williams said. "Which way is the wind blowing?"

"Southwest. Why?"

"We're okay," Breen said privately to Williams.

There was no need to break out the masks and frighten the pilot.

"We're going to step outside," Williams told him. "We'll be grounded for about an hour."

"How do you know that, then?"

"History repeats," he replied.

"Do you know something about what all this is?"

"Not enough. Not yet," Williams said.

Leaving the puzzled man behind, Williams and Breen removed the headphones and got out. There was an eerie silence. The distant sound of sirens made it seem even quieter than it was, in a strange way. Whoever was here had departed, and did so in a hurry. Blankets and even a baby stroller had been left behind, adding to the sense of desolation.

"Be right back," Breen said, stopping suddenly and turning back toward the helicopter. "I want to check something."

Williams got on the phone with General Krummeck. The South African wasted no time.

"Commander, where are you?"

"On the ground in an East London park."

"The target got away in a black SUV headed east, but that's all we know. We have nothing airborne, no one trailing them."

"Deaths?"

"Locally, so far—we think he did it to get away, nothing more."

"What is the response going to be?"

"The Minister of Defence is conferencing the members of the secretariat now. I suspect the senior military advisors will push for a missile assault."

Williams saw the future unfold precipitously. China in the South Indian Sea and now—

South Africa did not have a sophisticated missile defense and targeting system. No nation below Northern Africa did. The Southern African Development Community was organized in 2003 to promote mutual defense but the member states had been unable to fund the undertaking and it was largely on paper only. Fearing expansionism from Beijing, South Africa had secretly signed a pact with Russia for military support in exchange for limited diamond mining rights.

And thus is born the next superpower battleground, Williams thought. Never mind that Foster might seek refuge in a hospital or church. Putin would take him and his bioweapon out. Then, of course, a Russian team would be sent in to make sure the area was fully decontaminated.

And collect samples.

"There has to be a way to stop him on the ground," Williams said, searching the street for some sign of Breen. "Where might he go?"

"Teams have been sent to his home, not that we expect him to return, but there may be clues to other residences. The two surviving STF members said there was a woman in the office with him and they apparently left together. She may have a place to go. We're trying to determine who she was."

"Payroll records?"

"We're checking. She may not be staff—legitimate staff. The way they described her, young and attractive, she may have been one of his paid companions."

Williams was not surprised that Foster had more angles than a ziggurat. These smugglers and black marketers usually did. Just now, Williams missed his old Op-Center team. While he could call Berry, asking the deputy national security advisor to locate a nondescript black SUV somewhere in or near East London would take time.

"Hold on," Krummeck said. "Here's the defence ministry order." The call went silent for a moment. When Krummeck returned, he said gravely, "As soon as the SUV is located, it will be hit with a low-yield SLBM."

"General, the smallest submarine-launched ballistic missile in the Russian arsenal will still take out a half-dozen city blocks. I know. I prepared a lot of those reports."

"I agree with this decision, Commander. We also require help finding the SUV by satellite before he goes to ground and—air traffic, commerce, nothing is moving. It cannot go on."

"We can give you satellite support—"

"And a Tomahawk strike?"

"General, that may not be necessary. Give my partner and me a chance—a few hours. The collateral damage will be extreme."

"We call it 'severe deployment' and, unfortunately, our history is written in it."

"That doesn't need to be—"

"Are you telling me? I'm the man who tried and failed to bury this thing. The decision is made, Commander. Thank you for your assistance. I will let you know when it's safe to depart."

The general hung up and Williams looked around for Breen. He was still in the helicopter, sitting next to the pilot. Williams walked over. Breen had the headset on and was playing with the dial.

He removed the headset and stepped out as Williams approached.

"What's the latest?" Breen asked.

"Russian missile launch as soon as they find the vehicle."

"Our pilot is former air force. He said they'd blast whoever did this."

"I didn't come all this way to watch the good guys kill more people than the bad guys," Williams said. "It's insanity. Forty years under my belt and I'm helpless."

"Not necessarily," Breen said.

"Why? What were you doing?"

"Did you know that civilian ownership of police scanners is illegal in South Africa?" Breen said.

"No. How does that help us?"

"I've been listening to the radio," Breen said. "There's no public information about police movements anywhere on the public spectrum. Given Foster's business, he would need a scanner, don't you think?"

Williams brightened. "Those who track can be tracked."

Breen nodded. "Scan the area by sea or satellite, filter out the police, and all you have left are felons."

"What's the frequency?"

"Police dispatch is 407.94000," Breen said.

Williams punched Berry's number and stepped away from the helicopter. The pilot leaned toward the open door.

"Say, just who *are* you guys?" he asked.

"I'm a lawyer and he's a bureaucrat," Breen answered. "Just the people you want to gum up any operation."

CHAPTER THIRTY-FOUR

November 12, 9:20 A.M.

"Follow my lead" was as cloudy a guideline as Rivette had ever received, the language being Chinese with Grace's expression fully hidden behind a mask.

Just move when and where she does, he told himself.

The good news: the language of "9mm" is universal.

The dinghy, with its four armed, masked seamen, seemed a little thin in the dozen-capacity boat. That was probably because the Chinese did not have enough masks to go around for more. If so, that was useful information.

As the dinghy approached the open door, the QBZ-95 light rifles were raised by all but the man steering at the rear. He slowed when they were about two hundred feet away, the blue-ray boat swaying from side to side almost as much as it moved forward.

Grace had angled the door so that the sun was reflected off the glass.

She leaned out and spoke in Chinese, shouting through her mask.

The men in the dinghy were restless, Rivette thought. They probably had not gotten a lot of sleep since becoming an invading force.

One of the men shouted back.

Grace turned to Rivette. "I told them I am the translator for a South African defector who can help them. They want us both to come out."

"They're gonna see I'm armed."

"Why wouldn't you be?" she said. "Just hold up your hands."

Grace held the edge of the doorway and dropped the four feet to the float. She held one of the forward aluminum struts that attached the pontoon to the aircraft. The only place Rivette could go was behind her—as she intended.

"*Sawubona!*" the lance corporal shouted as he swung out.

The dinghy bobbed nearer as the Americans held tight to keep from slipping on the sea-slick access panels atop the float. There were two planks for seats in the roughly eleven-foot-long vessel. Two of the Chinese were looking up at the aircraft, trying to see through the glare.

Rivette's pulse rate jumped, as it always did. Just as involuntarily, his fingers wriggled beneath the thin, thermal gloves. In his mind, he was running through take-down options if the seamen suddenly decided to open fire. They shouldn't. Grace would probably want to get to the patrol boat without incident, as the guests of these men. However, if something went wrong, Rivette knew, through drilling more than from their one previous mission together, how Grace would move faced with three adversaries at this specific distance with fierce firearms.

The matter was decided when the propeller suddenly died. Blocked by the aircraft, so, for a moment, did the wind. The pilot howled behind his mask.

The Chinese jerked their weapons to the right and Rivette looked inside the cabin. The heel of the pilot's boot was pressed against a black knob on the instrument panel.

"Shit," he moaned.

The Chinese would investigate. The pilot would blab. The matter was decided.

Grace was already in motion as the Chinese were diverted. Her arms were open wide at her side in crane form as she literally flew onto the dinghy. She drove her stiff pinfeathers, her ridge hands, into the masks of the two seamen in front, knocking them back. Since she could not hope to retain her footing on the soft-bottomed boat, she went into a somersault.

Rivette had clear shots at the remaining seamen. Only one of them was armed. First blood was always politically dicey. The rules of engagement had always embraced a shoot-second policy. That approach got GIs killed. The lance corporal put a bullet in the arm of the armed man then turned on the seaman in back. That man—showing training or smarts—had drawn a knife and was about to disable the dinghy with a downward thrust.

Hold, Rivette cautioned, watching Grace.

She had seen it too, and panther-leapt on all fours, putting her shoulder into the man and knocking him overboard. Her jump brought her halfway over the back of the dinghy. She came down, cat claws extended, and grabbed the seaman before the currents could carry him away. Her knees braced against the inflated aft edge, she hauled him back in.

The first two seamen had recovered and Rivette shouted at them. They might not understand "Stop!" but he was sure they'd recognize his I'm-not-shitting tone.

The men froze. Grace crept back to the forward part of the boat, collecting weapons. When she got onto the float, she threw the knife and all but one of the guns into the sea.

"They'll be looking for military issue," Grace told Rivette. "You know how to handle it?"

"Competed with the Type 97 civilian variant of—"

"Good."

Grace returned to the seaplane and side-kicked the pilot in the cheek. The mask blunted the blow slightly but there was still an audible crack and a moan.

"Your balance is restored," she said to him. After lingering to unscrew the throttle and propeller knobs, Grace turned away.

"I don't know what that means, but next time we tie the feet," Rivette said.

"It means he hurt us with aggressive yang and will need yin to heal," she said as she went back to the float.

Rivette still did not understand, but he was accustomed to that with Grace. As long as she was happy.

The woman went back to the dinghy and, in Chinese, told the men to file into the aircraft. One assisted the wounded man, pressing a glove to the wound. Once they were inside, crammed in the small space between the door and the seats, she took a radio from one. The patrol boat probably would not expect a report, given the difficulty of speaking behind the masks. But they might give orders. Then she ordered the two men nearest her to remove their parkas.

The men hesitated. She doubled the nearest man over with a palm heel strike to the gut. He was straightened immediately courtesy of a knee to the chin.

"I am growing impatient!" Grace yelled.

The others undressed quickly. Rivette knew that she did not, in fact, ever lose her cool. But a blow was a blow and the seamen obeyed.

"Put one of them on," she told Rivette. Hers was a little large but it would have to do. After pulling the hood on, she walked up to the ranking seaman. "What is your ID?"

"We haven't one."

Grace drew the knife strapped to her hip. She hooked it under the strap of the mask. That was her way of asking a second time.

"Albatross," the man said.

"How many men left onboard?"

"Five."

"That makes nine. Your crew should be—"

"One man died," he said, shivering. "The sickness."

Grace stepped back to the float and Rivette pointed into the cabin. "You might want to tell them there's a first-aid valise in the back."

"Thank you," she said, and passed along the information. She told the Chinese it was all right to close the door. They did so at once.

"How do you know they won't fly after us?" Rivette asked.

She showed him the knobs before tossing them in the sea. Then she used her elbow to disable the radio. Two strikes in the faceplate did the job. The moves were cold but they could probably rig a replacement for the controls and at least sail over to the recovery site on Marion Island.

Grace entered the dinghy followed by Rivette, who was fussing with the too-small parka, jamming his hands down the front and into the pockets.

"You ready?" she asked.

"Yeah."

She handed him the seaman's radio.

"Remember this word: *xìntiānwēng*," she said.

"Shin-wan-weng," he said. "Is that the ID word?"

"Yes," Grace said as she sat beside the motor and made sure the radio was on. "Hopefully, they'll blame your mask and the engine noise for the muddle."

"I'd like to see how you would have done with *Sawubona*," he said, though his voice was drowned out by the throaty gurgle of the engine.

Grace was thoughtful, distracted as Rivette sat beside her.

"You think they saw the jets that brought us?" Rivette asked after practicing *xìntiānwēng* several times.

"The corvette would have." She nodded.

"So they'll be waiting for some kind of surprise, especially when they only see two of us."

"This will be your show. We've got to get the doctor and we can't let the Chinese get away with the bug. Not a lot of options going in."

"No," Rivette agreed. "We gotta do what it takes to make all that happen. Sting of the Wasp. Hey, you ever wonder if we'll get STFted?"

"Never," she replied.

Rivette did not know whether she never wondered that or whether she thought they would never get bloodied. He would ask again when he did not have the mask on. He liked and respected her Daoist beliefs and wondered what the ancient Chinese had to say about odds and luck.

Right now, though, he took the time to make sure the Chinese firearm was not frozen or stiff and that his own two weapons, under the parka, were in good working order.

Attracted by the landing of the aircraft, Commander van Tonder had gone to the western wall in time to see the action that took place some two hundred feet below.

Ensign Sisula had briefed him about the Americans

and the plan, and the commander was eager to be a part of it. This was about more than the sovereignty of his homeland. It was about preventing the world from getting and exploiting another weapon of mass destruction.

Those were, to him, not just duties. They were moral trusts, akin to his deep religious convictions. He was proud of Sisula and, more than that, grateful for the help of whoever the two heroic Americans were below. In all his years of military service, he had never seen someone run at a boatful of primed firearms. And not just survive but win. He had no idea what their plan was going forward. He hoped it was as brash and as successful as what he had just seen. Tired and hungry, with a partner who was ill and cold, van Tonder feared that if they did not get relief soon, Mabuza would die.

Returning to the helicopter to run it for warmth—more to help the pilot than himself, since the sun was rising higher and warming the ridge—van Tonder gave the Americans a few minutes.

He was surprised to find Mabuza awake.

"Unless . . . I was dreaming . . . we're in a war . . . with China," the lieutenant said.

"It's true," van Tonder told him. The commander was smiling. "Tito, it's great to have you back!"

"The sun . . . man . . . feel it." The lieutenant tried to move.

"Easy, fella—"

"No, I have to . . . my ass is asleep."

"You're back." Van Tonder grinned.

"What about . . . Ship Rock?"

"Still open, still toxic. Gotta find a way to shut that down before—there's a Chinese ship down there, wants it."

"Bastards."

"Yeah. Sorry I can't give you water—the mask. You have to keep it on."

The lieutenant nodded and shut his eyes.

"Hey, help is coming. Americans are on the island, cutting loose."

"You . . . helping?"

"About to." The commander picked up the Milkor BXP submachine gun. "Sit tight, there's a doctor somewhere around. We'll get him."

The lieutenant nodded again and, giving him a reassuring clap on the shoulder, van Tonder headed for the northern ledge.

His spirits were high and the step quick—until he neared the ledge and saw something he was not expecting or wanting to see.

The corvette was moving toward Ship Rock.

CHAPTER THIRTY-FIVE

November 12, 2:24 A.M.

Sitting in his office, the door closed, Matt Berry was a tired but caffeine-jittery man who wondered whether his boots on the ground would start or avert an international conflagration.

President Midkiff was asleep and National Security Advisor Harward had gone home. Both had received updates from the CIA about the latest "kill zone" in East London. The president had called to ask Berry what he knew.

"Williams and Breen are in the middle of that," Berry had answered truthfully. "I'm awaiting an update."

That was also true, as far as it went. What he was waiting for were results. So far, both teams were naggingly silent.

Reports were coming in from European and American intelligence services that Russia and China were both converging on parts of South Africa with tactical support or confrontational military assets. Some reports said that Pretoria had invited the Russians in. Other reports said that South African Naval jets had been seen in the skies over Marion Island, buzzing a Chinese corvette that was—according to Beijing—"on a legitimate regional patrol and prepared-to-assist status" regarding the South African airline crash.

In the middle of that was Black Wasp, and on their agenda—as far as Berry knew—was a request for information about police movements in the smallish beach resort city of East London. Hopefully, one of the two teams was in a position to collect samples of what everyone seemed to want.

The National Reconnaissance Office had the answer for Chase Williams about his curious interest in East London police activities. Berry texted the information to him in the form of a map, complete with patrol car numbers where applicable. Berry had texted a question at the end:

What is this going to get us?

Williams had replied:

The stuff that nightmares are made of.

Berry did not know if Williams had intended to pervert either *The Tempest* or *The Maltese Falcon*. In any case, the deputy national security advisor took it as a grimly hopeful sign that they were closing in on the target ahead of Moscow or Beijing.

And there was still the playing field to the south. The Department of Naval Intelligence and the NRO jointly reported that the Chinese corvette and patrol boat were still in their off-shore and near-shore positions, that a helicopter was still down in the ground zero quadrant, and that one of the civilian rescue planes had traveled from the crash site to Prince Edward following a communication from the SAN outpost on Marion Island.

"It is not clear whether Chinese or South African naval personnel are in control of the SAN station, or what the deployment status is," the report concluded.

Those two organizations knew nothing about Black Wasp. Yet even with that knowledge, he could not begin to theorize what Lieutenant Lee and Lance Corporal Rivette were up to.

That concerned him, but not as much as the idea that he might have overestimated their abilities and that the two were dead, captured, or floundering. Yemen had been all four Black Wasps together, each drawing on the strengths and abilities of the others.

Not this time.

He hoped the president got back to sleep. Berry would be getting none till this was over.

Williams was off, Berry thought as he drained the last of his coffee and turned to a sandwich that had been sitting on his desk for three hours. What was unfolding in South Africa was more than a night-mare. It was a fast-evolving, quick-burning flashpoint for a global confrontation.

CHAPTER THIRTY-SIX

November 12, 9:30 A.M.

One of Claude Foster's greatest assets was that he listened. Regardless of whether he was interested in what was being said, in his office or at a bar, in a steam room or at a sporting event, he let it in.

That was how he had found Katinka. She and fellow graduates had been up all night and getting coffee at a shop when he went there for breakfast. He heard her say she was going to start looking for a job that very day.

"There's no time to waste," she had said. "This is when the diamond concerns are scouting."

Unlike Dumisa, who encouraged his gun runners to report on what their fellows said and did, Foster had never wanted to create an environment of paranoia. That was what made people stop talking.

Foster had heard Katinka ask for an advance years before, to build her boat shed. That was why he had opted to make her home their first stop. He had to hide the van but not abandon it. He needed to communicate with Dumisa or Mila Merch. Dumisa would help him sell the core samples—for a large percentage, but still paying more than extortion. With her human trafficking network, Mila was best equipped to get someone out of the country. Foster needed to regroup and resume his negotiations.

Katinka was limp, staring at nothing in the passenger's seat as they pulled into the driveway. Foster had removed his mask but he had left Katinka's on. Her strong, stonecutter's hand was holding the breathing apparatus. He did not want to tinker with whatever made her quiet, secure.

Foster was not even sure what he would *do* with her. He wanted to bring her to keep her from prosecution. But he could not afford inert baggage—which she appeared on the verge of becoming.

He stopped at the shed, pulled up the door. Katinka's scooter was parked in the rear and he moved it through the back door to make room. Then he tried to turn the van around to back in—just in case he needed to hit a full-on exit. There wasn't enough room. But the shed was close to the street and he could slam out if need be. The shadows inside were deep and he left the shed door open.

Leaving Katinka, he lifted the rear floor panel and selected a handgun and a submachine gun. If they were found, he would use the core samples only as a final measure.

Feeling momentarily safe in the semi-darkness,

Foster sat on the edge of the van, listening to the sounds of occasional traffic—both on the road and increasingly in the air as the government no doubt issued an all-safe alert.

Either they have more hazmat gear than I suspected or they must know something about this thing that I do not, he thought.

It was time to take this in a new direction, and he finished placing the call that had been interrupted at the office.

"You asked who we were," Williams said to the helicopter pilot. "I'm going to tell you."

Still waiting outside the helicopter, the Op-Center director had just received the map from Berry. Removing the scanners from clusters of police vehicles, Williams was left with three blips. One was overlaid with the East London bureau of the *South Africa Post & Telegram* newspaper. Another matched the address of a home for senior citizens—more likely than not, a retired police officer. The third was on a residential street not far from Nahoon Beach.

"What's your name?" Williams asked.

"Vic Illing."

"Vic, I'm Chase, and we are working with the government to stop these attacks," Williams said.

"I figured."

"Oh?"

"A general's office booked me. And . . . you got a lot of clanky gear."

Williams showed the man the map on the tablet.

He pointed to the spot near the shore. "We believe the perpetrator is here." He dragged his finger to the beach. "I want to go here."

"I can do that, as soon as the authorities say I can."

"Well, that's it—you can. I wouldn't ask you to fly any place that isn't safe."

Breen came jogging back just then.

"I think I've narrowed the geography," the major said. "They've got traffic cameras at the major intersections but nothing along the tourist and recreational routes."

"So, the beach," Williams said.

"Right. If we follow the shore—"

"No need." Williams showed him the tablet. "Confirms what I just received." He handed Breen the tablet then looked back at the pilot. "What do you say, Vic? This toxin rises and it flows with the wind. Only has a life span of about an hour. We'll be going in the opposite direction." He pulled a roll of bills from his pocket. "Yours if you'll do it. Just take us to the beach and stay there until the all clear."

Illing looked at the money and then at Williams. "I don't need that. Just stop this loon—that's enough for me."

"Thank you."

The men boarded, the chopper rose to one hundred feet, and just five minutes later they were settling onto the beach.

"Made it, like you said," Illing said with open relief as he killed the engine. "God bless ya."

The passengers selected a mask and a handgun

each from their gear. Before getting out, Illing handed
Breen his card while Williams texted Berry:

```
En route to Plymouth Rd site to
try and buy.
```

"I'll wait for you, if it's all the same!" Illing said as
the men ran down the beach. "Come back safe!"

Williams raised an arm to thank him but did not
look back. The two men ran slowly from the beach
onto the asphalt that followed the coast.

Beach Road was devoid of pedestrians. An occasional ambulance passed, the EMTs wearing masks.

"They must have wanted everyone mobile," Breen
said.

"Smart—quick quarantine," Williams said.

It was warm going on hot as the sun baked the big,
open shoreline. Following the GPS on Breen's phone,
the men turned into the residential area.

"How do we approach him?" the major asked.

"Hands up, mask and gun visible. Tell him we want
to bargain."

"You think he'll believe us?"

"Why not?" Williams said. "He'll know from our
voices that we're not South African."

Breen nodded. He also didn't think the man would
shoot first. Foster might be ruthless, but he seemed
too cool an operator for that. Breen also did not think
there was any threat from his accomplice. He briefed
Williams as they ran. According to the research he had
done on the short flight over, the house belonged to a

gemologist named Katinka Kettle, twenty-five. She worked for MEASE and had no criminal sheet.

The men slowed as they neared the house. There was a walk to the front door and a driveway.

Williams was not breathing as hard as his companion but the old Op-Center had left him softer than he should be. Then he felt the weight of the gun in his hands.

That was not true in every way, he thought. He had, without hesitation, put a bullet in the forehead of a terrorist in Yemen. He wondered if he would do that again to be sure of saving lives . . . or let a negotiation play out. There was a line a person crossed where it was not just the rule of law but his moral compass that was at risk.

"I think you should talk for us, Counselor," Williams said quietly. "Starting curbside? I'll be watching the surroundings while you watch him."

Breen nodded. When they reached the house they stood at the curb, facing the walk unmoving, arms raised.

"Mr. Foster!" Breen said. "We're here about that item you have for sale."

The only thing they heard for what seemed dangerously too long was the wind from the beach. It carried a misleadingly pleasant smell of salt water and rose gardens.

"Americans?" a firm male voice finally replied.

"That's right."

Another hesitation. Then, finally, an answer.

"Come down the walk, slowly, hands up, single file."

"Understood," Breen said.

Breen shouldered in front of his companion and crossed the sidewalk to the flower-lined slate walk. He saw the shed to the right, set back a little from the house and hidden from the neighbor by a high hedge. That was where the driveway led. The door of the structure was open but all was shadow inside.

"Stop there," the man said when they had reached the part of the walk that turned from the house to the shed. "You came prepared, I see."

Breen looked from the man to the mask then back. "In every way."

"Ah," Foster said. "Good. Both of you toss the guns and masks and you come here—the other man stay where you are. In case of gunfire, you're a target."

"No one knows you're here but us."

"How is that, if you don't mind?" Foster asked.

"Our people tracked your police scanner," Breen said as he flung the handgun and mask toward the hedge. Breen tossed his onto the small front lawn.

"Damn. Clever," Foster said. He half turned. "Katinka, turn it off. Do you see it?"

"Yes," a voice replied faintly. It sounded beaten.

Foster turned back to the men. "You may approach . . . slowly."

Breen said, "Before we continue, may we confirm that you have what we want?"

Foster hesitated, then said, "Come."

"Thank you," Breen said.

Foster nodded amiably and Breen moved ahead, his eyes on the van. Foster had not been holding whatever the bacteria was in but it had to be near. As he neared he saw weapons and a backpack in the rear of the vehicle. A pair of cylindrical outlines was visible. He'd had the same feeling when he first set eyes on a tactical nuclear weapon at El Toro Air Base before it was shut down. Such a small package but with the power to destroy an entire population.

Strangely, he did not feel ashamed about any of it. No soldier should. His job was to protect the homeland and, in the end—as with the shot he put in the brain of Ahmed Salehi—he was prepared to do that.

Foster returned to the back of the van. "Thank you for the advisory, gentlemen."

"Anything to protect the transaction I hope to make," Breen told him.

The major was wondering if that was true, if he was serious about this. Paying off terrorists was anathema to him and to American policy. They had recently risked their lives to hunt one down.

If we don't buy it, some reckless nation might, he told himself.

Foster motioned him forward and Breen was about to enter the shed when Williams shouted.

"Hat up!" the commander cried.

Foster was alert and confused but Breen got the move-out message. He spun to look out at the street. When he saw what Williams was talking about, Breen's pale eyes died a little.

South Africa had finally, unfortunately, taken matters into their own hands.

CHAPTER THIRTY-SEVEN

PRINCE EDWARD ISLAND, SOUTH AFRICA

November 12, 9:57 A.M.

It was at once as beautiful and dangerous a thing as Lieutenant Grace Lee had ever seen. As the dinghy rounded the main island and reached Ship Rock, the gaping maw was an alternately melted and jagged display of bright gray rock and deep shadow. And there was an almost indistinguishable gossamer over it all—a faint, pale-lemon sash rising upward, like the sashes she had seen on high-leaping acrobats in the Beijing Opera.

Even Rivette was transfixed by the five-foot-high opening.

"It looks like a place where disease would grow," the lance corporal observed.

"And die," Grace added.

"If you've got a high-explosive non-fragmentation grenade."

Their attention shifted as the trip around the island

brought the stranded patrol boat into view. Two armed men stood on the prow, both by the ladder, which did not surprise her. Unfortunately, the approach of the corvette did.

"Crap," Rivette muttered when he saw the big boat just a quarter mile off and closing. "Ideas?"

"We still have to get on the boat, get the doctor, and find something to close that cavern," she said.

"That means taking the boat," Rivette said. "It won't last a minute against those 30mm cannons and antiship missiles."

"They may hesitate just a minute before killing their own sailors," Grace pointed out.

"If no one answers a hail, they'll figure it's a lost cause."

In combat, a minute could make the difference between death and survival.

As they closed in on the patrol boat, the radio came on.

"He wants the ID," Grace told her partner.

He raised the radio to his mouth. *"Xìntiānwēng!"*

The men in the prow seemed to relax slightly but they did not lower their rifles. The man yelled something back.

"He's impressed with the defector's Chinese," Grace translated.

Rivette snorted into the mask and raised the QBZ-95 in acknowledgement. "I'll give him some Chinese."

"Steady, Jaz."

"Yeah, but how far do we let this rope play out?" Rivette asked. "Somebody's gotta draw first blood."

Grace was distracted by something aft, on the sea. "Movement behind the PB." She listened. There were banging sounds. "Dammit. Repair crew—probably from the corvette."

"Gonna be a lot of shooting," Rivette warned.

Grace was rethinking the approach even as they reached the prow. She had wondered, after Yemen, just how the team was selected. Were she and Rivette tapped for their skills alone or because they also fit some kind of sociopathic algorithm, with Major Breen as a counterbalance and Williams as a colossus astride both worlds?

She both suspected—and feared—the answer was yes. She had to guard against it. Black Wasp was not a Triad hit squad, Hong Kong gangsters for whom murder and sometimes massacre was a way of life. But some of that wall they saw, the one that let loose the toxin, had been chewed away by hand. These people were here to harvest, refine, and distribute death. And perhaps to civilian as well as military targets. China was an overpopulated nation that enforced misogynic birth control.

What is the ethical center of the mission? Grace asked herself. The answer described the more difficult path. *Not to be like the enemy.*

"Major Breen may be rubbing off, but I'm thinking we return fire only," Rivette said. "We gotta be able to justify."

"You're a good man," she said.

"Nah, I can still outdraw them."

"You go first. Once they see I'm a woman—"

"They'll go for first blood." Rivette answered his own query.

"If you can take the bridge by surprise—"

"Yup."

The dinghy was just a few feet from the boat. Rivette grabbed the lowest rung of the aluminum ladder. The seaman just above had his rifle trained straight down on the new arrival. To that man's left, the other sailor had his gun facing Grace. She began to second-think her expressed tactic. Both men were trembling. It could be from the cold, exhaustion, or the knowledge that only a mask separated them from death. In any case, they projected a hair-trigger, shoot-first vibe.

From the dinghy, the only place she could conceivably move was into the sea, which would not help the mission and would leave her hypothermic, drowned, or shot.

Maybe we should have just taken these two out and boarded, she thought. There was a reason *The Art of War* and Daoism were quite separate studies.

The lance corporal ascended the five-foot ladder with his own Chinese weapon slung loosely across his back—an odd place since it seemed to be out of reach. He was also climbing slowly, as if sea spray had slickened the metal. He planted one hand and gripped firmly before reaching up with the other. He moved his left hand faster than his right.

Grace turned her face down and, finding the mooring rope, tied the dinghy to the eye beside the ladder. She listened, though. Part of her training as a young girl was to be able to fight in the dark. For that, you had to filter extraneous sounds and not just listen but visualize—in this case the boots on the rungs, movement of the fabric, the location and number of voices, of breath.

Also, gunfire.

A wave had tossed the dinghy and the hood of the parka flew back just enough to reveal her hair—which was short but not buzzed-short. The seaman watching her cried out.

"A woman!"

Grace looked up in time to see the man's gun discharge—and fire wide of her, but only by inches. When the man yelled, Rivette had thrust his free right hand into the deep pocket of his parka. It emerged with his .45 and, shooting from the hip, he put a bullet straight up under the man's chin. The seaman staggered back and Rivette simultaneously swung around to the left as the man above him fired. The trembling Chinese seaman missed, but Rivette did not. Before the sailor could aim and fire again, the Colt discharged a second time. The young sailor was forcefully bent over backward and flopped to the deck.

Grace was not in the clear, however, since the first two bullets that stitched the water had clipped the side of the dinghy. It was deflating quickly and she hurried across the wobbly boat to the ladder. *That was what he was doing with the parka,* she thought. And also why he was moving slowly. More time for the hands to be free.

Adrenaline washed away any regret she felt.

Above her, Rivette had wasted no time or movement. He pulled himself up and over the rail of the patrol boat, shrugged his left shoulder down, and dropped the Chinese gun into his left hand.

Grace was right behind him, watching her footing on a deck now slick with sea water and blood. She did not bother telling him that they were stranded.

"I'll take the crew, you keep the engineers in the water," Grace said.

Drawing her knife, she ran ahead along the port side, the smooth steel-gray outside wall of the bridge to her left. Rivette was close behind, slightly to her right so he would not shoot her or run into her if she stopped suddenly.

The door ahead was open, the gunfire having drawn everyone who was on deck: two of the three crewmen were standing shoulder-to-shoulder outside the open door, guns aimed ahead; a tall, pasty South African was half-inside; and two officers were running toward them. They had apparently been at the stern, overseeing repairs.

The two armed seamen subtly adjusted their positions, bracing themselves for recoil. They had been trained to shoot but not to avoid telegraphing their intent. Rivette fired his pistol twice—just as the South African pushed the seamen, hard, toward the side of the boat. The bullets clanged off the open door, ricocheting and hitting the tall man in the left leg. He went down, writhing.

While Rivette continued toward the two officers,

Grace relieved the fallen seamen of their guns, tossed them overboard, then entered the bridge. The helmsman was talking fast and low into the radio. The woman ran forward and hooked her right foot around his lower legs, twisted, and dropped him to the floor—both silencing and disabling him. She yanked the wireless headset away and dropped it on the flat instrument panel. She found and jabbed the green button that put the receiver on audio.

"Stay there!" she yelled in Chinese as she looked back at the South African.

The man was on his side, wincing and trying to examine the injury. She looked around for a medical kit. Outside was only silence—a good sign. It meant that Rivette had not shot the men, which suggested they had surrendered. A moment later they entered the small bridge, arms raised, followed by the two seamen.

Grace located a small plastic case with bandages and antiseptic. She knelt beside the stricken man and looked at the wound.

"I heard you speaking English," he said.

Grace nodded.

"Let me," the man said, taking the kit. "I'm Dr. Gray Raeburn, SAN."

Grace did not introduce herself. She got up and went to the helmsman.

"I was trying to knock them over," Raeburn said as he removed the scissors. Craning around painfully, he cut the fabric around the wound. "Whoever you are, there's an infected body below. I was up here trying to convince them not to bring the disease onto the corvette. I don't think anyone should have it."

"No," she agreed. "Are there explosives to seal that opening?"

"I don't know. I assume so."

Just then, the radio came to life.

"Captain Tang, what is your status? Over."

Grace knelt, her knee in the small of Tang's back, the knife point in the nape of his neck. "What will they do if you don't respond?"

"Board or sink," he said. "Probably sink."

"Not enough masks to come closer?"

He nodded anxiously. "Let me tell them we have control, please! If they assume we're dead, the boat means nothing."

Grace rose. "Go ahead. Say anything *but* that and you join your dead crewmen."

"Say nothing of the kind!" one of the engineers shouted in Chinese.

Rivette faced him. "Whatever you said, don't say any more," he warned.

The captain went to the instrument panel and Grace put the knife in the small of his back. He picked up the headset and put it on.

"*Shangaro,* this is Tang," he said. "We have fallen."

CHAPTER THIRTY-EIGHT

Before either man moved, Foster shot Breen a sharp, lingering look of unvarnished contempt. In it, the mass murderer had packed disdain for Breen and the corruption of what should have been a trusting, man-to-man process. Breen understood—and, improbably, felt wounded.

Then both men moved.

Breen did not want to waste time shouting. He turned toward Chase Williams and just pointed to where the man had thrown his mask. There was no need: the other man was already moving to recover it.

Breen did the same, literally broad-jumping toward the hedge. He landed on his knees and fell on his chest, grabbing the mask and pulling it on. He did not move, save to look back and ascertain that Williams had done likewise. Both hunkered down, out of the way of the eight masked STF officers who deployed into the yard with R5 assault rifles—all pointed toward the shed, once they realized that was where Foster was.

With the few seconds he had before the eight barrels converged, Foster had turned toward the back of the van, first for cover and then for a weapon. He managed to slam the door shut and smash the glass with the butt of his submachine gun.

Though he was in darkness, it was a narrow swath with eight barrels aimed at him with overlapping vectors of fire.

"I have the canister and will open it—" Foster shouted, then seemed, almost tragically, to realize that the men in the masks would not be slowed by that, that he himself would die if he made good his threat, and that the STF team was probably prepared to accept collateral damage to put an end to him.

Foster began firing.

Through the smoky lenses of the mask, Williams saw the red *sput-sput-sput* of the muzzle and then the red of Foster's body being pecked to shreds by the rifle fire. The submachine gun continued to fire into the roof of the van as Foster fell over, his finger locked on the trigger. The echoing drone was like a defiant roar, finally sputtering as the gun emptied.

When the confrontation was over, the STF members moved forward, a wave of camouflage green. Breen got up and removed his mask. He was still the closest person to the shed, and looked inside. Then he went over to Williams, walking wide around the unit.

Williams was still on his knees, his shoulders

slumped in defeat, his expression flat. Breen offered him a hand up. Williams took it.

Williams looked down. He was generally repulsed by self-pity but he was also unaccustomed to defeat. Now, in just over three months, he had managed to bungle the future of Op-Center and permitted the *Intrepid* to be firebombed . . . and this. They had not prevented any deaths and had lost the bug to South Africa. God alone knew what they would do with it.

"I guess they figured out the scanner thing too," Williams said, looking at the team.

"Perhaps. But why didn't they take us into custody?"

"I don't know. Maybe we look honest." Williams sighed. "Do you realize, Major, that we managed to accomplish absolutely nothing being here?"

"That's not true," Breen told him, "and maybe we're not so honest."

Williams's eyes snapped up. "What do you mean?"

"I had a look in the shed. Katinka Kettle isn't there. The STF may not even have realized she *was* there."

"Okay, felon on the run—not exactly our concern."

"It is if you think back to that initial distress call from the yacht," Breen said. "That was Foster on the call—he mentioned three sites, three samples. Foster showed us only two."

Williams did not realize he was slumping until he straightened. "Thank you, Major. I should have *thought*. There's a back door to the shed. She could have escaped during the gunfire."

"And maybe not empty-handed. As long as the STF doesn't seem interested in us—"

Breen did not have to finish. With their masks and guns, the men went to the street, along the hedge on the adjoining property, and looked for evidence of an escape. They found it in trampled roses out back.

They were crushed by the tracks of a bike or scooter having been walked across them. Beyond was a backyard and then another street.

Williams started running toward Harewood Drive but Breen stopped him.

"I have a better idea," he said, reaching into the inside pocket of his jacket.

"He's dead."

No matter how many times she said it, the reality was something else. Katinka Kettle still felt that she should could call or text Claude Foster and share news, get an answer, go to the office.

"But you saw him die."

Protecting her. That was the image that would last. She had been helpless in the front seat, her sole window to his heroic defense of the space under the headrest. Even as stuffing of the seat exploded into the air as fair-colored dust, even as glass cracked and fell all around her, on her, even as she dropped down flat, Foster was just a few feet away, defiant to the end.

"Even in death they were afraid," she said. "They crept toward you."

And while they crept, she escaped. During the fusillade she had opened the door and slunk out and crawled on the concrete floor of the shed, a floor one of the men at Foster's car dealership had poured at no charge. Protected by the shattered van, she had crept to the bag of fertilizer and removed the canister.

"The bag I was using to deceive you," she said apologetically.

It was easy to crack the back door and depart. Foster had even moved the scooter for her, which enabled her escape. Maybe he had even intended that—

"Just in case."

For all the man's monstrous acts that day he had still been looking out for her.

"He chose this death . . . but he did not deserve it," she thought aloud. "He merited a hearing, a chance to speak for all the poor."

The wind pushed Katinka's tears across her ringing ears as she raced her scooter west along Beach Road. She knew she would hear the gunfire forever, first the assault and then the dead hand of Claude Foster spitting bullets into the van.

"What good did it do?" she asked. "What did any of it do? Death! *Death!* How did it go so wrong?"

As she sped not *to* any place, just away, she looked at the street ahead, saw the houses and parked cars. Everyone was inside, hiding—

"Because of you," she said. "How many of them are in mourning because of the thing you brought among them?"

Yes, Foster had committed the mass homicides. Randomly, callously, with God alone knew what old hates driving him.

"You should have thought more clearly, though," she said. "Waited before giving him the samples."

But that was not the way they had worked. She had always become excited by every find, could not wait to deliver the news or the gems to him. A pleased expression, a wink, a complimentary word from Claude Foster meant so much.

"So you barreled into this like an idiot schoolgirl with a crush on teacher," she said, thinking back to *those* in her life. And each time she had tumbled up, from a professor to an assistant dean and naturally to Foster.

"How could you be so reckless?"

They weren't questions but laments. It seemed as if, in a day, her life had been put through a cyclone and landed somewhere else.

"But it wasn't a day, was it?" she asked.

She had been building toward this. She recalled the steps now, with hindsight. This was not just a crush but a partnership. And there was one thing more, one crucial evolution to come.

"You are not quite landed, not yet," she said.

There was the canister she carried on the back of her scooter. And a destination that occurred to her. The tears dried as she did some thinking. That was a good sign: something that made her less upset was worth exploring.

"You can get there," she told herself.

She was headed toward the R72 Expressway. The scooter was not permitted there, but that was not the only way to get where she wanted to go. Church Street was about four miles away . . . twenty minutes at the most.

The young woman did not know whether it was vengeance or a rising desire to join Foster that moved her. Now that *she* had the power, she began to understand what may have tempted him. The chance to craft a platform, to make a statement.

"All right," she said. "I will make one."

With the sun to her back and her destiny ahead, Katinka pushed the Sym Blaze 200 to its top speed.

CHAPTER THIRTY-NINE

Grace did not push the knife into the small of Captain Tang's back. His courage and willingness to give his life deserved consideration. More than that, she did not want to have to explain a revenge killing in her written debrief.

Or to revisit her own concerns about why she was tapped for Black Wasp.

She pushed him forward as she herself moved in on the console. She smashed the unit with the hilt of her knife then faced the others—before anyone had had time to move or even process what she had done.

She was about to go below in search of an inflatable raft and explosives when resounding fire erupted along the starboard side.

"They will sink us!" one of the engineers cried, turning to leave the bridge. Rivette was blocking his way.

"Get the hell back!" he said to the panicked officer.

The captain peeled himself from the instrument panel and turned to the engineers. "They will not. We have what is needed."

The body, Grace thought. *Goddammit.* There wasn't time. The gunfire was to rattle them, not the crew. She faced the second, calmer engineer. "Are there inflatable rafts below?"

"Yes, but you'll never get away. You murdered two crewmembers. They will hunt you."

He was right about that too. A bullet to the back of the head did not frighten her as much as the loss of face in a public trial.

"Let's get everyone outside," she told Rivette. "Maybe there's still enough dinghy to float."

Slipping past the lance corporal, Grace ran to the prow as, behind her, the sound and turbulence of the approaching corvette grew louder. Arriving at the railing, she looked down and saw the dinghy entirely underwater, hanging on by the mooring rope.

There was no way off except the water or a narrow isthmus of stone and ice to the south—and that led to a sheer wall over a hundred feet high. She was sure the corvette had the kind of inflatables that would bring a substantial landing party to the base of the peak.

No matter, she thought. *When there's only one way out you take it and chance the consequences.* They would bring the doctor. The Chinese seemed to want him. This could well end up hand-to-hand.

If it was not a way out it was at least a way to die.

To fail at a mission was shameful but to fail at dying would be worse.

She went to the side and waved at Rivette, pointed to the narrow causeway.

He nodded and, slinging the doctor's arm over his shoulder, backed toward the rail. The .45 was back in his pocket but the QBZ-95 was pointed directly at the Chinese. He need not have bothered. As one, the seamen swarmed to the stern to try and signal the corvette. Grace came forward and swung herself over the railing. She dropped the five feet to the slippery rocks and Rivette—still pointing the rifle with his left hand—passed the doctor over the side with the right.

Grace grabbed the man's legs, but he still screamed as he hit the ground and fell on his seat, the bandaged thigh having crumpled with the impact. Rivette fired a burst in front of the Chinese to back them up then slung the weapon over his shoulder, straddled the railing, and lowered himself down.

The three moved slowly forward across a surface of both ice and slippery seawater. The corvette continued to plow forward, Rivette keeping one eye on the rocks and the other on the vessel.

"That turret can rotate," he said.

"They won't shoot me," the doctor said, wincing.

"Why? How're you special?"

"I created the disease," he replied.

Rivette looked like he wanted to punch the man in the temple. *Maybe later,* he thought. He might knock his mask off due to overenthusiasm.

Suddenly, when they were halfway to the sheer ledge, Grace saw what she was not expecting:

Salvation.

Van Tonder had watched the attack with hope and pride followed by sudden grave concern. The latter occurred when the 76mm gun turret unleashed a barrage just north of the ship, along the starboard side.

There were several people standing outside the long, narrow bridge. He could not see who they were or exactly how many, since the bridge and its twin satellite dishes and radar installation threw long black shadows across the deck. The commander had seen others go inside, though he could not tell what was happening—until the corvette fired and figures began to move.

One of them ran forward and looked briefly at the submerged and flopping dinghy. Then, in less than a minute, the three outsiders onboard were going over the side.

I can help, he realized.

Leaving the gun and racing back to the helicopter, van Tonder began pulling the rescue net from the back.

"What's . . . happening?" Mabuza asked.

"Chinese closing in and we have allies stranded. Rest up. I'll get them, then we figure out how to close that damn disease pit and send everyone home."

The commander bundled the yellow vinyl package in his arm and hurried back. He knew the line would fall short—it was one hundred feet and it would take at least four or five feet of that to secure it to the ledge. But with a boost, two of them might be able to get up. A jump from a rock—maybe the third.

The line had a mesh basket at the end, a seat of sorts. It was designed to be suspended from a hook at the side of the AH-2. He and Mabuza had used it once, to pull a science team member from a rowboat that had been carried south by currents. There were several sharp, flat boulders on the ridge line: one of those would support the weight of a climber.

Skidding to a stop and selecting a rock with cracked edges, he ran the hook line through them and gave it one turn. Then he threw the rest of the line and the basket over the side.

The trio was about fifty feet away. If they did not look up, they would not see the mesh. Grabbing the submachine gun, he fired a burst to get their attention.

The three stopped and looked up. They saw van Tonder and the line. The man with an SAN cap raised a hand as they moved forward. The others were too busy watching where they stepped. A slip would send them into the icy, churning breakers that struck the cliff and rolled back out to sea.

The basket was blowing side to side like a pendulum about three feet above Grace's head. She feared it might rip if she tried to reach up and grab it. She was looking for flat rocks as the other two arrived. There was nothing to stand on.

"You go first," she told Rivette.

"Nah, the doctor—"

"He can't climb. You can. When I get him in you can pull him up and also cover us."

"Ah, shit," Rivette said, knowing she was right and moving to the face of the cliff. He was immediately struck at how the rock climbing they did was something of a fail: the gloves had gripping surfaces, there was no wind, and Chinese weren't chasing them. Other than that, he felt a sense of comfortable familiarity as he grabbed a knob on the wall.

It was an easy transfer to the net. Standing, Rivette grabbed the line, though he was forced to wrap it around his hands to get a grip on the slender nylon. He went up, wrapping his feet in the rope as they'd trained to do.

Grace kept watch on the Chinese ships. The crew of the patrol boat did not go for any weapons. Two men had gone below, presumably to get the body . . . and the sample of the bacteria. She regretted not having disposed of that. This entire mission had been an inglorious flop in her mind. She disliked failure. She disliked it even more than the Department of Defense.

Rivette was nearly to the top when Grace began to consider how she would get the doctor into the basket. He was leaning beside her, against the wall, propping himself up.

"If I give your free leg a boost from the heel, can you reach the basket?" she asked.

"I'm thinking that's probably the only way I'll get there," he said. "I can probably pull myself in if I get a grip. But once I do—the corvette has no reason not to fire on you."

"You're finally right about something, Doctor," she said. Bending, she formed a stirrup with her hands as she watched Rivette. When she saw him disappear over the ledge, helped by van Tonder, she crouched near the injured man. "Go!"

Letting go of the wall, Raeburn allowed himself to be hoisted up by his good leg. Though the other leg gave out, he was able to stay erect long enough to thrust his fingers through the mesh. He closed them, holding tightly.

"I can't pull up," he said through his teeth. "Have him pull!"

There was no time to try again. Even as the doctor tried to pull his knee up into the basket, she was signaling the men above to pull.

The line and the doctor rose in jerking concert. Grace watched his dangling legs rise, saw two pairs of hands working above them in tandem. It would be another twenty or thirty seconds before they had him and could drop the line to her.

In case they were delayed, and not wanting that man to be the last thing she beheld in this life, Grace turned, drew her knife, and faced the corvette.

As she did, she thought she heard someone shouting. But the voice, if there was one, was swallowed by a loud, cliff-shaking roar directly above.

CHAPTER FORTY

EAST LONDON, SOUTH AFRICA

November 12, 10:07 A.M.

As they made their way through the yard, Williams felt the phone in his back pocket vibrate. He took it out. It was a text from Matt Berry.

```
East London cops on Foster payroll
gave up address of likely accom-
plice. STF you are likely on-site
for Gen. Krummeck. Caution.
```

God bless TAC-P, Williams thought.

The Timely Alert Circulation Protocols were designed to be an electron-fast, laser-sharp interagency program, created to prevent what just happened—the delay of information reaching those who most need it.

Black Wasp might not end up being the security secret weapon the military wants, Williams told himself, *but when it comes to field-testing flawed systems, we are right on the front line.*

He would share it with Breen later. Right now, the major was busy texting a location for Vic Illing to come and get them.

"I told him the lot at the corner of Logan and Beach, just east of here," Breen said, pointing.

The men started out, Breen working on his tablet.

"We should be able to spot her from the air," Williams said.

"That, plus I have an idea where she may be headed."

Williams didn't pressure Breen to explain. As they walked, Williams noticed the major looking up information on the East London Web site—a public site. In the end, what intelligence work really needed was not lightning-fast strikes of data but the right mind looking in the right places.

The helicopter landed just as the men arrived, and Illing's smile was as bright as the sun on the big windows. His relief was also apparent.

"We just got the all clear," he told the men as they boarded, "so your timing was perfect. Everything work out?" He pointed at the radio. "There's a lot of talk between the pilots and dispatch, and on the news channel—"

"A big piece of the problem was solved," Williams told him.

"Wow. And *I* know it before all those reporters I saw rushing over. Can't wait to tell my wife."

The chopper lifted off as the two passengers were still pulling on their headsets.

"Where we headed?" Illing asked.

Breen was looking at his digital map. "We're going in the same direction as the R72 but to the shoreline side. Somewhere a scooter or bicycle could travel."

"That would be Old Transkei Road, coming right up!"

"No, another way," Breen said. He switched to private mode and said to Williams, "She might avoid that. MEASE is there, so the roads are likely buttoned up."

"Galway Road," Illing said. He cocked his head to the right as they rose. "We're actually right there."

"Good," Breen said.

"Destination?"

"We'll keep a lookout but let's head toward Church Street," Breen told him. "We're looking for a woman driver with a backpack or large parcel."

"The accomplice," Illing said knowingly. "The wife will *never* believe!"

"Vic, keep your height and follow my instructions," Breen cautioned. "This accomplice may be more dangerous and determined than her boss."

What little traffic there was seemed to be headed away from Katinka. Police, paparazzi on motorcycles, probably reporters rushing to the sites that were newly notorious: her home and the MEASE complex.

"My *home*," she said, a sense of profound loss having given way to a rising sense of violation. For all his faults and crimes, Foster had been welcome. The men with the guns were not.

"They could have talked to him, like those first

two," Katinka said. She believed those Americans were as surprised to see the police as she was. "How did they know? Claude Foster was *so* careful!"

That didn't matter now. Nothing did. Her new plans, her old plans, *all* her plans were finished. She could not even go home and—

"I will be hunted," she said knowingly.

Katinka did not want that. She only wanted one thing right now. The police had done nothing to the Kettle family except harass her father and then her boss before finally executing him.

"They'll be hailed as heroes, those eight who cut down one man trapped in the back of a van."

The more she thought the angrier she got until all Katinka wanted was to send those men and women in uniform after Claude Foster one more time.

CHAPTER FORTY-ONE

November 12, 10:16 A.M.

When she heard the blast, Grace Lee flattened herself against the wall, arms stiff at her side. She had felt the rock tremble, assumed it had been struck with artillery from the corvette, and waited for the rain of stone to batter her. Hopefully, the concussion would have sent it flying outward and more of it would land in the sea than on the foot of the causeway.

But there was no rockfall and the sound did not echo and vanish. It continued.

She looked up.

The sound was not an explosion but the roar of a helicopter. The black Denel AH-2 roared across the ledge and out to sea, more missile than aircraft. It did not appear to be aerodynamic; it wobbled from side to side as it plummeted toward Ship Rock. It was a short ride but Grace was not sure the aircraft would even make it, nosing forward well short of its goal.

But in the last moment, just twenty or so feet from the water, the AH-2 suddenly steadied, charged forward, and attacked Ship Rock with self-destructive vengeance. It hit the jagged rock hollow with a crush of glass and metal and dislodged rotors that spun briefly at an angle before sparking to a stop against the stone and then flying apart.

The tail assembly cracked and fell on the patrol boat just as the surviving structure above exploded in a vertical column of fire. Grace wondered if the flames were riding the same gasses as Williams had mentioned. She felt the heat where she stood and almost at once the ice turned to slush beneath her feet.

There was pandemonium at the stern of the patrol boat, whose prow was ablaze. Apparently fearing an explosion, the crew vaulted into the sea—even as life preservers were thrown into the water from the approaching corvette. Moments after the last man had gone over the rail, the boat erupted from somewhere in the middle, the prow and stern going down in snapped pieces, tumbling onto their sides as they went down in the shallow sea. They stuck there, the broken ends burning like torches, black smoke chugging east with the prevailing wind.

Grace hoped that whoever had sacrificed himself to seal the cave had succeeded in immolating the bacteria. Otherwise, there was a good chance that everyone on the ship would perish.

The lieutenant heard a shot from above. She had been so wrapped up in the assault on Ship Rock that she had forgotten about the net that was swinging above her. Grabbing the rock as Rivette had done, she took off her mask and pulled herself up to the mesh and then onto the line. She was arm-weary from taking the outpost and the patrol boat, but she would be damned if she'd give Rivette bragging rights that he climbed and she did not.

Reaching the ledge, she saw a solemn assemblage. The man she assumed was van Tonder was on his knees, halfway between the ledge and where it looked like struts had flattened the grass.

"Dude just took off," Rivette said when she arrived.

"That was Lieutenant Mabuza?"

Rivette nodded. "Commander heard the rotors but couldn't stop him, couldn't let go or we would have lost the doc."

The South African was leaning on a boulder, eyes downcast. She had no desire to go to him. There also wasn't time. They had to contact the outpost and arrange to get out of there.

Rivette still had the Chinese radio. She took it and went to van Tonder.

"Commander, I'm very sorry," Grace told him.

"I'll miss him, but I'll say this—he died where he belonged, behind the controls. Just too bloody soon, because people have lost their goddamn way."

"Amen to that. But if fire was the answer, he definitely managed to destroy every particle of this thing."

Van Tonder pulled off his own mask and rose. "Bless you, Tito," he said to the smoking cliff beyond the ledge.

Just then, all eyes turned to the western cliff as a new arrival trudged up the last segment of ridgeline. Ryan Bruwer approached the others, his eyes falling on Dr. Raeburn, then shifting to Grace.

"You did it," he said. "You actually got him off the boat."

"Somehow," Rivette said, walking over.

"Who is this man we pulled up?" van Tonder asked.

"The man you rescued is the man who invented the bacteria," Grace told him.

She watched van Tonder walk toward his fellow South African. For a moment, Grace would not have put money against the commander using the submachine gun that was still in his hand.

Raeburn seemed uncertain, then afraid.

"I couldn't save my mate because I was saving you," the commander said to him.

Grace had never heard a whisper so full of fire.

"I came here to help him," Raeburn said helplessly.

"You did a shitty job of it, *Doctor*. You can thank whatever pig god you worship that judgment will be in the hands of the military and the Lord, not me."

Van Tonder turned and walked to the cliff, where he knelt facing the smoldering ruins.

Rivette looked at Grace, who was uncommonly somber. He was glad he didn't have her cosmic Daoism complexities as an algorithm. To him, this doctor, the Chinese, Black Wasp—they were no different than the street gangs he grew up around. The only difference was the size of the turf and the stakes that came with winning or losing. Plus, this time, the bad guys lost bad.

He faced Bruwer. "So what happened to our chilly-ass friends in the plane?"

"The pilot managed to get the engine going, not to fly but enough to trudge back to where he started. The Chinese are with him."

"Beijing's going to *love* trying to explain that," Rivette said.

"You want to see if you can raise Ensign Sisula at the outpost?" Grace said. "You've got the radio and—I don't want to bother Commander van Tonder right now."

"No—sure. I'll call him, get us a ride home. I think we all wrecked enough aircraft and seacraft for one day."

Grace nodded.

"But you know what'll make this okay when I finally sit down and take off my boots?"

She shook her head.

"The most important ones are still flying," he said. "A pair of Wasps."

CHAPTER FORTY-TWO

EAST LONDON, SOUTH AFRICA

November 12, 10:18 A.M.

There was no mistaking the target. It was a woman, speeding, with a large platform mounted to the back of her scooter. It was probably there to hold mineral samples. At the moment, it had what appeared to be a cylinder on the back. From about 150 feet up, it conformed to the size and shape of what seemed to have been in Claude Foster's backpack.

The scooter was on Esplanade Street, right along the seashore. The rider did not seem to be aware of the helicopter about an eighth of a mile behind her. Or if she was, she probably assumed it was part of the entourage of law enforcement and press that were the only people driving, boating, or flying.

"Up ahead," Breen said to Williams, pointing.

"What am I looking at?"

"Big, long, rectangular building right on the expressway. The East London Police Station."

"Where that team originated?"

"Yeah."

"We've got to warn them," Williams said.

"She may be going there to turn the sample in. They may not give her the chance."

"We'll tell them that," Williams said. "Major, that's an urban center—churches, six-lane highway, offices, schools—"

"Which is why they may shoot first."

Williams was experiencing a sharp sense of déjà vu. Once again, they had a terrorist in their sights. Last time, Williams had learned something about his priorities when he pulled the trigger. He went to confession after that—and didn't bother mentioning it.

He had a similar feeling now.

"Whichever side street she takes, she has to turn onto the expressway to go inside." Breen folded Illing into the conversation. "Vic, big favor."

"Go!"

"I want you to land on the R72. Not a lot of traffic—I think you can scare them away."

"Sir, uh—I could lose my license and spend a very long time in prison."

"You could also be a hero. The lady below has the last container of bacteria. I want to stop her from opening it in the police station and keep her from being shot."

"Hold on," Williams said. He regarded Breen. "You drop down like God Almighty, how do you know you won't scare her into opening the damn thing right there?"

He took the gun from his pocket. "If she tries, I'll shoot her. No hesitation."

"I like *that* idea," Illing said.

"Will you do this, Vic?" Breen asked him.

"I'm not a hero, gentlemen, but I *am* crazy. I guess—I guess I can tell them I had engine trouble."

"Good man," Breen said.

Plunging toward the largely deserted expressway, Illing came in west of the police station. He hovered some fifty feet above the street as the scooter was making a left turn from Buffalo Street to the east.

"In front of her," Breen said as Katinka raced forward.

Two cars had already rushed to switch lanes as the helicopter dropped. It came down right in front of the police station, causing Katinka to swerve and officers to rush out—though all but two armed police stayed inside. The pair had handguns. They were on Williams's side of the helicopter.

"I'll deal with those two," Williams said as the aircraft set down.

"Vic, kill the engine," Breen said.

"Long as that's all that gets killed, like you promised," the pilot reminded Williams—only partly joking.

"Stay cool," Breen cautioned, his own voice calm.

"Sure, sure, I'll just wait here, then. Right behind this big glass bubble that isn't bulletproof."

Breen was not listening. Each man got out from his own side—without having coordinated it. Breen had his weapon tucked in his belt, in back, out of sight. Williams left his gun in its holster. Neither wanted to antagonize the objectives. Breen hesitated then placed his gun back on the seat.

"Major?" Williams cautioned.

"If she opens it, bullets won't help," Breen said. But it was more than that. He believed in a process and gunfire was not a part of that.

Either you believe in it or you don't, he thought.

Breen raised his empty hands and walked toward Katinka. His dark eyes were fixed on the woman's face, the way they had locked on the expressions of countless plaintiffs and defendants in depositions. He had learned to read the truth before he heard a lie, a confession, or a half-truth.

The woman who was still astride the partly turned scooter was homicidal. Not by nature but by circumstance. He had seen that in killers talking about their crimes of passion: planned, committed, and regretted in under five minutes.

"Katinka, I'm the man who was at the house before the shooters arrived," he said, choosing his words carefully as he continued to approach. He wanted her to understand that he was on her side.

"Did you betray us?" she asked, dismounting and throwing the kickstand. She walked around to the back.

"No!" Breen assured her. The tail rotor stopped and it was suddenly funereally silent. There were no distractions. He lowered his hands and held them imploringly before him. Every word, every gesture carried the future on its back. "I did not approve of what Mr. Foster did. But I did not want to harm him."

"He was driven to this terrible thing!" she shouted. "More than I understood . . . more than I wanted to believe."

"Katinka, you were not responsible for his actions. You don't have to answer for them—"

"I should never have turned those samples over," she said, sobbing now. She stood beside the canister. "I thought . . . he would see what I could do. He would be pleased."

"You did nothing wrong," Breen said. "Do you hear me? I know what happened at Prince Edward, on the *Teri Wheel*. It was all an accident. Don't do anything now that you *know* will harm others. I saw in the van—that isn't you, Katinka."

Her strong fingers and tearful eyes came to rest on the canister. The two armed police were moving to be clear of the helicopter where they would have a clear shot.

Breen saw them. He continued to approach and began to move so he was between the officers and their target. Williams had the same idea and had moved forward, toward Katinka and Breen.

"Sir, step back!" one of the officers said.

"I'm SANDF Intelligence and *you* will stand down!" Williams ordered without turning.

The police hesitated then continued forward silently.

"Katinka, take my hands," Breen said. "Let me help you."

"I thought *he* would," she muttered as she removed the straps from the core sample.

"He did. He gave you time to get away."

"He did that," she agreed, nodding, then crying. "Everything is lost, gone."

"Only the past, not your future." He was nearly opposite her. "Come with me, please."

"Where? I want to be with Claude."

Uncertain what Katinka would do, what the police would do, Breen threw himself over the container, pushing her back with his right shoulder. She stumbled, fell, and clutching the sample like a football, he turned away.

"Go!" the police yelled as they ran forward.

Williams was ahead of them, preventing them from firing, and was the first to throw himself on top of Katinka.

He half turned toward the police, who were now approaching in a flood. "All of you get back! I am in charge here!"

With their focus on Katinka—and this was, Breen realized, part of Williams's ploy—the major was able to reach the helicopter.

"Start her up, Vic."

"That was . . . *amazing,* sir!"

"Rotors—now!"

"Yes, sir."

The helicopter hummed to life and Breen watched

through the bubble window as Williams stood and helped Katinka Kettle to her feet. His arm around her shoulder, he walked her back toward the helicopter. He spoke to a woman in a sharp uniform and cap who had come through the crowd of police. He handed Katinka to her and the woman waved everyone else away as she walked her toward the police station.

Williams turned, then, and ran to the helicopter.

"Let's get out of here," Williams said, slamming the door.

The commander's eyes fell on the container that Breen was examining. He had not expected to find any breaches. If there were, they'd be dead.

"I take back what I said about accomplishing nothing," Williams said quietly as they rose.

Below, officers were swarming the scooter, realizing, as they searched, that the men in the helicopter had not just the toxin but their evidence.

"What did you tell her, the arresting officer?" Breen asked.

"I told her not to cuff the woman or she would answer to General Krummeck of Intelligence," Williams said.

Breen smiled thinly. "Thank you."

"No. Thank *you*. If *I* had been in command—"

"Yeah. Way to go Black Wasp," Breen said dryly.

"Speaking of way to go—?" Illing said.

"You got enough fuel to get us back where we started?"

"Just about. If not, you got guns—we'll score some on the road." He half turned. "Kidding. Gentlemen, you got me pumped. I will never have a day like this again if I live to be a great-great-great-grandfather."

"I hope you do," Williams said.

"I hope we all do," Breen replied, looking at the canister as they turned toward the sea.

CHAPTER FORTY-THREE

November 12, 11:15 A.M.

Upon arriving unheralded in Illing's helicopter, Major Breen had immediately gone to the refueled C-21 that was still waiting to take them home.

Williams gave Illing all his South African money for fuel, which the pilot gratefully accepted.

"I'll take my wife to dinner with this," he said gratefully. "In Paris."

Williams smiled as he went to join Breen. En route, he had received a text from Lieutenant Lee stating that their mission had been accomplished and that they were returning to Pretoria with "the man who made this all necessary."

While the two men waited, Williams contacted General Krummeck. He put the man on speaker so Breen could hear.

"Congratulations. I heard you had arrived," the general said.

"Mr. Illing was an able pilot. You should use him again."

"Yes, I've heard about his talents. The police aren't sure whether to give him a legal citation or a medal."

"I think he'd be happy with both. So you've heard from East London, then?"

"Just. We were discussing Katinka Kettle. It seems she was apprehended by 'two of my people,' as they put it."

"A convenient stopgap. What do they intend to do with her?"

"That depends. They're waiting for a court-appointed barrister to take her confession."

"Consider interceding," Williams urged. "She was not an accomplice and appears to genuinely regret what her employer did."

"There is a sense that she intended to attack the police station," Krummeck remarked.

"She could have done so, if that was her true intent. She had time to open and throw the container. And keep in mind, General. She had, not more than thirty or so minutes before, been subjected to a deadly barrage by the STF. I've seen enough combat to know the effect that has on seasoned warriors. A young gemologist is something else again."

"True," Krummeck agreed. "And I would be willing to help in light of the service your people provided here and at Prince Edward. I understand they are going to return on a SAN helicopter."

"Along with Dr. Raeburn, whom I believe you know

well," Williams said. "I understand this bacteria was his work? Team work?"

Breen frowned at that.

"Sir," the general said, "if it is your intent to try and intimidate me while you are still on South African soil—"

"You wrong me, General. Dr. Raeburn appears to know more about this bacteria than anyone. He has told my people he wishes to find a cure. It is my *intent* to encourage you to help him do that. I am prepared to offer any assistance he might require. That includes anything our people discover by researching the sample I have with me."

"Dr. Raeburn will require that for his work," Krummeck said. "It is my understanding all other samples have been destroyed."

"I doubt that," Williams said. "You have dozens of victims with dormant samples. Samples, I might add, which can be reconstructed and replicated. No, you do not need this active set of specimens."

"But Washington does? You're an old military lion, I saw that the moment you walked through the door. You'll do what Beijing was prepared to do—find a cure for what you will weaponize."

"That may be. But you also opened the door to Moscow. I'll bet they have already hacked the phones and computer of the chief forensic pathologist in East London. Beijing has probably done so as well, along with our own Department of Defense. We at least— and you have my word on this—will share with you and Dr. Raeburn anything we find. No one need know where this came from, only who was the key to making sure it never happens again."

Breen frowned a second time.

Williams smirked and muted the phone. "Okay, it *was* a threat. But I knew where I was going with it."

General Krummeck sounded appeased and agreed to what Williams had proposed. The Americans had no doubt his sudden urgency to get off the phone was to secure the devices of the East London CFP.

Williams ended the call and sat back in the thinly cushioned seat. Breen still had a disapproving look.

"You don't think we should take the sample back?" Williams asked.

"Actually, I do," Breen said. "Mutual assured destruction is an arguably necessary attitude. I just don't have to like it."

"No argument." Williams rose. "But we have a few hours until Grace and Rivette get here—I'm going to see what they've got to eat in the galley and then take a nap."

"I like when we're in agreement, Mr. Williams."

"Yeah." The commander smiled.

Williams bit off the rest of what he wanted to say. Agreement was a diplomatic idea. Wrong was an ethical one. With Salehi, and now with Katinka, any course of action they might have chosen had legitimate moral weight.

I like it when we're in agreement, but I learn a helluva lot more when we're not, Williams thought as they made their way forward.

CHAPTER FORTY-FOUR

November 13, 6:50 P.M.

"Does anyone remember this line from my first inaugural address?" Midkiff asked the three men sitting with him at the conference table. "'The mailed fist of power must always yield to the whisper of compassion'?"

Governor John Wright and Matt Berry nodded. Chase Williams was noncommittal. It was a rhetorical question, anyway.

The president regarded Williams, who sat across from him, beside Berry.

"Commander, your team performed brilliantly. I'm looking forward to meeting Major Breen, Lieutenant Lee, and Lance Corporal Rivette."

"They are looking forward to meeting you both," Williams said, looking from Midkiff to the tall, graying, square-jawed president-elect.

The team had flown home and were met by Berry,

who took them directly to the Hay-Adams Hotel across Lafayette Park from the White House. Berry also took charge of the core sample, which was placed in a hazmat container by a team from the Centers for Disease Control and Prevention.

"I felt it best to locate this nonmilitary," Berry said. "Good thing we have an outgoing president who didn't care about crushed toes."

The team was surprisingly fresh. All had slept on the plane and did the same thing they had done after Yemen: debriefed one another. Not to corroborate or confirm matching stories but to air what they learned and how they felt. That was not something very many soldiers got to express in a relaxed, non-command environment.

Of them all, Grace was the most unsettled. She was not happy to have left Raeburn behind.

"I wanted to do Commander van Tonder the favor of putting him in a lock that caused unbearable pain—and keeping him that way for a ride across the ocean."

"Would you have?" Breen asked.

"I'd have shot him in the mouth," Rivette said.

"I don't know," Grace answered. "That commander—he was in just that kind of pain and it'll never go away."

"It shouldn't," Williams said. "Otherwise, you become a Raeburn instead of a Lieutenant Mabuza."

That failed to assuage the woman, and Williams suspected that what was truly at the core of her unhappiness was the same thing that had bothered him:

it took someone else to do what they were used to achieving themselves.

Hopefully, meeting President Midkiff and Governor Wright would help to mollify those feelings. It would also be the first time the team was together other than being on a mission. That would be validating, too. If they had not ultimately succeeded here, as in Yemen, there were likely to be questions about the Black Wasp program.

"Governor Wright, I am pleased that you will have this remarkable unit at your disposal," the president went on. "And more like it, if you can persuade the generals that they need to field more tactical and experiential skill and less redundant hardware."

"We *will* need more like it," Wright said—with great certainty.

"Why do you say that, sir?" Williams asked.

The president-elect had been sitting with his legs crossed. He leaned forward now, reminding Williams of the way he had looked directly into cameras with a gaze that commanded respect.

"Because your team just showed the Chinese, the Russians, and everyone else who was watching what you can do," Wright said. "That can hardly go unnoticed at the highest levels—or unanswered. I hope, Mr. Berry, that when your tenure here is through you will consider serving as intermediary of such a program."

"I'm honored," Berry replied.

The president rose. "I'm sure, Commander Williams, your teammates are getting restless in the anteroom. Why don't you bring them in?"

"With great pleasure, sir," Williams replied.

And it was.

And the old military lion felt a refreshing spring in his walk as he went to the doors of the Oval Office with two presidents and Matt Berry rising to their feet behind him.

Read on for an excerpt from

TOM CLANCY'S
OP-CENTER:
THE BLACK ORDER—

the next exciting title in the
Op-Center series,

coming in trade paperback from St. Martin's Griffin!

PROLOGUE

January 15, 11:18 P.M.

In the two years since retiring as commander of Naval Support Activity Philadelphia, Captain Richard "Atlas" Hamill had been dedicated to three things.

The first and most important was his wife, Sophia. They had recently celebrated their forty-second wedding anniversary, and their love and friendship were "eight bells strong," as he put it. Hamill had met the Texas native when he was stationed at Naval Station Corpus Christi. That was where she gave him his nickname, after the moving van he had stopped beside to give her their first kiss.

Hamill's second great passion was hunting, which he did every weekend during season. Absent sea air he required country air, the smell of leaves alive or rotting—he did not care. He ate what he killed, and always thanked God for His bounty. During the off-season he kept fit by walking the Western Pennsylvania woods.

The captain's third passion was spending at least several minutes a day in the company of his neighbors, the dead ones: the towering ghosts of Independence Hall, the birthplace of the nation that the captain loved and served.

Whenever he was in the city, whatever the weather, the sixty-year-old walked two blocks from his Spruce Street town house to the historic compound. His knees never failed to weaken as he stepped on that holy ground. Even when he had the flu a year before, Hamill had dragged himself to the rooftop of his four-story home to gaze upon the iconic building. His wife, her gray hair whipping in the wind, had gamely helped him up the steep staircase—to argue would have been futile—then hustled him back inside before he could catch pneumonia.

"I thought I heard the Liberty Bell up there," he had said, smiling in his feverish state as she tucked the comforter under his chin.

"I hit my head on the door helping you," Sophia had replied. "Now we are *both* hearing things."

In all the years he and Sophia had been together, the captain had never confided that it was more than love of country that compelled him to lay eyes on the landmark. It was a sailor's superstition that bordered on obsession. Richard's father, Captain Martin Hamill, was XO of the USS *Yorktown*. He had refused to board the aircraft carrier for its decommissioning until his lucky silver dollar flipped heads up into his left palm. He had done that every time he'd boarded for the past quarter century. To the elder Hamill a successful flip meant he would not go down with his ship.

Martin Hamill lived to be eighty-nine, his wife, Carol, ninety.

On the day of the decommissioning, the coin flip had accomplished one thing more. The ceremony that had transferred the *Yorktown* from active duty to the Atlantic Reserve Fleet, the "Mothball Fleet," gave them their permanent home. After the event, the elder and younger Hamills had decided to walk for a while and let their emotions settle. They took an out-of-the-way turn and strolled onto Spruce Street, right past the For Sale sign outside the corner building. Martin Hamill bought the four-story town house that afternoon.

Richard Hamill did not become overly superstitious until his mandatory retirement after thirty-eight years. That was only his "public" retirement, as the retiree called it, because he had immediately gone to work as a consultant for the Office of Naval Intelligence. Major Becky Lewis of the Transnational Threat Department remembered him from a logistics conference years before and booked him a train ticket. She recalled him having spoken about his love of hunting, and it was not Hamill's years in the navy that interested her but his unique knowledge of the game lands throughout the state—and fellow hunters. Hamill had recently celebrated the twenty-fifth anniversary of PAVE—Pennsylvania Venison, a loose collective he had cofounded and which helped feed veterans suffering hard times. Hunters dropped off food at his home, and he brought it to veterans in his station wagon. His own kills were among those hand-delivered to the group.

Now, most days, Hamill was busier than when he had been running the supply and support services for naval operations at NSA Philadelphia. His reconnaissance for the Office of Naval Intelligence was dangerous work, as it turned out. Much more dangerous than bear or bobcat. His job was to circle ever closer over five hundred acres to a target that his handler only suspected was real. Its possible existence was something she surmised based on information from "Taikinys," a debriefed arms dealer. The gun-and-explosives runner had kept using the words "black order," though neither Major Lewis nor Atlas Hamill had ever heard of such a thing. Initially, she had taken those words to describe a secret purchase agreement. But then she wondered if it might be part of a name. Just yesterday, when he returned from his latest "walk in the woods," as he downplayed his activities to Sophia, he began to have a feeling that he was not just looking and watching but being watched. A hunter's instinct, nothing more, which he communicated to Major Lewis.

If Sophia knew how risky the work was, she would have dragged her husband to safety, just as she had put her small arms around him and hauled him to and from the rooftop. All he had said, in passing, was that if Sophia ever needed anything from the navy she should press two on speed dial. She, of course, was number one.

Well, he thought, *America was born in danger and would always face such challenges.* Philadelphia's native son Benjamin Franklin had risked his life just by showing up for meetings and affixing his name to an immortal document. *Should I do less?*

Just a half hour before, after walking to Walnut Street to remind the Founding Fathers that yet another American presidency was soon to begin, Captain Atlas Hamill lay on his back and shut his eyes. He did not lament his fears but welcomed them. He was proud and content thinking about the few tourists who had stood with him in the cold, amidst the skeletal winter trees, looking up at the bell tower, its famed contours set emphatically against a gibbous moon.

He was somewhere between wakefulness and sleep when a bus growled three floors below, on the corner of Spruce and South Third. Sophia had never liked the sound and the faint whiff of fuel, but it made her husband smile. Both had a comforting, almost narcotic effect on the system. Diesel was in the noses of most seamen. Functioning machinery was in their ears. This was especially true when they bedded down in bunks stacked three or four high. At lights out, the olfactory and auditory senses were undistracted.

Sleep came just as the point of a knife stung the throat of Captain Hamill, its straight edge going deep under his Adam's apple and causing blood to gush into his windpipe. He gasped, the flood burbling as it poured into his windpipe and rose in his throat, backing into his mouth.

* * *

Sophia Hamill woke when she heard gurgling and wheezing sounds to her right. It was faint enough so that she thought, at first, a homeless person was regurgitating in the street. Then she was aware of it being closer, much closer, and rolled toward her husband. She saw his dark shape trembling violently against the glow of the clock on the night table.

"*Richard!*"

The woman jerked upright, her right arm flinging out to find the light switch.

She was pushed back by a masked figure who was looming above her, his weight on her chest and shoulder pressing her arm deep and helpless in the mattress. She reached up with her left arm to push back, and he smacked it away with his free hand. She snaked it up again, and he struck it again, harder. Fully awake and terrified she looked up, saw her attacker silhouetted against a portion of the ceiling that was lit by a streetlamp just below the window.

The woman screamed with violence that rocked her entire body. The hand on her shoulder jerked to her mouth. A leather glove, pliable with age, trapped the cry in her mouth, causing her cheeks to expand. The attacker's fingers closed tightly and gripped her jaw. He leaned his weight on her mouth, jamming her head into her pillow even as her husband flopped freely, weakly to her left. She was now aware of blood soaking her back starting at the shoulder and creeping down along her ribs. The sensation was warm, wet, and impossible. Her eyes were wide as she sucked air and the smell of leather through flared nostrils.

The killer was not oblivious to the death rattle of the man beside her and the blood spilling with weakening spurts from the dying man's wound. He simply did not care. The intruder had committed an execution, not a murder.

"The devil is not as black as he is painted."

He had withdrawn the gory knife with his right hand, the hand that had rapped her left arm hard. He moved the double barrel fixed blade hunting knife over, put the point against the widow's left side. The pinch of the blade was in line with her racing heart. Her chest struggled against his weight as it expanded, hard and fast with each short, sharp breath; her breath, along with her small struggles, made the corpse beside her rise and fall grotesquely. The rapid beat of her heart caused the blade to pulse. The man on top of her could feel it throb through the metal.

The killer gazed down through a black ski mask. It was good to feel the random strands of wool on his lips, his own hot breath warming his cheeks, his hair damp with perspiration despite the cold. The smells here were unfamiliar, yet the mask brought back the past. The feeling of service blended with the more satisfying sense of power. He took a moment to savor it, as he always had.

The Iranian bomb maker in Basra. The young war widow on her way to pick up a suicide vest in Tikrit. The Iranian spy in the Green Zone who gave him a gift: the location of an American hostage, who was liberated that night.

Every one of them had been a personal triumph of surveillance and bribery, stalking and eavesdropping, and finally isolating and killing. Civilians would never understand the balance of patience and urgency an undercover operative required in country.

The others did.

The killer saw the pinpoint gleam of her eyes directly below his own. Those eyes were large and frightened, and they widened even more as he pressed the tip of the knife a little harder. He smiled under his mask. It was a look of terror, open and pleading.

The man waited a moment before lowering his face closer to hers. She was just an animal now, afraid and without dignity or shame. The light in her eyes died as his head blocked the source. He spoke, his voice a whisper, his breath warm on the woman's cheeks.

"You will deliver a message, Mrs. Hamill. Nod if you understand."

Sophia Hamill nodded obediently, more from horror than understanding.

"You are to tell your husband's employers that the war has begun. Inform them that those who move against us will die, whether it is one or one thousand. Is that understood?"

This time she did not nod. The command did not make sense.

The man leaned closer, his full weight on the hand pressing her back. "Mrs. Hamill, will you communicate what I told you, or must I write the message in your husband's blood?"

The woman tried to replay the words, to process them. Comprehension did not make it through her terror.

The man relaxed his grip on her mouth but did not raise his hand. "One last time, you are to tell the people your husband worked for: the war has begun. The war has begun. You will tell them that, yes?"

This time the simple phrase stuck. The woman nodded vigorously.

In a single, fluid movement the intruder drew the knife from her side, raised the hand that held it, and brought the steel hilt down on her forehead.

The woman let out a grunt as she felt an electric shock race from that point around her skull. She squeezed her eyes shut and saw circles of rusty red that slowly turned to black.

With the woman unconscious, the intruder went back to the dead man's side of the bed. He turned on the light and snatched up the man's cell phone. It was locked.

That wouldn't matter, Poole had said. The manufacturer's theft-deterrent software could be tricked into entering recovery mode with signals from cloned servers. A new password could then be furnished and used to access everything stored on the phone.

"I hope so," the man muttered.

Checking to see that the woman was still out, the man went downstairs. He removed his ski mask, changed into the clothes he had left on a chair, and exited by the front door.

Upstairs, after what may have been seconds, minutes, or even longer, Sophia realized that the man's hand was no longer on her mouth. She drew a long breath, felt it fill her lungs, and yelled it out until her chest had deflated and her face had twisted into something barely human.

Driven more by instinct than thought, she pushed herself from the bed. Her forehead screamed with pain and she fell stiff armed against her night table.

She felt her phone. She had to call—

No, not 911.

Just a few days before, Atlas had put a number into her phone. Someone at the navy. Someone he said she should turn to if she ever needed anything. Sophia asked him why, and he said that there had been security concerns, nothing to worry about, but to call if anything—*anything*—happened out of the ordinary.

Her finger shaking, Sophia unlocked the phone and pressed the saved number.

Sobbing and fighting back nausea from the blow to her head, she heard a woman's voice, sobbed out her name, then did the only thing she was capable of doing.

She screamed.